PRAISE FOR *SUCKER PUNCH*

"Blake's twenty-seventh outing (after *Serpentine*) is a crafty murder mystery wrapped in plenty of fur and fury. Fans of the series will be pleased to see Anita Blake's return."
—*Library Journal*

"Well written, very descriptive, and a fast-paced read."
—The Reading Cafe

"Deliciously evocative, compelling, and a well-rounded story!"
—Fresh Fiction

"Laurell K. Hamilton continues to deliver an original, fast-paced, captivating story. It is edgy, twisted, suspenseful, and touches on quite a few emotions."
—Literati Literature Lovers

"A very nice new novel. . . . I had a great time with this volume!"
—Between Dreams and Reality

PRAISE FOR LAURELL K. HAMILTON AND THE ANITA BLAKE NOVELS

"Hamilton remains one of the most inventive and exciting writers in the paranormal field."
—#1 *New York Times* bestselling author Charlaine Harris

"If you've never read this series, I highly recommend/strongly suggest having the Anita Blake experience. Vampires, zombies, and shifters, oh my! And trust me, these are not your daughter's vampires."
iterati Book Reviews

T0020245

"A sex-positive, kick-ass female protagonist."

—Starburst

"Number one *New York Times* bestseller Hamilton is still thrilling fans . . . with her amazing multifaceted characters and intricate multilayered world, a mix of erotic romance, crime drama, and paranormal/fantasy fiction. Her descriptive prose is gritty and raw, with a mosaic of humor and horror to tell this complex, well-detailed story. But it's her enigmatic stable of stars that continues to shine, managing their improbable interpersonal relationship dynamics."

—*Library Journal*

Titles by Laurell K. Hamilton

Anita Blake, Vampire Hunter Novels

GUILTY PLEASURES
THE LAUGHING CORPSE
CIRCUS OF THE DAMNED
THE LUNATIC CAFE
BLOODY BONES
THE KILLING DANCE
BURNT OFFERINGS

BLUE MOON
OBSIDIAN BUTTERFLY
NARCISSUS IN CHAINS
CERULEAN SINS
INCUBUS DREAMS
MICAH
DANSE MACABRE
THE HARLEQUIN
BLOOD NOIR
SKIN TRADE

FLIRT
BULLET
HIT LIST
KISS THE DEAD
AFFLICTION
JASON
DEAD ICE
CRIMSON DEATH
SERPENTINE
SUCKER PUNCH
RAFAEL

Merry Gentry Novels

A KISS OF SHADOWS
A CARESS OF TWILIGHT
SEDUCED BY MOONLIGHT

A STROKE OF MIDNIGHT
MISTRAL'S KISS
A LICK OF FROST
SWALLOWING DARKNESS

DIVINE MISDEMEANORS
A SHIVER OF LIGHT

Specials

BEAUTY
DANCING
WOUNDED

Anthologies

STRANGE CANDY
FANTASTIC HOPE

Zaniel Havelock Novels

A TERRIBLE FALL OF ANGELS

RAFAEL

LAURELL K. HAMILTON

BERKLEY
New York

BERKLEY
An imprint of Penguin Random House LLC
penguinrandomhouse.com

ISBN: 9780593332917

Jove mass-market edition / February 2021
Berkley mass-market edition / March 2023

Printed in the United States of America
9   11   13   15   16   14   12   10   8

So many of you told me that you wanted Rafael, Claudia, and all the rest of the wererats to have a book where they were center stage; well, this one's for you and all the other readers who told me they wanted more stories faster. Write faster, you say! So here's the next book just in time for the Year of the Rat! As the old year slips away and the Year of the Ox begins, may it be full of hope, happiness, good health, and prosperity for the whole world.

1

I WAS WORKING out in the weight room with Claudia, who was a more serious weightlifter than I would ever be, but she was teaching me how to trust my new supernatural strength. In the movies you become a vampire or a werewolf or whatever, and you just automatically know how it all works. In real life it wasn't automatic, or at least it wasn't for me. In all honesty, lifting some of the weights scared me, which meant I couldn't lift them, because my mind convinced me it was impossible, which was why I'd started spending part of Saturday in the gym with Claudia. She was helping me work through my nerves and had patiently explained that a lot of people had the same issues when they first became shapeshifters. I wasn't exactly a shapeshifter, but close enough. What were we talking about between lifting heavy objects? Men. You can take the human out of the girl, but you can't take the girl out of the wererat, or something like that.

"But Rafael is literally tall, dark, and handsome. His house is beautiful, and the pool is so nice I'm beginning to want one. He's polite, well-spoken, a gentleman."

"All that is true," Claudia said.

"So why doesn't he have more lady friends?"

"Ask him," she said, and lay down on the weight bench and started to wrap her dark hands around a truly frightening amount of weight. She was six feet, six inches tall and already had enough muscle visible around the sports bra and double shorts that I knew she could lift it. I'd seen her lift that much before, but it still sort of scared me for shoulder press. I'd owned cars that didn't weigh as much as she was about to lift on the specially reinforced bar. If she were merely human and it fell on her neck, she'd have a crushed larynx and be dead before medical help could arrive. If it landed on her chest, I might be able to call for help before she suffocated from not being able to expand her chest enough to keep breathing, but I couldn't lift it off her. I could not spot her at these weights. I'd pointed that out to her, and she'd replied with, "This is the weight I'd be doing if you weren't here." She had a point, so I let it go.

I thought I lifted respectable weight for being five foot three and female, but trying to lift in the same room with Claudia always made me feel sort of puny; of course, the Hulk might feel kind of puny trying to keep up with her, so I guess I shouldn't worry about it.

She got the weight clear of the bar. Lowered it slowly and with perfect control. The only sign of strain was the way her muscles corded and the sound of her breath as she did a sharp exhale and pushed the bar upward again. I knew we were doing pyramid sets, so she'd be doing three to five reps on this last weight, but part of me just wanted her to put it back on the rack and be done. It wasn't that I thought she couldn't handle reps with it, I just wasn't sure my nerves could handle watching her do it.

She did five reps, her muscles working smoothly, showing no effort except for her breath being a little more serious at the end. She set the weight back in the rack, and

I realized I'd been holding my breath, because it came out in a *whoosh*, as if I'd been the one lifting.

She sat up and smiled at me. "You know I'm not in any danger when I lift. If I thought it was dangerous, I either wouldn't do it, or I'd have someone in here to spot me."

"I know you're very safety conscious in the gym, but I don't know if I'll ever get used to watching you and the other shapeshifters lift so much more than human-normal."

"You can lift more now, too," she said, reaching for the towel she had to the side of the rack. It was just good manners to wipe off the bench after you were done.

"Yeah, but not that kind of weight."

"You're smaller than me."

I laughed. "Most of the male guards are smaller than you."

She smiled, a fierce baring of white teeth in the deep brown of her face. "Your turn," she said with that smile that was fierce and happy at the same time, as if a panther could smile like a person, though that wasn't her flavor of wereanimal, but somehow rat just didn't convey the dangerous beauty of Claudia.

She let me help her put most of her weights back on the weight racks because I insisted on helping, but it was a workout just to do that part. I let her help me put my weights on the bar because it was fair. "Just so you know, I wouldn't lift this by myself without someone to spot me."

She gave that fierce smile again, with a small deep chuckle. I'd only recently learned Claudia was a throaty alto when she sang, and that she could sing. It had been worth going to karaoke just to hear her.

I lay back on the bench and centered myself under the bar. I hadn't been super strong long enough to really believe it all the time. I looked at the weights and thought,

I'm about to press three times my body weight, which was ridiculous, except that I'd done it before. Claudia put her hands over the bar, ready to help if I needed it; without her there I would have been scared to do it.

I wrapped my hands around the bar, using the roughened part of it to help me decide on hand placement, and then I couldn't put it off anymore. Lifting this amount of weight off the rack wasn't about strength really, it was about believing it was possible. I'd learned that I couldn't look too hard at the weight on either side of the bar, because it made part of my head start screaming, *Impossible, I can't lift this!* I could do the inhuman weights for most of the exercises and just marvel at it, but the chest press and the squat rack both spooked me, because if they went wrong, I could end up crippled or dead, if I'd been human, and of course that was the other part that rattled around in my brain. How human was I? How much did the metaphysical connections to the vampires and the shapeshifters help me here? They made me stronger and harder to hurt. They helped me heal faster than human-normal from cuts, stabs, bullets, a brain injury, but did they cover being crushed? Did I really want to find out just to lift in the gym? Saying it that way made it sound stupid.

"You can do this, Anita, you know you can," Claudia said, leaning her face a little more into my line of sight.

I looked up into her true brown eyes, the utter surety in her face. She was right, I knew she was right. "I can do this," I said.

She gave that fierce smile again and leaned over to whisper, "We got company, make me proud."

I didn't point out that whoever had come into the weight room would have to be a shapeshifter, which meant that they would be able to lift this and more, but as I'd learned in the weight room when I was merely human, it wasn't always about who was stronger, it was about who wanted it more. I wanted it, because if the

guards who just walked in had been ones she liked, she'd
have yelled it out, teased them about me being tougher
than them. That she'd whispered it meant she didn't like
them, which probably meant neither would I.

I suddenly wasn't afraid of the weights; Claudia was
there, she could catch anything I could lift, and besides,
I wanted to make her proud. She'd started being my
weight-lifting partner even though I wasn't strong enough
to spot for her. She was teaching me how to use the new
supernatural strength, and without saying it out loud she
enjoyed having another woman who worked out hard.

I cleared the weight off the rack, took in my breath,
and started lowering the bar down. My body had a moment of going *You're joking, right?* when my elbows bent
and the bar touched my chest, not resting on it, but just
touching it. My arms trembled as I started pushing upward. The elbow on the side that had the most scars hesitated a second, and then I was pushing up, using my
breath to help push the weight up, as if I could blow it
away from me. I could feel the muscles bunch and move
in a way that no other exercise made them do, or maybe
weights made me more aware of it. I loved the feel of my
body fighting to lift it, and then I was up, all the way up.
I'd done it! The thrill of adrenaline, the relief, and then
the thought *Can I do it again?* I fought my arms to make
sure the weight went down steady and controlled. I
touched my chest, this time a little more solidly, and there
was that moment when the weight didn't want to be lifted.
I pushed and the elbow on my left arm hesitated again
like the joint was thinking about it, and then the muscles
kicked in and the bar started to rise. I fought not to arch
my back and cheat with more of my body than I was supposed to use. There was a little more tremble in my arms
as I got the bar all the way back up. I debated on trying
for a third rep, but the fine tremble in my muscles said no.
All I had to do now was put it back in the rack. My arms

were trembling visibly now. Claudia started to put her hands on the bar, but I snarled, "No, don't touch it!"

She moved her hands wide so the room could see she wasn't helping.

I couldn't seem to sink it on the rack—it was like trying to thread a needle that weighed a ton when your arms were starting to do the spaghetti wobble. I thought I was going to lose it for just a second and really regretted not letting Claudia help me, but then the bar sank home on the rack with a satisfyingly soft clank. I was breathing hard but grinning up at her as she grinned down at me. She offered me a fist to bump. It took me two tries to manage with my arms a little wobbly. "Personal best for you," she said.

"Two reps, that's all she can do at that weight, and she's supposed to be our queen," a male voice whined from across the room. It was Kane, one of my least favorite people. Perfect.

"Come over here and prove you can do better," Claudia said.

I sat up, careful not to bang my head on the now safely racked weight bar, and if you think that doesn't happen, you haven't been in enough weight rooms. I sat on the bench with my arms still shaky. We'd already done a full round of weights before we started with the pyramid sets, so I'd earned the sweat along my spine and the noodle arms. I sat there letting my pulse and breathing get under control. The fact that I was breathing as if I'd done cardio meant I'd really pushed myself for that personal best on the chest press. Yay, me! Staring across the room at Kane, I didn't feel personally victorious, I felt defeated. Kane was a problem that I didn't know how to fix, and he was right, technically I was about to be everyone's queen, and Kane wasn't the only one who thought I wasn't up to the job. He was just the only one who was this vocal about it. I'd kicked his ass twice, once with magic and once without. I'd put a gun to his head that last time because there was only so much I could do against shape-shifters that could grow their own claws and fangs. I was almost as fast and strong as they were, but I couldn't grow my own weapons.

The other man with him said, "Kane, we're here to work out, just leave it."

"She's too human to be in charge of all of us, you said so yourself, Helios."

Helios gave me a look that was almost pleading. "I didn't say it to her face, though. I'm sorry, Ms. Blake, and I'm really sorry, Claudia."

"Why are you sorrier to me than to Anita?" she asked.

"She may be queen someday, but you'll beat my ass in combatives." The moment he called fight practice *combatives*, I knew he was one of the former military that we'd been hiring as guards. Popping hot for lycanthropy—sorry, Therianthropy—was still an automatic discharge from all branches of military service, which meant we'd been picking up some well-trained talent courtesy of Uncle Sam's shortsighted policies.

"I think Anita could win on the mat," Claudia said.

Helios, who was blond and six feet tall, in obvious good shape, grinned. "I didn't say she couldn't win on points, but she can't pound me into the mat, and you can."

"Anita can't win unless she sucker punches you first," Kane said as he strutted his way through the full set of free weights with a few machines and big metal frames of the squat rack. He was six feet even just like Helios, but where the former teams guy was starting to let his blond hair grow out, Kane still had his hair shaved down to dark stubble with that high widow's peak at the front so that the skin went back from it sharply, which always made me want to ask if he'd started shaving because he was going bald, or if it was just a fashion choice. I knew it wasn't a military buzz, because Kane had never worn a uniform, he didn't have the discipline for it.

"Kane, we're here to work on your form in the weight room, not make trouble," Helios called after him.

Kane blinked big, dark brown eyes at me, because he was close enough for that kind of detail. "It's not going to be any trouble," he answered the other man, but his attention was all on me. The lack of hair left his face unadorned so you could see he had good bone structure and was handsome, almost prettily so; the body that showed around the tank top, exercise shorts, and jogging shoes wasn't bad, but it was more a body that was lean because he was built that way than lean because he worked out and watched his nutrition.

Claudia handed me my towel, and I used it to wipe down the weight bench. She started taking the weight off the bar.

"I thought I was going to do reps with that," Kane said.

"It's three times Anita's body weight. She did two reps with it after a full workout with me in the weight room, and then starting back with pyramid sets. You can either do a full workout with weights of my choice for you, or you can just jump right to doing chest press with three times your body weight." She gave that smile that was more a snarl again. Claudia didn't like Kane, because he was supposed to be one of the guards and she didn't think he was good enough. I agreed, but Kane and I were feuding over a man, sort of. It's always hard to be the ex-girlfriend when the new boyfriend is a jealous bitch.

I picked up my water bottle and started trying to rehydrate.

"That's not fair," Kane said, and that handsome face scrunched down into the sour lines that were usually how he looked, at least around me. It stole all his pouty good looks and showed him for what he was—unpleasant.

Claudia stopped taking weights off the bar long enough to give him a look. "Not fair, really?" There was a dangerous undertone in her voice. I don't mean dangerous as in violence, but in the you've-just-mouthed-off-to-your-coach/martial-arts-instructor/drill-sergeant/dad way.

Helios was hurrying toward us, saying, "He didn't mean it."

Claudia turned her head enough to aim the look at Helios. He stopped moving toward us. "Are you his baby-sitter today?"

"I don't need a babysitter," Kane said; he hadn't understood the look or the tone in Claudia's voice.

"No, ma'am," Helios said, both of them ignoring Kane's comment.

I started taking weight off the other side of my bar. If I was careful, I wouldn't drop anything on myself. My arms were still letting me know that I'd used them, but they weren't trembling anymore.

Claudia put up the weight in her hand. Her side was clean, so she could turn her full attention to the men. I kept putting up the weights on the other side of the bar and staying out of it.

"Who told you to bring Kane to the weight room?" she asked.

"Bobby Lee." Helios looked uncomfortable for a moment, and then he stood to attention, shoulders back, hands at his sides. He looked at the far wall of the room, rather than directly at Claudia.

"What were his exact orders?" The bodyguards were a lot less formal than the military, but we had so many of them now that it just saved time and confusion to use some of the military jargon.

"Take Kane to the weight room, work on his form,

because it sucks. If it still sucks after you've worked with him, I'm going to personally smoke both your asses." I'd never heard Bobby Lee say anything that harsh to me, but then he never had to tell me to work harder in training.

"So, you're Kane's battle buddy today," Claudia said, still in that you-done-fucked-up tone.

Helios swallowed visibly, but stayed at attention as he answered, "Yes, ma'am."

"What's a battle buddy?" Kane asked.

Claudia said, "Anita, tell Kane what a battle buddy is." She didn't even look behind her, she just assumed I'd answer.

I didn't come to attention, but I did pause in the middle of putting up the last weight. "A battle buddy is a military term for someone who has your back as a friend and/or has seen combat with you, so they have your back as a brother in arms. It also means someone that an officer, or drill sargeant, has assigned to a soldier who is a screwup or lacks training. Their battle buddy is supposed to help train them, or make sure they don't screw up."

Helios's eyes flicked to me and then back to the invisible point on the wall. The eye flick meant I'd either surprised, interested, or impressed him with my answer.

"You were never military. How do you know that?" Kane asked.

"I asked someone," I said.

"Anita, what happens if the screwup the battle buddy is supposed to be babysitting continues to screw up?" Claudia made it sound like an order, and technically I was *her* boss, but in the weight room and in fight practice she was the expert—that made her the boss.

"The battle buddy gets punished along with the screwup."

"I am not a screwup," Kane said; he almost yelled it, his hands already in fists at his sides.

I sniffed the air before I could stop myself. His anger smelled like food. I could feed like an energy vampire on two things, lust and wrath, two of the deadly sins. I'd met real vampires that could feed off fear, violence, even death. In the grand scheme of things, I'd gotten lucky on my menu.

"Ma'am, may I intercede before he does anything more that we'll both regret?" Helios asked.

"You may," Claudia said.

"I don't need your help," Kane snarled, half turning toward the other man.

"I'm helping myself, not you," Helios said, and he dropped out of attention, just relaxing into himself, or his ordinary stance.

"We're werehyenas, we shouldn't have to take orders from rats!"

"Narcissus, our Oba, told us to train with the other guards; that means taking orders from whoever is higher rank. That includes Claudia, Bobby Lee, and Fredo."

"It's not natural for different animal groups to work together," Kane said, but at least he wasn't yelling. His anger was fading, too, which was just as well. I'd fed off him once, and that was enough. I'd done it to make a point that I was dominant over him, but the lesson hadn't sunk in for Kane, just like a lot of lessons didn't sink in for him.

Helios stepped not just closer to Kane, but so he moved the other man back a little from Claudia. I don't think he wanted to know what the punishment would be if Kane took a swing at her. "I'm learning a lot from all the training here in St. Louis. I'm a teams guy, I came in here with serious skills, but Jake has hundreds of years of fighting practice. I'm learning things from him that no one else could teach me. I don't care if he's a werewolf."

"Jake has only lived that long because he's tied to his vampire master. He's a slave to the vampires."

"Oh, come on, you're Asher's *moitié bête*, his animal to call, just like Jake and his master," I said, and instantly regretted saying anything.

"You stay out of this!" Kane said, and he was instantly angry again. I had that effect on him.

Helios tried to move him back away from both of us, but Kane went wide around the bench toward me. I wasn't armed, not even with a knife, because I was in the gym underneath the Circus of the Damned. If I wasn't safe in our inner sanctum, then something was wrong. I hoped that something wasn't six feet of tall, dark, and stupid.

Helios moved so fast it was just a blur and he was between me and Kane. The military trained the special forces to be better than the best; add to that the extra speed of a wereanimal and they were scary good.

"Back it up, Kane," Helios said.

I used Helios's body to hide the fact that I was backing up and around the weight racks. I did not want Kane to take a swing at me with me pressed up against the weights with nowhere to go. I'd beat him once hand to hand, but I'd sucker punched him while he was still arguing about the rules. Professionals act while amateurs are still asking what the fuck just happened. Sometimes being a professional doesn't mean throwing the first punch, it means avoiding the fight altogether.

"Are you going to hide behind one of your guards, Anita?"

"She's supposed to hide behind us. We're her bodyguards," Helios said.

"Then why does she train with us? Why is she always down here training?"

I was far enough out into the room now. I figured between Claudia and Helios they could wrestle Kane without involving me. He'd been training harder in the fighting part of things since I kicked his ass. He didn't work harder anywhere else; I think he wanted a rematch, but I didn't. He was at least cruiserweight, or even heavyweight, and I was bantamweight at best, and if two fighters are equally trained, size matters.

"I'm a U.S. Marshal for the Preternatural Branch; I train so I can go up against the monsters and survive."

"She just called us all monsters, the kind she executes."

"I've seen what happens when one of us goes rogue," Helios said. "We *are* monsters. We need people like Blake who can take us out when we go full beast mode."

"Why are you taking her side? Did she fuck you like she fucks all the other men?"

"That's out of line," Helios said.

"So, you did fuck her!"

"Oh, for the love of God, Kane, it's not my fault that Asher is bisexual and not just gay the way you want him to be," I said.

"He'd be gay if it wasn't for you," Kane said, and he had moved so he could see me around the other man.

"Asher is Asher, he's over six hundred years old, I didn't change any of his sexual preferences."

"Liar!" He screamed it at me.

"I'm not sleeping with your boyfriend, Kane."

"But he still wants you!"

"And that is not my fault," I said.

"Lying bitch!" Kane moved toward me and Helios stepped in between us. Kane pushed him hard enough to make the other man stumble. Helios made a fist, and part of me wanted him to take the swing.

Kane seemed to see it, too, because he calmed for a second and said, "Sorry, Helios, it's not your fault, it's hers." And the calm was gone as if it had never been, he was right back to being furious—at me.

"Let Asher sleep with other women, and maybe he'll get me out of his system."

"No! It's not women he wants, it's just you, he's only hetero for you." I tried to see something in his face that I could reason with, but there was nothing but the jealous rage. It pinched his features down so that the handsome was all gone. Some people really are pretty when they're angry; Kane wasn't one of them.

"You act like I'm the only woman he ever slept with, Kane. I know he slept with Dulcia, the leader of your old hyena clan."

"Only because Jean-Claude told him to seduce her."

"What about Belle Morte and Julianna?"

Kane made a sound low in his chest, and an eerie high-pitched growl spilled out of his human lips.

"Anita, just go, hit the showers. He'll calm down once you're gone," Claudia said.

"Asher is bisexual, Kane. You can't change that about him."

His human words came out with that hyena squeal threading through them, so the sound raised the hairs at the back of my neck. "I can love him enough so he won't need anyone else."

"You sound like a woman who marries a gay man convinced she can love him straight." I shouldn't have said it, but I was just so tired of him.

He started rushing me, but Helios was there wrapping his arms around him from behind. I expected Kane to fight Helios then, but he just kept staring at me, trying to get at me like a dog on a chain.

I looked at the big man who was almost foaming at the mouth with rage. The anger didn't smell good to me now, as if he'd gone past healthy anger into something more, or worse. Whatever was twisting Kane up inside was nothing I wanted to feed on.

Claudia got close enough to me to lower her voice over Kane's yells. "Go, I'll make sure he's got a battle buddy with him at all times." There was a very serious look in her eyes; she was acknowledging that I might not be safe alone with Kane.

I didn't argue, just took my towel and left my water bottle by the weight bench. I didn't want it badly enough to get that close to Kane when he was having one of his fits. I was beginning to believe that his possessive jealousy of Asher was just that insane, as in something was broken inside Kane that needed either talk therapy or medication, or both. *Crazy in love* wasn't just a phrase for Kane and Asher, which was one reason I wasn't sleeping with Asher. Under other circumstances we would have fired Kane and sent him to another city to be someone else's problem, but thanks to Asher having made him his beast half, if Kane left, then so did Asher, and though I wasn't sleeping with him, there were others who were, or who were working their way back to it. There were people here who were in love with Asher; too bad we all hated Kane, and he hated us right back.

2

I TURNED A corner toward the locker rooms and nearly ran into Rafael. He had to catch me in his arms, or I'd have smacked face-first into his chest. I was more bothered by Kane than I'd thought, since I didn't sense Rafael's energy with his main bodyguard, Benito, right beside him. Even without the otherworldly energy they were both tall: dark, muscled, and handsome for Rafael, more sinister for Benito. They both had short black hair and brown eyes, but Benito had deep facial scarring from something that looked like more than acne, but it wasn't just the scars. I had other people in my life who had facial scars, and none of them seemed like a villainous henchman in a superhero movie, but Benito did. Maybe it was the fact that he worked so hard being scary as Rafael's main bodyguard.

I started to push away from Rafael, partly because I was startled and partly because that had been my reaction to getting close for so long. Luckily for all of us I'd worked on my issues enough to let myself realize that a hug might be nice, not for romance, but because Kane's hatred of me was beginning to be unnerving. It never feels good when someone hates you, but when it's for things you can't change, like being a woman and having a past relationship with someone's boyfriend . . . you can't fix that.

But there was another reason not to take a hug from Rafael; he wasn't one of the loves of my life. He was supposed to be powerful food for the *ardeur* and that was it, but because I didn't know how to be regularly intimate with someone and not date them, the lines were getting blurry between us and I didn't know how to handle it. If he was just my friend and sexual snack, was it fair to turn to him for emotional comfort? Where is the line between friend with benefits and boyfriend?

Because I didn't have an answer, I let myself relax against Rafael's body, let the strength of his arms wrap around me. Honestly with my back to the room with Kane in it I should have moved so I could see him coming, but with Rafael looking in that direction and Benito with us, if Kane tried anything, I was betting on us. Then I wondered, was I trying to bait Kane? I hoped not, because that would be childish and dangerous for both of us.

"I hear someone ranting in the weight room," Benito said.

"It's Kane," I said, as Rafael said it with me. He hugged me tighter to his body and I slid my arms around his waist to find his back wet with sweat, and the chest where my cheek tried to nestle was a little damp, too. It made me pull back a little, laughing.

"I was working out, too," he said, laughing with me.

"Let's move toward the locker room," Benito said. "I don't want us in his sight line when he exits the room."

Neither of us argued. We just put my arm around Rafael's waist and his arm across my shoulders and let the bodyguard herd us away from the sound of raised voices. We'd been lovers long enough that we knew where all the arms and legs and noses went when we did most anything. I'd never been this physically comfortable with anyone that I wasn't in love with before. It felt weird, because some part of me had still believed that this level of physical comfort was supposed to come only after the in-love part; that it could come just through being together often enough sort of bothered me.

Kane wasn't shouting anymore, but then he couldn't see me or any of the other people he was jealous of; once the object of his hatred was out of sight, he was better.

"He's dangerous," Benito said, almost like he hadn't meant to say it out loud.

"Agreed," I said.

Rafael hugged me one-armed as we walked. "You need to have a guard with you at all times, Anita."

"So I'm not the only one that thinks Kane's jealous rages are getting scarier," I said.

"They are getting worse," Benito said.

"If he were not Asher's hyena to call, I might urge something more permanent be done before Kane hurts someone I care about," Rafael said, kissing the top of my head.

"I even agree with you. We wouldn't even have to do anything but let Kane get all ragey at the wrong person and let nature take its course," I said, "except if Kane dies, Asher may die with him."

"It is admirable that Asher has taken his therapy so seriously, Anita, but he tied himself to Kane before the therapy," Rafael said.

Benito said, "I do not approve of therapy or medication, but the change in Asher since he went on the meds is impressive."

"I'm not a big believer in finding a happy pill either," I said, "but seeing the difference in Asher, I might have to rethink that for certain things."

"My understanding was that it is a biochemical imbalance," Rafael said.

"Yeah, which means that Asher really couldn't help some of what he was doing."

"How do you feel about Jean-Claude having taken Asher back as his lover?" Rafael said, kissing the top of my head again.

"If you're wanting to know if Jean-Claude has asked me to take Asher back, then we've talked about it. Nathaniel and I have talked about it, too."

He turned us outside the locker rooms so he could see my face as he asked, "And how do you feel about Asher?"

I had to look away from those big brown eyes while I tried to sort out my feelings and how much I wanted to talk about them. "I miss him in some ways, but I'm a big believer that if you can't handle someone at their worst, then you don't deserve them at their best, and I can't handle him at his worst."

Rafael put his finger under my chin and gently raised my face so he could see my own brown eyes. His brown eyes and black hair were from his Mexican heritage just like mine. I had my German father's pale skin, but the rest of me was my mother's, so I was told, and so pictures showed me. She'd died when I was eight, so I didn't remember that much of her, and what I did remember was filtered through the child I had been when she died, which meant I could never see that I looked like her without the pictures.

Rafael was like my parents—first generation born in this country. I was second generation. We both thought of ourselves as American, and most people didn't even realize I had Hispanic heritage. I could pass, as they say, though I'd never been pale enough for my blond stepmother, but that was a sad racist story for another time.

I looked up into Rafael's face, dark brown skin to match the hair and eyes. He couldn't hide what he was, and I didn't try to hide, I just didn't think about it until

something made me think about it. Planning the wedding
with Jean-Claude had made me have to think more about
my family; so far my father wasn't going to walk me
down the aisle, because I was marrying a vampire, which
meant I was damning myself for all eternity in the eyes
of the Catholic Church. My family were devout Cath-
olics.

"So many serious thoughts going through your eyes,"
he said.

I shook my head. "Nothing worth sharing."

He gave me the look that all my semiserious people
got eventually, the one that said they didn't believe me
when I said it was nothing. "It's okay if you love Asher. I
don't see what any of you see in him, but I don't have to,
he's not my boo."

"He's not my boo either," I said, and wondered if I was
protesting a bit too much.

Rafael gave me a look, as if he was wondering the
same thing, which pissed me off and made me draw my
face back, so I wasn't resting on his hand.

Benito said, "If he is so unimportant to you, then why
do you risk Rafael's life because of the mess Asher has
caused with the local werehyenas?"

"Benito, it is not your place . . ." Rafael started to say.

"If not mine, then whose, my king? It is my sworn
duty to keep you safe, but I cannot fight your challenges
for you. If Anita would make you her rat to call, you
would gain enough power to win against any challenger."

"Why did you get another challenger this soon?" I
asked.

It was Rafael's turn to look away from me, as if he
wasn't sure what I'd see in his eyes. I grabbed the tank
top and used it to pull him toward me. "You just fought a
duel out of town two weeks ago. You're a good king, a
great leader, why is this one challenging you again so
soon?" I'd learned that any challenger for rulership among

the wererats, the rodere, had to give a reason for it, and the reason had to make sense to enough of the wererats for them to vote on it. If a challenger had a bogus reason for the fight, then they could just vote that the reason wasn't good enough to risk their king.

"Tell her, Rafael," Benito said.

"I am king here, not you!" His anger brought his beast like a line of heat across my skin. I had to let go of him and step back so I could do a few deep, even breaths. I couldn't change shape for real, but I still carried the beasts inside me, and one of those was rat.

"You are my king, but she needs to know what is happening."

"One of you tell me, because it's starting to make me nervous."

Rafael motioned at Benito. "You want to tell her, tell her."

Benito looked startled as if he hadn't expected that, but he recovered quickly and gave me very serious eyes. Whatever he was going to say, he didn't expect me to like it. "The reason given for this challenge is that they are afraid that once you make Rafael your rat to call, all the wererats in the United States will be slaves to the vampires through Jean-Claude's ties to you as his human servant."

"The local clan here would know that's not true," I said.

"But I am no longer just the king of the St. Louis clan. I am king to all the wererats in this country, so they are all voting."

I frowned at him. "How are all the wererats voting in time for the fight tonight?"

"Online, we created a poll online," he said.

"How's the voting going?"

"I am losing."

"Jesus, I guess I can understand that if they don't

know me or Jean-Claude personally, they'd be worried. They have no idea that we're not evil bastards."

"They know your reputation as a legal executioner of us, and they have seen the videos that people took in Colorado when you raised a zombie army," Rafael said.

"If I say the bad necromancer raised his army of the undead first and I had to stop him, does that make it any better?" I smiled, hopefully playing to the fact that I was small and if I was willing to stoop to it, I could be adorable. I'd hated it for years, but some of the women in my life had taught me that feminine wiles weren't just about sex, cuteness was its own superpower. If only I'd known about it years ago, or been willing to stoop to use it.

Rafael laughed, but Benito was made of sterner stuff. "Your reputation is fearsome, Anita. If you were Rafael's mate, it would make him powerful, but you are engaged to Jean-Claude, you will be queen to the vampire king of this country. It frightens our people."

"I carry just as much shapeshifter magic as vampire inside me," I said.

"But they have seen you with your zombies online from people filming you with their phones. They have seen you on Jean-Claude's arm in the engagement video and more and more interviews as the wedding gets closer, but you do not change form, and they have not seen you with us. They have not felt your power as leopard queen to Micah's king. They have not felt the pull of your inner rat. They feel you feed on them through Rafael, and that scares the hell out of them."

"I think that's the longest speech I've ever heard you make," I said.

"I must speak up for Rafael, for he will not."

"The threat has to be serious for you to push like this, Benito. Is this new guy a really good fighter or something?"

Benito nodded.

"How good?" I asked.

"Good enough that I am frightened for my king and my friend."

That scared me because Benito didn't talk that way.

"Do you have so little faith in me in the fighting pit?" Rafael asked.

"You are good, incredibly good, my king. You were fierce today in practice."

"But you do not think I am fierce enough to win against Hector."

"I think you can win, but if the vote goes against you, then all the next challenger has to do is use the same excuse and they can simply challenge you time after time. No one is good enough to withstand that; eventually everyone loses. In a fight to first or even third blood it is a loss of reputation, but it is not fatal."

"Can fights for the crown be to just third blood, the way lesser challenges are?" I asked. I couldn't help looking at the black crown branded into Rafael's forearm. It was the mark of kingship among the rodere and gave the St. Louis clan its name, the Dark Crown Clan.

Benito just shook his head.

"Is there anything else I need to know, while we're being chatty?" I asked.

"Yes," Benito said.

"No," Rafael said.

"Benito," I said.

"Please, my king, my friend, she must know that you broke one of our most sacred rules."

"She does not change form, she is not a true wererat, so the rule does not apply."

"Someone tell me the rule, so I can decide if it applies to me or not."

The two men glared at each other. Claudia called from down the hallway. "Anita deserves to know." I looked to see if Kane was with her, but she was alone. She must have seen me look for him, because she added, "Helios is taking Kane through a new weight routine. I've got two extra guards with them. They'll all get their weight lifting in for the day, and Kane will have enough people to sit on him if it's needed."

"If Kane is that dangerous to Anita, he must be put down," Benito said.

"We can't risk killing Asher," I said.

"But you will risk killing Rafael," he said.

"Benito, enough," Rafael said.

"Please, Rafael, please, Anita needs to know," Claudia said.

Claudia didn't plead with anyone for anything. My stomach was suddenly tight with anxiety. Then I realized that Benito and Rafael had already given me enough clues. "I know that other than a few attack survivors or freak accidents, there is only one way to become part of the rodere. You must fight for it. I didn't think about that applying to me, because I wasn't asking to join the rodere."

Claudia said, "Yes, if you were a normal human being who wanted to be one of us, you would have blades and fight one of us in half-beast form."

"Not fight, Claudia," Rafael said, "simply draw blood once, before one of us can bloody them three times."

It was interesting that Rafael didn't think of that as a fight, but I didn't debate it, just said, "That's one of the reasons you are all such bad-ass fighters, because you have to be to even get into the clan."

"Exactly, but our king brought you over as if he was a leopard, or a lion, or any other animal group with a lover," Benito said.

"It's the only form of Therianthropy that I volunteered to take on, all the others were accidents or attacks."

"I hate the new politically correct vocabulary," Rafael said.

"The idea was that lycanthropy meant just were-wolves, but Therianthropy means all forms," I said.

"I know what the words mean, but we all understood that *lycanthrope* had become the generic for all of us."

"Therianthropy is pretty straightforward, too," I said.

"Yes, but they didn't stop there, the social justice warriors, they had to create new names for all of us. Arouraiothropy is impossible to spell, and most of us can't even agree on a pronunciation."

"I agree that the new vocabulary is ridiculous, but as a marshal I have to use it, or I get written up."

"Did you get written up already?" Claudia asked.

"Yes."

"By whom? Because it wasn't one of us that complained," Rafael said.

"Another marshal," I said.

"If Anita would fight in the pits to just first blood with one of us, then she would have earned her place and that would slow the challenges," Benito said.

"As her bodyguard, I can't agree," Claudia said.

"You guard her, but you are sworn to serve Rafael."

"If we let them bully us into making Anita fight in the pit, our enemies could maneuver us into Anita being forced to fight a true battle. Not against one of us, but against one of our kind who could take the chance offered and hurt Anita badly."

"Are they allowed to kill the human who's fighting them?" I asked.

"No," Claudia and Benito said.

"But the wererat is within their rights to demand that the human draw to third blood just as they must," Rafael said.

"What happens if I lose?" I asked.

"Normally you would simply not be allowed to become one of us. If the next full moon doesn't see the defeated human turn, then it is over," Rafael said.

"And if a defeated human turns on the full moon?" I asked.

"They are hunted down and killed," Benito said.

"Because they didn't earn it," I said.

He nodded.

"That is our way," Rafael said.

"I don't turn, I can't turn, so even if I lose, I should be fine."

"Jean-Claude will never allow you to risk yourself on the sands of our fighting pits," Rafael said.

"He's not the boss of me yet," I said.

Rafael smiled. "I am not certain anyone will ever be the boss of you, Anita Blake, but I would not risk the alliances we have built up between all of us on something that will not stop the duels for kingship."

"It would show that you still honor the ways of the rodere and that Anita respects our ways. That would calm some of the worst fears that you are abandoning our culture in favor of Micah and his leopards," Benito said.

"Why Micah in specific?" I asked.

"He travels the country as head of the Coalition that is bringing unity to all the animal groups," Benito said.

"Yeah, Micah is the poster boy for the cause of better relations between humans and Therianthropes, and all the flavors of shapeshifter," I said.

"Some among my people think it should have been me in charge of the Coalition."

I looked at Rafael. "You travel for the Coalition almost as much as Micah does now."

"But I am still not the head of it, which has led to some saying I am his second-in-command. That Micah is becoming high king to all the beasts, as I became high king to all the wererats."

"You run the wererats. Micah stays out of rodere business unless you ask for his help."

"You know that and I know that, but the fearful among

my people do not believe that, and my enemies actively tell the fearful that I am but a puppet for Micah and his lover Jean-Claude."

"They are not lovers," I said, automatically, but not like I expected anyone to believe it. You can't prove someone didn't do something, especially if it's a really good rumor.

"Everyone standing here knows that," Rafael said.

"It's not if Micah is fucking Jean-Claude that is the problem, it is that our enemies say that Rafael is fucking him," Benito said.

I stared up at him. "That's a new rumor," I said.

The three of them shook their heads.

"Okay, it's new to me."

"It reinforces the idea that if Rafael becomes even more closely bound to you and Jean-Claude, we will all be his for the taking," Benito said.

"Jean-Claude isn't into rape," I said, and in my head I thought he'd suffered too much and too often at the hands of more powerful vampires over the centuries; it had left him with no taste for forcing himself where he wasn't wanted, though admittedly he was around six hundred years old, so his idea of seduction was a little less than politically correct, but he did not do rape. Somewhere before the last deed was done the person had to say yes.

"Again, we have seen how fair Jean-Claude is, but our enemies have not," Rafael said.

"Make Rafael your *moitié bête*, Anita. Give him enough power to defeat our shared enemies so decisively that they will fear to challenge him to the pits," Benito said.

"You know why I haven't."

"Because Narcissus has sworn to kill Kane if you make me your rat to call before you make him your hyena to call," Rafael said.

"Which risks killing Asher," I said.

"I say again that Rafael is more important than the vampire," Benito said.

"That is not your decision to make," Rafael said.

"Wait, if I make Rafael my rat, won't that just invite more challengers for the same reason as tonight's fight? I mean he really will be more closely tied to Jean-Claude afterward."

"They will challenge him afterward, but once they see what his new power level can do to an opponent, that will be the end of the duels," Benito said.

"There is no way to know that for certain, Benito," Rafael said.

"I am certain of it."

"That whole Asher problem," I said.

"Then make Narcissus your hyena to call and then Rafael your rat to call. You are not like most vampires, Anita, you can have as many *moitié bêtes* as you have beasts inside you."

I'd have liked to argue the whole vampire question, since I didn't feed on blood, but I did have to feed on either anger or lust, or I stopped healing as well. I didn't make the legal definition of vampire, but then no energy vampire met the legal criteria. "I don't want to tie myself to Narcissus, he's almost as crazy obsessive with Asher as Kane is, so no thanks. I don't want that much drama llama tied to me for all eternity."

"Then tell Narcissus that and seal your bargain with us, Anita," Benito said.

"It's not that simple, Benito."

"Everything is simple if you do not complicate it," he said.

I wasn't sure what I would have said to that, because Rafael said, "I would take your kisses and more with me tonight. I do not want to argue away the time we might have."

"You're really worried," I said, studying his face.

"Let me go into battle with the feel of your body like a shield. Let my challenger smell you on my skin. Let him be as intoxicated by the mere breath of you on my lips." He touched my face, raised it up for a kiss. What could I do? I went up on tiptoe to meet him partway.

I moved back from the kiss to say, "That's still the plan, but we were going to all work out, clean up, and then have our . . . date before the fight." It wasn't really a date, but I just couldn't make myself call it a hookup, or a fuck date, at least not in front of Benito and Claudia.

"We could be very efficient and use the shower together. We could clean up and start our date early."

I knew that Micah and Nathaniel were having their own "date" currently, and Jean-Claude was in the sword class he'd started with some of the older vampires and shapeshifters. In fact, everyone I might have spent time with was either exercising, working, or otherwise occupied.

"Unless you are expected elsewhere by one of your other lovers," Rafael said. He managed to be almost neutral as he said it.

"No, nothing scheduled but cleaning up, and you're right, sharing the shower would be efficient and it would conserve water." I tried to be serious as I said it, but a smile crept in at the end.

The smile he gave in return was worth saying yes. It chased all the gloom and doom away and left him looking happy. We started walking hand in hand toward the showers, and this time we didn't stop to debate anything.

3

RAFAEL AND I were holding hands and all romantic until we got close enough to the showers to hear the rumble of male voices and realize that the four of us weren't the only people showering. If I'd been by myself, I'd have used the shower in the room I shared with Nathaniel and Micah, but it seemed a little awkward to use their shower when I was planning on getting a different man out of his clothes. Also, I wasn't sure where they were on their date, and since Micah was still working out his issues about it being just the two of them without a girl in sight, I didn't want to crash their rendezvous. Nathaniel was for Micah what Kane kept trying to make me for Asher—the one person who had changed his sexual orientation, except in this case Micah had been heterosexual until he fell in love with Nathaniel.

"What's wrong?" Rafael asked.

I realized that I'd stopped moving forward, so he was a little ahead of me with our arms stretched between us. "Showers are a little crowded for romance."

He looked up as if he'd only just heard the water and the male voices raised in good-natured shit giving. It was Claudia who said, "We are wereanimals, Anita, we don't notice nudity."

I looked up at her. "You all keep saying that and most of the time it's true, but all it takes is one guard noticing the naked girl in the room and suddenly it's awkward as hell."

"Who noticed and made you uncomfortable?" she asked, and her voice was back to that drill-sergeant/boss-from-hell/parent you're-in-deep-shit tone again.

"The werewolf, Ricky," I said.

"Which is why we fired him," she said.

"He was also not good enough to be part of our guard," I said.

"He did not train hard enough to get better," she said.

"No, he whined almost as much as Kane," I said.

"If this Ricky is gone, why are you so apprehensive?" Rafael asked.

"I could just shower with the other people in there, and I have, but you and I were going to get each other out of our clothes and have at least foreplay in the shower. I don't like an audience."

"Nor I, but we can use one of the closed showers with curtains," he said.

"Like Claudia said, you're wereanimals, so it's not just sight that's the problem. To most of you smell and hearing are as intimate as a visual."

I liked the curtained shower stalls, and I wasn't the only one. It hadn't been just me among the women that didn't like showering with the men. I'd even come in more than once to find men in the curtained stalls. Men like more privacy than you think, or at least some do. It's not only women who are modest; another double standard bites the dust.

He took the step back to me and used our still-clasped hands to draw me into a hug. "That is true, but I want as much of you as I can have today, Anita. I am willing to use the showers with curtains."

I put my free hand on his chest where it showed above

the tank top. The skin was smooth and warm, the sweat already drying. "The other thing is that having sex while the other guards are in the room might make them all wonder if it's okay for them, too."

"They would not dare approach you," Rafael said.

"Probably not, but the other female guards might have a harder time in the showers."

"I won't have any problems," Claudia said.

"They're afraid of you and me for different reasons, but they're not afraid of most of the other female guards. Also do we want to encourage everyone to have sex in the public showers here?"

"It wouldn't be the first time for you and one of your . . . people," Claudia said, and then looked almost embarrassed, which didn't happen often. She was like most bodyguards—nothing their clients did fazed them.

"Yeah, but that time you made sure it was just Nicky and me, and I almost drained him to death," I said, frowning.

Rafael hugged me closer. "I am not your Bride of Dracula to be drained of life by the *ardeur*, Anita."

"And I have better control over the *ardeur* than I did back then," I said.

"We can kick everyone else out," Benito said.

"They're in the middle of showering," I protested.

"I'll go in and tell them all to hurry up and finish." Claudia nodded. "Yes, do that."

"Wait, no," I said, as Benito started to move past us. He turned and looked at me.

"What is wrong, Anita?" Rafael asked.

"It just seems, I don't know, high-handed to kick them out of the group showers."

Rafael laughed and kissed me on the forehead. "It is adorable that you keep forgetting that you are both their employer and a queen."

I frowned up at him. Most short people hate to be

called adorable; even *cute* can be problematic. "I'm their boss, but technically Jean-Claude pays their salaries so he's their employer, and I'm not a queen yet, not until I marry Jean-Claude."

"You are the queen of tigers," he said.

"That's only because I didn't like being called the mother of all tigers," I said.

"Most of the ex-Harlequin guard call you their dark queen," Benito said.

"They're used to following a queen, as in thousands of years of being the elite guard for the Queen of All Darkness." I shuddered when I said her name. I'd killed the vampire queen of the old council, if you could kill something that didn't have a body. I'd killed her as dead as humanly and inhumanly possible.

"Anita did try to break them of calling her their dark queen," Claudia said.

I sighed and leaned in against Rafael's body a little, resting my cheek against his tank top and the solidness underneath it. "I did break most of them from calling me their evil queen."

He hugged me close, kissing the top of my head. "I am sorry, Anita, I did not mean to bring up something that makes you uneasy."

"That's a good word for it," I said, still with my head on his chest. I didn't say out loud that *afraid* was a better one. I'd killed the Mother of All Darkness by absorbing her essence while she tried to take over my body and use it for herself. It had been sort of the immovable object meeting the unstoppable force, and most people had been betting on her. She had been the very first vampire, maybe, so old that her original body had been lost and the last body she'd had had been one that she'd successfully possessed. That body had been blown up by a group of mercenaries hired to assassinate her, but all they'd done was destroy the body that had trapped her for a thousand years. They had freed her from her prison to wander like a nightmare to try and find a new body. She'd wanted mine.

Rafael stroked my hair and murmured, "She is dead and gone, Anita. You do not need to fear her."

I moved out of the circle of his arms. "You never had her try to take over your dreams, or your body."

"You are quite right," he said; his face was closed down, reasonable, and blank, hiding what he was feeling and thinking.

"I feel like I should apologize to you, but I don't know what for," I said.

He gave a very small smile, but it left his eyes sad. "If I were truly a gentleman, we would shower separately and I would prepare for tonight's battle, but I want to be with you too much to play such games."

"I want you, too, Rafael," I said, because that's what you're supposed to say when someone declares that kind of attraction. It's like when someone says *I love you*; you're supposed to say it back if it's even remotely true, unless you're willing to have that most awkward of modern dating talks, the one where you try to explain that it's not about love.

"I can only take your words at face value, search your face to see if it matches them, because I cannot read your mind, feel your emotions."

"You can smell my emotions on my skin, all shapeshifters can," I said.

"In this moment I know you are not feeling lust, because you are right, I would smell it on you."

I fought not to look embarrassed or even uncomfortable. I looked at the floor and then forced myself to look up and meet his gaze. "I can't smell your emotions, but I can read your face and you're not feeling very lustful either."

"I cannot disagree, and if this were any other day, I

would let you go to shower in the room where you shower with your other men, or perhaps that huge bathtub that Jean-Claude has in his rooms, but it is not any other day. I want you as a man wants a woman, but I also want you to feed the *ardeur* on me."

"Won't that weaken you for the fight tonight?"

"If you fed off only me, perhaps, but you will feed off the strength of all who call me king. If it is to be the last time, I want you to take as much power from us as possible for Jean-Claude to share among your people."

I touched his arm, studying his face, trying to read him. "I asked if you thought you would win tonight, and you said yes. Am I missing something? Am I not asking the right questions?"

"He is me thirty years ago, Anita. He has less to lose and more to gain. I have far more to lose and nothing to gain except his death, which I do not want. I think he believes that you will enslave us all, you and Jean-Claude. He is righteous in his goal to tear me from the throne. I am defending what is mine, and I am decades too late for that righteous surety of youth."

"I don't understand what that means."

He smiled down at me, putting his bigger hand along the side of my face so that I could rub my face against the weight and warmth of his hand. "Of course you don't, you still have that righteous surety."

I moved away from his hand, frowning. "Not as much as I used to have."

"You are starting to grow into the next stage of your life, Anita. Your job as a vampire executioner and now as a marshal has aged your attitude faster. Hector knows nothing but his clan. He has risen as high as he can within the local clan, so he sets his sight on the highest seat among my kind."

"You said he's you thirty years ago."

"Very much so."

"So how old is he?"

"Are you asking how old I am?"

I stared up at his raven-black hair, the unlined face. If I hadn't looked into the wisdom and patience in his eyes, I'd have put him at no more than thirty, but his eyes gave it away almost like some of the vampires' did. They were ageless, but their eyes could show an echo of the great weight of all those years, as if there were ways to grow old that had nothing to do with the body.

"I know that shapeshifters age slower than humans," I said.

He smiled. "I am over fifty."

I must have looked as shocked as I felt, because he laughed. "Sorry, it's just . . . I'd have never guessed."

He drew me into another hug, still laughing.

"We'll clear the showers for you," Claudia said, and she and Benito started toward the entrance, but there was a small crowd of guards hastily dressed coming out. They mumbled, "Anita, Rafael, Claudia," and a few mentioned Benito but he wasn't their boss, or one of the people who trained them, or a king of any kind. He didn't take offense, like all good bodyguards, he knew being invisible until needed was part of the job.

"I think they heard us," I said, not sure how I felt about the fact that Rafael and I just suggesting we might want them to give us the showers was enough to get them to do it, or maybe it was Claudia and Benito starting to clear them out? I knew that Claudia intimidated a lot of them, and if Benito wasn't as scary as he looked, then he wouldn't be Rafael's main bodyguard.

When the exodus of tall, athletic men clutching clothes and weapons trickled to a stop, Rafael offered me his hand. "Shall we?"

What else could I say but "Yes"?

Claudia insisted on going through the doorway first, even though we were supposed to be safe as houses down here. There were bodyguards I might have argued with; she wasn't one of them. Benito trailed behind his king and incidentally me, but I had no illusions about whom he'd protect if the flags went up, but then I had Claudia, so I was good.

4

THE SHOWERS WEREN'T completely empty, though; Pierette was still in there with her dark hair still damp and her only clothing one of the supersize towels that we kept in there for everyone. The towels were designed to cover people close to seven feet tall, like Claudia, so for Pierette, who was only a few inches taller than me, the towel covered her to the ankles like a formal evening gown. On me I had to fold the top of the towels down, so I didn't trip over them. One size does not fit all.

Pierette dropped to one knee and managed to make the movement look graceful, as if the towel were a real dress. I'd have knelt on it wrong and ended up flashing if I'd tried it, but then I hadn't had hundreds of years to practice being graceful and she had.

"My queen, King Rafael, how may I serve you?" She looked at the floor as she said it, so I couldn't even see her expression, which might have helped me know what the hell was going on.

"Pierette, I told you I didn't like the whole bowing and scraping thing," I said.

She raised her face up to look at me then, and without any makeup at all she was still pretty. Her eyes dominated her face even without eye makeup, but without eye-

liner or shadow the brown of them seemed paler, lighter
than mine or Rafael's. Her face was a delicate triangle
with her lips pale but still kissable without the red lipstick that she usually wore to match mine, but then I
wasn't wearing any right now either. I thought about
leaning over and giving her a kiss, but I wanted to know
why she was kneeling before I did anything. She was my
lover and I liked having her in our poly group, but sometimes she puzzled me.

"You did, my queen, but I was not certain how to approach both you and King Rafael, so on my knees seemed
to be a good place to start." She looked up at me as if that
made perfect sense.

"Approach us about what, Pierette?" I asked.

"For joining the two of you in the shower." Again, she
said it as if I should know what she was talking about,
and I was getting a clue, but I wasn't happy about it.

I felt Rafael's stare on the side of my face before I
turned and met it with my own. He raised eyebrows at me
and said, "What is going on, Anita?"

"Give me a minute, okay?"

He nodded but let go of my hand, as if I might need
both to handle the woman kneeling at our feet. "First, get
up off the floor," I said, and offered her my hand. She
took it and even let me take some of her weight as she
stood, though she didn't need a hand up any more than I
would have.

She stood with us still holding hands, and again I had
that urge to kiss her. If Rafael hadn't been standing right
there, I might have, or if she'd been one of my primary
partners, or . . . oh hell. "I want to kiss you, Pierette."

She smiled and started to lean in toward me, but I
stopped her, using my hand in hers to sort of stiff-arm
her. "But first I want to know why you think you're joining us in the shower."

She stopped trying to lean into me and looked puzzled. "I thought those of us that wished to sleep with King Rafael were supposed to make that known to him."

"What did she just say?" Rafael asked from behind me.

I sighed, closed my eyes, and tried to think of a good way to say the next part; nothing came to mind. I let go of Pierette's hand and turned and faced him. "So, I was wondering why you don't date more."

"Are you trying to say that you're tired of me?" he asked, face blank, but I knew the tension in his shoulders well enough to see it.

"No, not at all; God, this sounded way less awkward in my head. I love being with you, the sex is great, the friendship is, as it has always been, wonderful. I know that you have not just my back, but all of our backs, as we have yours."

"This sounds like a 'let's be friends' speech."

I made an exasperated sound and tried again. "It's not, I swear, but you're great and I sort of assumed that you were dating other women in a more serious way, but that you were just very private about it."

"You thought I was sleeping around on you?" he asked, frowning, clearly puzzled.

"No, no, that's not what I meant. Fine, I talked to my poly group about the fact that you were only having sex with me and I couldn't give you more time because I'm already sort of overcommitted relationship-wise, so I asked the group if they'd be okay with you maybe sleeping with any women in our group that were interested in you that way."

He looked even more puzzled. "Have I done or said anything to make you think that I need more sex from you?"

"No, but . . . I would need more sex. I would want more, so I was going to talk to you about it, but I wanted to make sure that some of the women in the poly group were okay with it first."

Pierette dropped back to her knees. "My queen, I am so sorry, you have not spoken with him yet."

"Nope," I said.

She started to try to press more of herself to the ground at my feet, but I caught her arm in time. "Please don't grovel, Pierette, that really bugs me. We've talked about this."

She got up without me telling her to this time. "I am sorry though, truly. I did not know that you had not spoken to him."

"I just talked to all the rest of you two days ago. I hadn't seen Rafael yet."

"My deepest apologies to both of you," she said.

I sighed and turned back to the man in question. I couldn't read the expression on his face, because it was a new one. "You're fighting for your crown tonight; I wouldn't have brought it up today."

Pierette started to drop back down, but I yelled, "Pierette!" It stopped her in midmotion, and she stood there with her towel, looking truly contrite, and still sort of adorable. It was weird for me to think of other women as adorable, but there it was; I was starting to think I might owe some men an apology for getting angry with them when they'd called me cute or adorable over the years.

"I am sorry that I do not please you, King Rafael." She said it eyes down so she couldn't see the emotions that flew across his face.

He smiled. "You are beautiful, and I am sure delightful in many ways; please do not think that it is lack of charm that makes me hesitate."

She looked at him then, and I knew the look, because it worked on me. She was trying to be cute for him, interesting. "Then I do not understand, Your Majesty."

He frowned, I think at the title, but he didn't correct her, or maybe he, like me, wasn't sure if it needed correcting, or if it was accurate. "Anita, are you saying that if I said yes, this would be happening now?"

"You mean the three of us sharing the shower and maybe more?" I asked.

"Yes, that is what I mean."

I sort of shrugged. "Like I said, I was going to talk to you about it."

"So that's a yes," he said.

I nodded. "Yes, I hadn't planned on it happening this soon, but yes."

He shook his head. "It's a trap."

I frowned at him. "What's a trap?"

"The offer of a three-way."

"Um, a trap for what?" I asked.

"I've had this offer before from other women that I've dated, and it's always a trap."

"How is it a trap?" I asked.

"Either the girlfriend uses it as a test to see if I'll cheat . . ."

"It's not cheating if she tries to get you to have a three-way with her and another woman," I said.

"That's not how she saw it," he said.

"That's so not fair," I said.

He smiled. "Thank you, I agree with you."

"That would be a trap," Pierette said.

I looked at her and then we nodded together.

"Or the three-way happens, the sex is good, everything's good that night, but in the morning one or both of the women decide that it was an awful idea and it's my fault somehow," Rafael said.

"Your fault how?" I asked.

"Being a man, I think, somehow being lusty enough to want and satisfy two women. I don't know, Anita, Pierette, it didn't make sense to me at the time."

"So, every time any woman has offered you a chance

to sleep with her and another woman, it's been a trap?" I asked.

"Yes," he said.

"Well, Pierette is my girlfriend, so . . ."

He shook his head. "Tried that, ended up with them being jealous of the time I had with each of them and it broke us all up."

"Were they polyamorous?" I asked.

He thought about that. "No, bisexual, but not poly."

"Then there was your problem," I said.

"I believe that you mean what you say, Anita, you usually do, and I do appreciate the offer, but no matter how well it begins, it has always ended in drama, breaking up, and sometimes violence."

"What kind of violence?" I asked.

"One of them stabbed me."

I stared at him. "Shit, that's . . . tell me you pressed charges. I hate the double standard that if a woman hurts a man, she gets a pass just because she's a girl. Equality means just that; you do something awful, you get the same punishment."

He shook his head. "It was a steak knife, no silver in the steel. There wouldn't even be a wound by the time police could arrive; besides, I am a king and a wererat, it would have made me look weak."

"Did you feel she was justified? I mean not stabbing you, but did you cheat on her or something?"

"The morning after the three-way that was her idea, with the woman of her choice, she woke up third in the bed. Her friend and I were kissing."

"You thought you had her permission," I said.

"We both did, but she got out of bed obviously upset, so I went after her, trying to understand what I'd done wrong."

"Which was what?" I asked.

He smiled. "I think when it was all over, her complaint was that I hadn't kissed her awake first. She wanted to share me with her friend, but she didn't want me to like her friend better."

"Wow, I understand why you're leery of being with two women at once now. I'm like totally sorry that Pierette sprang it on you like this, and we can skip it, or talk later, or whatever makes you the most comfortable."

"Thank you," he said.

"Wait a second, what did you do to the woman who stabbed you if the police weren't involved?"

"I broke up with her; why, what did you think I had done to her?"

"Trying to kill the king for most shapeshifter groups is an automatic death sentence outside of a formal challenge."

"It was suggested by some of my people, but she didn't really want me dead. She was horrified as soon as she saw the blood. She begged my forgiveness, professed her love for me. I think she even meant it."

"Abusers are always sorry afterward, but it's still not love," I said.

He studied my face. "You consider what she did the same as a man hitting a woman?"

"If you stab someone because you're jealous of them, that's crazy and abusive no matter what sex you are—it's not okay for a man to do it, or a woman to do it, or anyone to do that to another human being because they're jealous of them."

"Very practical," he said.

"You look and feel like you're not outraged by it, like it was okay. You know it's not okay, right? You know that was not your fault, or justified in any way, right?" I asked.

"I do now, but it would take me years after it happened to understand that."

"How can you not know that's not okay, Rafael?"

"I am attracted to sexy, crazy, unstable women, and that is my fault."

"Should I be insulted?" I asked with a smile.

It was his turn to look embarrassed. "No, no, you are the most stable relationship I've ever had."

I didn't know what to say to that, because it seemed sad. "Really?"

He laughed. "The look on your face, Anita, and yes, really. No matter how sane and together they seem, if I'm attracted to them, they are seriously unstable. Some hide their insanity better than others, but it's always there. The harder I am driven to pursue a woman, the crazier she will prove to be."

"Even your ex-wife?" I asked.

He nodded. "Oh, yes. I learned not to marry in haste after that one."

"I'm so sorry," I said.

"Don't be, I've learned my lesson. I simply don't date unless someone else chooses the woman for me."

"Are you serious?" I asked.

"Very serious."

"Your taste in women is that bad?"

He nodded.

"That is a terrible burden," Pierette said.

He looked at her. "Thank you for understanding that it is exactly that."

"So, with me you get sex, but don't have to worry about the relationship part."

"You do sex like you're the crazy girlfriend, but you do relationships as logically and as pragmatically as any woman I've ever met."

"Thank you, I think, but I'm not sure about the last part. I don't feel very logically when I'm in love."

"No one does," Pierette said.

He turned to her with a smile. "Thank you so much for being willing to try this with us, Pierette. It is a lovely offer and you are a lovely woman, but for tonight Anita and I need to talk about what it might mean for our arrangement, and she has to convince me that it won't blow up in my face." He took her hand in his and laid his lips across her knuckles as it was meant to be, not an actual kiss. Jean-Claude had taught me the difference, just as he'd taught me to let him raise my hand to his lips and not to try to raise my hand to him and smack him in the mouth.

Pierette got her clothes and her weapons out of the little locker, and then she left the way some of the other guards had, with her belongings in her arms, as if we wouldn't have waited for her to dress. It was awkward, but not as awkward as the conversation had been.

When we were alone, I said, "Sorry that she sprang that on you."

"It was a lovely thought, Anita, but thank you for understanding that I am gun-shy about it."

"It's not just the one who stabbed you that offered a threesome, is it?"

He smiled, shrugged, and finally said, "I am attracted to women who are willing to try anything once, or who are already doing nonstandard sex, but also I am king of the rodere. Our women used to fight over who would be in my bed."

"Do you mean really fight for the privilege?" I asked.

He smiled, looked embarrassed, and then nodded. "If the king has a clear choice, then there is no need, but once I stopped trying to date seriously within the rodere, the fights began. It is part of our culture that a great many things are settled with fights. Except for the battle for king, it does not have to be to the death, it can be to just first blood, but it is a way our people settle many things."

"I've never heard of any of the women in your clan fighting over you," I said.

"It was hurting us as a clan, so I ruled that if they

fought for me, neither would win a place in my bed. I finally had to simply not date anyone within our clan, and then as I became king of more rat clans, I just ran out of dating possibilities. The power and stability were more important to me, and as I ruled over more people and land, I found that I didn't have time to pursue a relationship, and here we are."

"Wow, now I'm sort of embarrassed that I brought the topic up with our poly group, because it's going to hit all sorts of issue buttons for you."

"Who else besides Pierette agreed to it?" he asked, and the fact that he asked it at all meant that he was still intrigued by the idea.

"Angel's arm went up so fast I thought she'd pop a ligament."

He laughed.

"Fortune was interested, but I think Echo is feeling that they're spreading themselves too thin now."

"They have been a couple for hundreds of years, that must take precedence," he said.

I nodded. "Yeah, till death do you part can last a hell of a long time when one of you is a vampire."

"Only if the vampire makes you their human servant, or their animal to call, so you share their ageless immortality," he said.

"If I make you my rat to call, I can't promise I have any ageless immortality to share. I'm not a real vampire, I just share some of the powers of one."

"I know, it is not for that reason I wish you to mark me."

"You want the power," I said.

He nodded. "I do."

"It's not that simple, Rafael."

"Some of the people in your life are afraid that tying yourself to me will take time and attention from them," he said.

I must have looked surprised, because he added, "I

have spoken with Micah at length. He told me that some of your secondaries already feel they do not get enough of you."

"I guess that's another reason I thought about you sleeping with some of the other women. I thought that might take the pressure off the just-you-and-me dynamics and calm all the insecure people down," I said.

"It is a good idea, Anita, but one thing I've learned dating crazy, passionate women is that logic and good ideas cannot reassure an insecure person. No matter what you do, it is never enough, because the insecurity is inside them and only they can fix it."

"Wise words," I said.

"I try, but I would like to leave wisdom behind now."

"What did you have in mind?" I asked, smiling.

"Fuck me like you're one of my crazy exes."

I laughed.

"Then feed on me, feed on all the rats, take as much energy as you can."

"You don't want me to take that much," I said.

"No, but take what you can, just in case."

"I'll have to alert everyone that I'm taking that big a feeding, so no one is driving a car or something where they need to concentrate," I said.

"Benito has already sent out the text chain to let my people know."

I could have argued that he should have asked me before the text went out, but I didn't. He'd been proactive, I sort of liked that. Competency and confidence were sexy, and Rafael had both of those in spades.

5

WE GOT OUR clothes off in a rush of hands and eager kisses, but once we got into the shower, it slowed down to hands gliding over and exploring smooth, wet skin.

Rafael drew back to gaze down at me, water running from his hair, down his face. I had to move back enough that I was in the void his body made in the pattern of the water drops so that the only water hitting me was a few stray drops as it poured over him.

"I want time with you, Anita. I'm not in the mood for a quickie," he said, raising his voice a little over the sound of the water.

"Okay," I said, "probably better not to hog the showers from everybody anyway." I tried to make it a joke, but his face stayed solemn and the weight of emotions in his eyes was almost too heavy to lift.

"Unless you need to go to one of your other lovers?" He smiled at the end, but the only thing that lifted was the edges of his lips; his eyes and expression stayed heavy and closed down. Not in a hiding-his-thoughts-from-me way, but as if his thoughts were too dark to hide from me.

"I already answered this question, Rafael. No, no one

else is expecting me. We're all supposed to be working out or have plans with other people."

"If you need to exercise more . . ."

I touched his lips with my fingers. He looked at me with eyes that looked like wounds, so full of defeat. What the hell was going on? Why was this fight different from all the others?

"I'm here for you, Rafael."

He wrapped his arms around me, holding me so that our nude bodies were as close as they could be without having sex, but it wasn't erotic. His body was still against mine. The earlier heat was just gone as if the shower had washed it away along with the sweat of the workout. I put the side of my face against his chest, using his body and my own head to direct the water away from my face so I could breathe if I was careful. If you took in a big gasping breath with water on either side of your face in a shower, you could inhale water, but I knew better.

He murmured into my wet hair, "Will you come watch me fight tonight, Anita?"

"I thought it was wererats only," I said.

"Usually, but I am allowed a mate who is outside the power structure."

"What does that mean, outside the power structure?"

"I am not the only king in our history who had problems dating within his clan. I am allowed a girlfriend, even a spouse who is not a wererat."

I rubbed the side of my face against his chest, carefully, so that I didn't end up with a face full of water. "If it won't cause more problems for you and the rest of us, then sure, I'll come and cheer you on tonight."

"I want you to see what a challenge is like, and I want you to see Hector before the fighting starts."

"Why do you want me to see him before the fight?" I asked.

He held me tighter, closer, and I wrapped my own

arms around his waist and held him harder as if just that would make things better. It didn't, but it didn't make them worse either.

"You should see him clean and strong before I hurt him."

"You're going to kill him, Rafael, what does it matter what he looks like alive and healthy?" I asked. I wanted to see his face, but we were holding each other too tightly; if I raised my face up, I'd drown.

"If I win, yes, but if he wins, then you need to seduce him, Anita. You need to do everything you can to protect those closest to both of us in my clan."

"That's it," I said, and tried to pull away from him, but he held me in place. I raised my face to try to see him and got a face full of high-pressure water. At least I hadn't breathed in, I thought as I tucked my face back against his chest. "Rafael, why are you talking like this?"

"It is always a possibility that I will lose, Anita, you know that."

"Damn it," I said, and fumbled behind him for the shower controls. I turned the wrong one and we were suddenly covered in icy water. I cursed and found the correct knob. The water stopped and it was suddenly quiet. He held me close, putting one hand against my head so I couldn't move enough to even see his face. I could have struggled and maybe made him let me go, or maybe he would have let me go just because I struggled, but in that moment I felt the strength of his arm around my body like iron made flesh and coated in a smooth, wonderful brown skin. His hand was like steel holding me in place, my face pressed against his chest. I could hear his heartbeat now, thick and sure of itself.

I let him hold me but didn't hold him back. I rested my hands on his hips; under other circumstances it would have been sexy, but not now. "What is going on, Rafael?" I felt ridiculous talking like this, all pressed to his chest, but I wanted him to answer my question more than I wanted to fight him over where I was standing.

"I have told you what is happening tonight," he said, his voice rumbling up through his chest against my face.

"I've seen you before other fights, Rafael, and this is not right, you're not right tonight. I don't know what is wrong, but you have to delay the fight."

"Why?" he asked, and he kissed the top of my wet hair.

"Because if you are convinced you will lose, then you will, that's true of all fighting."

"I will do my best for my people tonight, Anita."

"Tell me you will win tonight. Tell me you will kick his ass. Tell me you will kill him, Rafael."

"I will try." But his voice made a lie of it. He would try, but he didn't believe it would work.

I started pushing against him then. I couldn't stay pressed to him like this; I needed to see him, I needed to move. "Don't make me force you to let me go, Rafael."

"Do you think you could?" he asked, and there was just a hint of amused arrogance that a lot of the big athletic guys had. Good, at least that sounded like someone who planned to win, though I didn't really want it aimed at me.

I said, "I'd have to hurt you badly, but unless you were willing to hurt me back, yes, I can make you let me go, but I don't want to hurt you." Then I had an idea. "Would you being hurt postpone the fight?"

He laughed then and let go of me, stepping back as much as the shower stall would let him. His face was alight with laughter even as it faded. That was better already in so many ways.

"Do not hurt me to keep me from the fight tonight, Anita. If they thought that you were able to injure me that badly, it would be another weakness on the long list that my enemies have collected."

"Could you say that you were injured in training?" I asked.

"Why should I lie?"

"Because this is the most confident I've seen you in the last few minutes, and I don't want to send you into battle unless you know you can win."

He looked me in the eyes, probably the best eye contact he'd ever given me when we were both naked and alone, but this moment wasn't about sex, so the nudity truly didn't matter.

"I did not care about the first few challengers, they were no great loss to the rodere, or the organization I have built, but now we are starting to lose the future of our people. I have had my eye on Hector for a few years now. I was thinking of bringing him here and starting to train him, groom him to take over from me someday."

"Won't he have to kill you to do that?" I asked. I hugged my arms, because without the hot water it was starting to get chilly.

"No, he would have to kill the challenger who just killed me."

"I don't understand."

He handed me one of the towels from the hook outside the shower stall. I took it and started to dry off as he continued to talk. "I wanted to find a young wererat to train up to be my successor. Hector was on the list. In another five to ten years he could be what the rodere need, what the Coalition needs, but now he is too new, too inexperienced to lead us. It would be a disaster if he wins tonight."

"Yeah, you'd be dead," I said, and had to carefully towel-dry my hair without rubbing it or wrapping the towel on it, which breaks the curl. I and Micah had had the towel lecture from Jean-Claude for weeks as the wedding got closer. I'd be the bride, but Micah would be standing with us and God forbid our hair not look fabulous for the day. Even listening to Rafael now, I was careful to remember. So stupid, but it made Jean-Claude happy.

"My death would be a disaster now with no one to lead us, but someday I will lose, Anita. Someday all warriors grow old and weak, or when two people are of the same size and equally well trained it is sometimes luck that chooses the winner of a fight. In boxing or MMA, the loser lives to train harder, to learn from their mistakes and come back and win another day, but tonight will be a final loss for one of us."

"Before you were talking as if you couldn't win tonight. Is he really that much better than you?"

He shook his head. "No, I don't believe so, but I see his death as a waste of potential. I will mourn his loss to the rodere, but he will celebrate my death. I cannot afford to think like a king tonight and see a great warrior and the potential for so much more. I must be the fighter I once was not just in body, but in mind and attitude. I need the tunnel vision that Hector has, because he believes in his cause. He believes that I am selling us into slavery to the vampires through you and Jean-Claude."

"That's not true, you know it's not."

"And yet I cannot prove it to Hector or to any of my enemies. Even now I want you to feed on me tonight and take power from all of them."

"Proximity makes vampire abilities stronger, Rafael. If Hector has never been this geographically close when I fed the *ardeur* on you, then it's just going to convince him even more that I'm going to give you all to Jean-Claude as food and slaves."

"Sex slaves," Rafael said.

"Excuse me?"

He smiled, but not like it was entirely funny. "The rumor says that Jean-Claude's seductive powers will turn us all into sex slaves for him and his vampires and those wereanimals closest to him and you."

"I've heard that rumor that everyone who joins any group in St. Louis has to sleep with one of us, but the whole sex slave thing is new. Do they think we're pimping people out, or how will it work?"

"I do not know and neither does Hector, but he is homophobic, so the fact that I'm supposed to be sleeping with Jean-Claude seems to threaten him and other young men in our clans. The last fight I won was someone like Hector, someone I saw as a potential next king. Even if I win tonight, Anita, I am starting to destroy the future of all I have built, for a kingdom is only as good as its leader. If the person who follows after me is a bad king, then he will destroy everything that we have worked so long and hard for, and if I keep killing the best and brightest of our young men, then I will win the battles, but eventually the war will be lost. Do you understand what I mean?"

I nodded, wrapping the towel around me, and having to fold it at the top so that I'd be able to walk later without tripping. "I think so, you've defeated all the would-be kings who would have been bad leaders, but now you're starting to fight the ones that you think could rule, just not now and not yet."

"Exactly, even if I win tonight, it is still a loss for the future of my people."

"I don't care if it's a loss for future generations, Rafael. I don't give a flying fuck if Hector would age into being a great king. He doesn't get to kill you tonight. He doesn't get to wear your crown a decade too early. He isn't a fit ruler tonight, and tonight is all that matters, Rafael."

"So fierce, would you miss me that much, or is it only as an ally and a part of your power base that you will mourn me?"

"You know I care for you as more than a friend and ally."

"I'm attracted to crazy bitches, Anita; that means that love to me is about drama and screaming and horrible behavior. That makes me feel loved; as fucked up as that is, it is still the truth, and before you ask, I am speaking with the therapist that Micah recommended. I even know that I was raised by someone who was that kind of unstable crazy, and that is why I chase it. Knowing why doesn't change that it makes me feel loved, or that it tears down my life and breaks my heart again and again. I am a king and I cannot afford any more unstable would-be queens, but you are so sane, Anita, so pragmatic at times that I don't know what you feel, or what I feel."

"Therapy takes time," I said.

"I hope someday to be able to love a woman who doesn't play games or burn my belongings in the driveway."

"Or stab you," I said.

He smiled. "Yes, that, too, but I still miss the women who go with that kind of insanity."

"Do I say I'm sorry, or do you want me to pick some of your stuff that I don't think you'll miss much and plan a bonfire for you? We could roast hot dogs and make s'mores."

This time he smiled at my joke. Brownie points for me. "That will not be necessary, but perhaps a summer cookout in the backyard, around the pool, with s'mores toasted over the fire pit would be nice."

I smiled. "That sounds good."

"It does."

I handed him one of the other towels. "If you don't dry your hair soon, you'll have to wet it down and start over, and if I don't put in all the leave-in conditioners, Jean-Claude will make me start over on mine."

He started drying his hair, still smiling. "Let us find a bed and do more things that put a smile on both our faces."

I was about to agree with him when Jean-Claude

whispered through my head, "*Ma petite*, how close are you to feeding on Rafael?"

I very carefully thought back, "Why?"

I could suddenly see Jean-Claude still dressed for fencing practice, though the way he and the other older vampires practiced it was more traditional combat arts. I did mostly kali, which was Filipino martial arts, though my main instructor, Fredo, was helping me incorporate the knife skills I'd been using for years, so it wasn't a pure style of Sinawali, but as Fredo taught me, *What is kali? I am kali.* Which basically meant that you should do it the way that works best for you. Kali isn't just a martial art, it's a combat style, and that means you do it the way that keeps you alive. Martial arts have referees and point systems. Combat arts have, did you live? I liked all the blade classes, from the various types of sword and knife work to the axe class that Truth and Wicked had just begun teaching. Some people thought blades weren't practical for modern day, but they should look up the Tueller Drill. A regular human being with no supernatural speed can still stab you before you can draw, aim, and fire a gun if they're within twenty-one feet of you. Between twenty and eighteen feet you may shoot them as they stab you and die together, but eighteen to sixteen feet and they will stab, or club, or smash your brains in, faster than you can shoot them. But honestly even without the practical statistics, I just seemed to like anything with an edge. Saturday's class was vampires and were-animals that had lived when the sword was *the* weapon at a gentleman's side. It was one of the few blade classes I wasn't trying to take.

Jean-Claude smiled up at me, because my visual was looking down at him as if I were a hovering camera; it was always the view from the mind-to-mind peeks. His black curls were back in a loose ponytail, but with or without the hair to frame it his face was still almost too lovely to be real. Once I thought it was vampire wiles that made him so beautiful, but it was just him.

He said, "I am soon to take my turn upon the field, and I need my concentration. The sweetness of your combined release will be most distracting."

I didn't try to talk anymore; I just lowered my shields enough so he could see Rafael and where we were in the process.

Rafael said, "What does Jean-Claude want?"

It made me startle and look at the other man, which made me lose the visual of Jean-Claude. I started to ask him how he knew anyone had contacted me, let alone knew it was Jean-Claude, then I realized he was rubbing at the goose bumps on his arms. "You felt the energy," I said.

"I know when Jean-Claude is in your head."

I didn't have to file it away to share later, because Jean-Claude just knew what I knew, because he was in my head. "Interesting," he whispered, and then was gone so that Rafael and I were alone again in the showers. Our thoughts and our feelings private and ours again.

"He's at the new sword class the older vamps and shapeshifters are doing. He doesn't want us to be feeding the *ardeur* while he's on the practice mat."

"I didn't think they used live blades," Rafael said.

"They don't, but you can still get hurt even with a dull practice blade."

"True enough," he said.

"I know that the wererats like to use live blades for most of their practices," I said.

"If it is not silver, then it will heal almost instantly if you are a powerful enough shapeshifter."

"Yeah, you're powerful as fuck, so you'll heal, but I've seen some of your people after the wererat-only practices and they don't all heal like you do."

He smiled and it had that arrogance, or maybe confidence, that he hid most of the time behind a diplomatic, almost humble demeanor. But since I'd been his lover, I'd seen him when he wasn't so controlled, and you didn't get to be king without being confident or even arrogant.

"You do not always heal as quickly as I do, and yet you participate in knife practice with us."

I shrugged and felt both embarrassed and proud. "I was surprised when Fredo invited me into the private lessons."

"You should be honored, Fredo includes only the very best in his private classes."

I smiled and then felt myself blush. It usually took something sexual to get me to blush, which meant that being invited into Fredo's private lessons meant even more to me than I'd thought. It was stupid to risk myself with real blades, and even in the private classes we used practice blades most of the time, but not all the time, and sometimes we used silver-edged blades, which meant that even a shapeshifter or a vampire would heal human-slow. The wererats and the golden tigers both believed that if you didn't practice with silver blades at least part of the time, you didn't really know how good you were or how you'd react when you got hit for real. I'd been cut up in real fights before, so I knew what it felt like and how I'd react, but the theory was sound.

Rafael laughed. "I am sorry that I have not been able to be in the practices since you were invited into them."

"What's so funny?" I asked and felt prickly like an old reaction that I hadn't quite outgrown.

"I did not mean to upset you."

"Sorry, I know you didn't mean it that way, but for a second it was like you were laughing at me; that whole smallest-kid-in-class, only-woman-in-a-man's-profession thing, it's put a serious chip on my shoulder."

He touched my still-bare shoulder, very gently, almost as if he wasn't sure I'd be okay with it. I didn't tell him not to touch me, but I didn't smile either. He had hit a serious issue by accident, but it was still hit.

"I would never laugh at you, Anita. I have benefited too often from that chip on your shoulder. It is what let you stand up to the Master of Beasts when he had me skinned alive. I will never forget that you risked yourself to save me. I never dreamed that we would ever be more than friends then, but if we had never been lovers, I would still owe you for that moment of bravery."

I put my hand over his where he was touching me. I could still see the back of his body red and raw where they'd had him chained. They'd left his skin nailed to a door as a message. I could still see him bound facedown to the table with silver bands at wrist, ankles, and neck. Bands that were bolted to the table itself. He was nude, but more than his clothes were missing. The entire back of his body was one raw bloody mess. I'd found the owner of the skin on the door. Rafael's darkly handsome face was slack, unconscious. It had been one of the worst things I'd ever seen done to another person.

"You were strong enough to withstand the torture until we could get to you, Rafael. If you'd done what they wanted and given them control of the wererats, they'd have had enough firepower to take over the city."

"I could not give my people over to a such a monster, no matter what they did to me."

I didn't say out loud that most people, even strong ones, would have caved under that kind of torture. As my friend Edward says, everyone breaks eventually. Out loud I said, "I'm only sorry I didn't get to kill the Master of Beasts before he left town."

"You killed his only son; for a vampire as old as the Master of Beasts, that is revenge enough."

"Yeah, his chances of ever having another child at his age is pretty slim."

"Have any of the Harlequin found the Master of Beasts yet?"

I shook my head. "We freed him from the Mother of

All Darkness, but after that he vanished. I think he's afraid of what we and all his enemies might do to him when we find him."

"All the old council members have many enemies, made over centuries," he said.

"Yeah," I said, and stepped away from his hand. "Let's get dressed and find a bedroom."

"I have spoiled the mood talking about old enemies," he said.

I took a deep breath and let it out slowly. "A little, okay, maybe a lot, but let's find a bedroom and see if you can get me back in the mood." Honestly with the memory of him tortured dancing in my head, sex was the furthest thing from my mind. If he'd been an ordinary lover, I'd have just said, *Let's skip it today*, but he was going to be fighting for his life later tonight. If I'd been in love with him, I'd have wanted sex just in case it was the last time, but that wasn't what made me suggest the bedroom. If it was the last time I could feed on him, the last time I could share the energy of a country's worth of wererats with Jean-Claude and all our people, then I needed to take it, but that wasn't the only reason. If Rafael died tonight, I'd regret saying no. We'd been friends years longer than we'd been friends with benefits, but friendship is a type of love and I would miss him.

6

WE GOT DRESSED, put our weapons in place, and were
going hand in hand down the hallway with Claudia and
Benito trailing us. I tried to get them to stay and shower,
but they insisted on escorting us to the bedroom. Rafael
took it as business as normal, so I stopped arguing about
it. He was their king, and that trumped anything I could
say or do.

Rafael and I moved well together; there was none
of that awkwardness you have with some people that
you date where walking hand in hand is a challenge in
rhythm, as if your internal music doesn't match, and yet
it didn't feel romantic. Again, I found it jarring that I
could be this physically comfortable with a lover and not
be in love with them. It hurt that tiny wistful part of me
that had believed most sincerely in that white-dress, one-
great-love-of-your-life ideal. I'd accepted that I had more
than one love of my life, but apparently part of me was
still holding on to the thought that some things only came
when you were in all-caps LOVE. Another illusion shat-
tered.

Rafael swung my hand in his, which was something
he did when he thought I was thinking too hard about
something besides being with him. I knew that he would

say something now, because that was what the hand swing meant.

"Do you have a preference on which of the empty guest rooms we use?" he asked.

In my head I thought, *A room I've never been in with anyone else*, but that seemed less than diplomatic, so I said, "Two of them have showers now. I think one of those."

"I thought you wanted us in a bed tonight," he said, smiling down at me.

I smiled back and said, "I do, but now we can clean up afterward without having to kick anyone out of the main showers."

He raised my hand and brushed it lightly with his lips as we walked; he did it smoothly with no broken motion. "You are always so concerned that others are not inconvenienced. You will be a queen soon, Anita, you must embrace it."

I shook my head. "I don't think the official title is going to change me all that much."

"If you were my queen, I would want to dress you as befits my lady and shower you with gifts."

I laughed then. "Jean-Claude is lucky he's getting me into the bespoke designer wedding gown. He knows not to push his luck on dressing me fancy every day."

"You think the wedding will change nothing?" he asked.

"It better not," I said, and there was an edge of threat in my voice that I didn't try to hide.

"I wish you better luck than I have had with such things."

I looked up at him then, studying his face. I don't know what I would have said next, because I felt the energy coming down the hallway toward us. Happy, wonderful energy of two of the loves of my life.

Micah and Nathaniel came walking up the hallway,

hand in hand, and suddenly it was like the sun had risen in my chest so that it was hard to breathe. My reaction felt over the top, ridiculous. I'd never been one of those people who let myself get carried away, until Jean-Claude and these two walked into my life and stayed. Micah was my height, the only man I'd ever dated who was as short as me. Nathaniel was taller at five foot nine. He'd grown three inches taller and suitably broader through the shoulders since I met him. His auburn hair had also been down to his ankles; now it fell just past his shoulders, shining and perfectly straight. Micah's hair was the same length, but his dark brown hair was so curly that it was inches longer when it was wet. I didn't usually think of Micah as the more delicate of the two men, maybe because I was usually beside them and didn't see them together from a distance that often.

Micah was built like a swimmer with that upside-down *V* of shoulders down to narrow waist and hips. He could spend as much time as Nathaniel did in the weight room, but he didn't muscle up like our shared man did. They were both strong, but in T-shirt, jeans, and boots Micah could hide it, Nathaniel couldn't. Nathaniel was the male equivalent of an old-fashioned pinup, lush and masculine, but with a face that was closer to beautiful; before he'd filled out with more muscle and extra growth, he'd been beautifully androgynous, and now he was still beautiful, but even from the back with the long hair he was finally and completely male. Micah on the other hand still treaded that androgynous line, and he sort of hated it. We were both over thirty, so there wasn't going to be a growth spurt for him or me.

Rafael squeezed my hand, which made me look at him. I had a second of wondering if I'd dropped a poly-amorous ball by ogling my men this way, but he smiled. "Go to them. It does my heart good to see all of you so happy together, gives me hope that I'll find my own crazy happy someday."

He didn't have to tell me twice. I left him with Benito and Claudia and almost ran toward them. We'd been together five years now, and I still wanted to be as close as possible to them every time I saw them. I didn't run to them, but I might have power-walked, and I was in their arms, because it was their arms. We'd been a threesome from the beginning, never just a couple. We put our faces together before we kissed, forehead to forehead for Micah and me, and Nathaniel bending over us so that we touched, our arms interlocked in a circle of just us. Then Micah kissed my cheek, which made me move so that he could kiss me on the mouth. It was a good kiss, soft and complete but still okay for public consumption. We could have kissed like that standing on the sidewalk and not offended anyone. I drew back from the kiss to stare into his chartreuse eyes, green and gold at the same time the way a cat's could be, because they were the eyes of his leopard trapped forever in his human face. Too long in animal form and sometimes you don't come back all the way. It was why he needed glasses, because leopards don't see distance that well; if it's too far to hunt or attack, then it's far more important to see up-close movement. The sunglasses he still wore to hide his eyes in public were prescription, and I'd never known. It had explained why he'd worn them inside so often.

I looked at him almost eye to eye, though my boots were more combat/police, so his club boots gave him a couple of extra inches of height. He didn't wear them to be taller, he wore them because Nathaniel had picked them out for him. Left to his own devices Micah was running shoes and nice dress shoes. We both had things in our closets that our third had bought for us.

Nathaniel used our joined hands to turn me toward

him as if there was music in his head I couldn't hear, and it was the beginning of a dance. Micah let go of both of us and stepped back to give him room to do what he was going to do, because just that one dancelike move said he had something planned that was less tame than Micah's kiss.

From a distance Nathaniel's eyes looked deep violet blue, but up close you realized they were just violet. He had to put blue on his driver's license because purple wasn't a choice. His normal color was a paler lavender; the eye color alone let me know his mood was up. He put one hand at the small of my back and the other in my hand and he literally started to waltz. I had a moment of awkwardness that I almost always did when I danced, but I stopped trying to shield so hard at the connection between us and suddenly I could dance, because Nathaniel could dance.

We danced in the hallway with him smiling down at me, his eyes shining with happiness, and along with the dancing skills came his mood. I laughed out loud from the joy that was bubbling through him. I wondered exactly what had made him this happy. He used his hand at the small of my back to press us closer together, so I could feel that there were other things up besides just his mood. The feel of him pressed so hard against the front of me made me miss a step; I got a string of visuals from the afternoon he and Micah had shared that made my knees so weak I would have fallen if he hadn't caught me. I loved being in the middle of the two of them for sex, but as their own wedding approached, our mostly heterosexual Micah was trying to work on issues he was having with two men and no girl in sight.

I managed to say in a voice gone hoarse with just the memory feedback, "Sorry I missed it."

"Next time," Nathaniel said, and then he picked me up off the floor and spun me around, laughing.

"This is not just the shorthand of a couple, you shared what you are feeling and thinking," Rafael said.

Nathaniel set me down, but kept his arms around me, and I kept hold of him. My knees weren't weak anymore, but we hadn't kissed yet. He'd wanted to share his delight, but he wasn't done.

"Yes," Nathaniel answered him, but kept looking at me. He leaned in to kiss me and I went up on tiptoe to help.

My eyes were closed, but I still knew that Micah had crossed behind me toward the wererats. He wasn't bound to me like Nathaniel was, but he was still my Nimir-raj and that was its own magic. Then Nathaniel was kissing me, and I forgot about everything else.

It was like a continuous feedback loop of his mouth on mine, mine on his, his hands so strong on my back, and my smaller hands on the smooth muscles of his back, his hands having to find their way around the shoulder holster with the Springfield EMP nine-millimeter and the big knife in a sheath along my spine, the extra ammo on the right side of my gun belt, the inner pants holster of the Sig Sauer .380. Nathaniel even got the thought in there that I still felt like I was cheating on my old Browning BDM by carrying the Springfield nine-millimeter for every day, and the Springfield .45 when I was on duty as a marshal. I got that he missed my body under his hands without all the straps and weapons. There was a moment when I wasn't sure whose thought, hands, mouth, body was whose. I was trying to climb back into control or something when I felt Damian wake for the night. Suddenly it was three of us and I felt that first gasp as he woke like a swimmer who had almost drowned and was fighting back to life.

Then we were looking down at him; the brightest green eyes I'd ever seen in a human being stared up at us, set in the milk-white skin of a natural redhead who had spent a

thousand years in the dark. It meant his hair had no gold
highlights like most redheads, so it looked darker, a true
red instead of the orangey color it might have been.

Rafael said, "What is that?"

Micah said, "Damian's awake," as Nathaniel and I broke
from the kiss and looked at each other. Nathaniel's eyes
were green, and because I could still see/feel through him,
I knew mine were, too. I had a moment to be truly creeped
out by it, and Damian shut down the link and we were left
alone in our bodies in the hallway, knowing that the vampire third of our triumvirate of power had his feelings hurt
that it had bothered me to see his power in our eyes.

7

"IS THAT WHAT it would be like if Anita made me her rat to call?" Rafael asked.

"No, it's a more complete bonding because we have Damian hooked up to us. Only the triumvirate with Jean-Claude, Richard, and I can come close to this level of . . . intermingling. It's not like this with any of the other animals to call unless we work at it."

"At least if Anita's power shows, we both have brown eyes, so it will not be so obvious," Rafael said.

"Did we miss something?" Micah asked.

Nathaniel studied my face. "I didn't see the decision in your mind."

"You got distracted," I said.

He grinned. "You always distract me." He reached for me again, and Micah stepped in the way.

"I love you both, but this is serious. If Anita is going to make Rafael her rat to call, I need to know and so do Jean-Claude and Asher."

Nathaniel wasn't smiling as he shook his head. "She hasn't decided yet."

"And you know that how?" Benito asked.

"It wasn't in her head just now." He said it as if it was a perfectly reasonable answer.

"Do you know everything she's thinking?" Rafael asked.

"No, but a decision that big would have been in the front of her thoughts, and it wasn't," he said, again so reasonable. Nathaniel had taken the new power level between the three of us in stride a lot more than I had, or even Damian had.

"I have never seen your eyes blaze with Jean-Claude's blue when he wakes for the day," Rafael said.

"He has more control over it," I said.

Nathaniel said, "It's not just that, some of the Harlequin's eyes change when their masters wake and they have control."

"It's a shorthand for them to know everything that's happened during the day while they slept. We can just tell Jean-Claude or Damian."

"Why does it bother you so much when it happens?" Nathaniel asked. His eyes were fading from the deep violet of happiness toward the normal lavender.

"I don't know," I said.

"Do you know everything that your *moitié bêtes* know?" Benito asked.

"No," I said.

"But you could read their thoughts if you wanted to," he said.

I thought about it and then nodded. "But it's more sharing memories than thoughts."

"Perhaps I have not understood all the possibilities of our king becoming your *moitié bête*, Anita," Benito said.

"Unless you have a vampire who shares rat as their animal to call included in the mix, it won't be as intimate as what Anita shares with Nathaniel and Damian," Micah said.

"How do you know?" Rafael asked.

"I've talked to Jean-Claude at length about it."

"But Damian is not a master vampire, so he has no animal to call," Rafael said.

"One of them is the master vampire," Micah said, motioning at Nathaniel and me.

"So, Anita," Benito said.

"I'm not so sure," Claudia said, and she was looking at Nathaniel as if she saw something in him she'd missed or hadn't noticed before.

"If we take this step together, Anita, will our secrets be safe from one another?" Rafael asked.

"I won't peek on purpose, but to say anything else is too close to a lie. The truth is, I'm not sure. What's happening between Nathaniel and Damian and me is different than how it feels to be with Jean-Claude and Richard, so I just don't know."

"Richard hates being a werewolf too much to be a full third in your triumvirate," Nathaniel said.

No one argued, and Rafael had been Richard's friend and ally before he was mine. Rafael asked, "So you think that your comfort level with being a wereleopard is what makes the difference between the three of you?"

"Yeah, I know now that Richard's conflicts cripple the power that Jean-Claude could have from their triumvirate, well, that and . . ." Nathaniel stopped in midsentence.

"He was about to say that Jean-Claude is too careful of Richard and me to bind us as powerfully as he could," I said.

"You finished his thought?" Rafael asked.

"No, we've had the conversation before," I said, not like I was entirely happy about it.

Rafael looked at all of us, including Micah, who was trying for a blank face. "What am I missing here?"

Surprisingly, it was Claudia who answered, "Nathaniel's not conflicted about what he is and what he wants."

We all looked at her. "I didn't know you were paying that much attention to what I wanted," Nathaniel said.

She looked uncomfortable, but said, "You almost picked a fight with Bobby Lee when you came into the power of your triumvirate. He told the other bodyguards so we wouldn't underestimate you."

Nathaniel looked embarrassed, which you didn't see often. "I didn't understand that power could be like drugs. It was like being high and I'm not good when I'm high, which is one of the reasons I got clean and stayed clean."

"The powerless are sometimes only good because they are not strong enough to be evil," Rafael said.

Nathaniel gave him startled eyes and then looked away and nodded. "The temptation was there, but Damian and Anita deserved better than me acting like an asshole."

"But you're the only one who isn't conflicted about your supernatural powers, and . . . the sex," Claudia said, like she wished she hadn't had to say it. "I didn't realize that it limited Jean-Claude's power with Richard and Anita so much until you showed us all how much power could be gained without that hesitation."

"Being nicer about it limits the power, too," he said.

"Maybe," she said, "but it still shows us what the other triumvirate could be."

"I want the power of being your rat to call, Anita, and I am not conflicted about it."

"Without a vampire in the mix to make this a three-way, metaphysically speaking, that's not as important."

"I am glad that Jean-Claude calls only wolves."

"So am I, because I think you would have been far more willing to compromise in ways that Richard wasn't," Micah said.

"What do you mean?" I asked.

"I mean if Jean-Claude had needed a rat instead of a

wolf to call, well, Rafael just said it, he's not conflicted about wanting power and being a wererat, so he would be closer to how Nathaniel is with you and Damian."

"More power," I said.

"And no room in your life for other people, maybe," Micah said.

"I don't understand."

"Our king would not have allowed Jean-Claude more liberties than the Ulfric allows him," Benito said, and he was angry enough that his beast flitted along my skin, but standing this close to Nathaniel, it didn't bother me like it had before.

"Hush, Benito, there is no shame in loving who you love," Rafael said.

Benito seemed to realize that he'd just insulted several people in the hallway by implying that guy-on-guy sex was shameful, because he tried to fix it. "I did not mean . . . what the Nimir-raj does is his own business and Nathaniel is Nathaniel. I just meant that . . . I . . ."

Claudia fought to turn her laugh into a cough.

"For the kind of power that Jean-Claude has now, I might have done many things years ago."

I think Rafael had just admitted he'd been willing to have sex with Jean-Claude to cement a triumvirate with me and him. I think I was surprised, and then I remembered something that Richard had told us years ago.

"Richard said you were the one who urged him to come back to Jean-Claude and me once, that if you could have offered yourself in his place to keep us all safe, you would have done it."

"Richard has thrown away more power than most of us in the supernatural community are ever offered," Rafael said.

"You wouldn't have thrown it away," Micah said.

Rafael looked at him, and they had a long moment of understanding between them. I wasn't sure exactly what they were understanding, but I knew that was what they were doing.

"Through Anita I now have a chance for some of that power."

"You started to gain power when Anita started feeding on all of the wererats through you," Micah said.

"As Anita and all of Jean-Claude's people gained through the feeding," Rafael said.

Micah nodded. "It is an amazing amount of power that you offer through the rodere, but you have gained and offered even more power together since Anita added rat to her beasts."

"It has exceeded expectations," Rafael said.

Since I hadn't realized there were any expectations to exceed, I kept my mouth shut and let Micah do the talking for us. He was a better diplomat than I would ever be. "We will solve the puzzle that Narcissus has set us, and then you will be Anita's rat to call."

"But will you solve it in time for me to win the duels that are coming as the rodere begins to rebel at the power we are building?" Rafael asked.

"I am sorry that it is Hector that you are fighting tonight, Rafael. I know what he means to you," Micah said.

"Have you met Hector?" I asked, turning to look at Micah.

He nodded and reached out to touch me, not in the way that Nathaniel had, but like I was his comfort object; it let me know that he was worried about the fight, too. Shit, how good was this challenger? "Rafael wanted my opinion of some of the up-and-coming wererats. I agreed that Hector was one of the most promising for a future leader, but I'm not convinced that he will ever grow into being a worthy successor to Rafael and what we have built with the Coalition."

"You did not like Hector as much as I did," Rafael said.

"No, I liked Luca better."

"Hector is the better fighter," Rafael said.

"But Luca is the better thinker," Micah said. He hugged me a little tighter and reached around to touch Nathaniel and then pulled away from us to go to Rafael.

"If I may speak freely," Benito asked.

Rafael nodded and said, "Of course."

"Nestor was the best fighter we saw."

Rafael and Micah both nodded. Claudia scowled almost as hard as she had earlier in the weight room. She didn't like Nestor at all. "He fights like a beast," she said.

"But he wins," Rafael said.

"Only if it is a death match," Claudia said. "If it is only to blood, we have seen him lose."

"His temper can get the best of him," Rafael admitted.

"If he controls his emotions, I would not want to face him," Benito said.

I looked at him, because I knew that other than Rafael himself, Benito was one of their best fighters. "I think Luca and Hector are more dangerous," Claudia said, "because they have more control."

"Maybe, but I'd rather face them across the pit than Nestor."

"What do you say, Micah?" Rafael asked.

"I believe I could kill Nestor if I did it within the first few seconds of the fight, because he would see a small man who is not rodere, but if I did not make the kill quickly enough and Nestor could hold his temper, I agree with Benito."

"And the others?" Rafael asked.

"Hector is a good fighter, he's controlled and skilled, but if a fight goes on too long, he loses concentration and makes mistakes. Either kill him quickly or stay out of reach until he grows impatient."

Rafael nodded. "Good advice."

"It's why you wanted me to see all the young warriors

that might threaten your leadership. I am surprised that Hector challenged you first. I expected Nestor to be the first."

"I agree," Rafael said.

It was my turn to walk toward the group. Nathaniel kept my hand loose in his and followed me, but he wouldn't have asked the question I did. "So why is it Hector tonight and not Nestor?"

"Because he challenged me first."

"Yeah, but why? Why him first?"

"Nestor is arrogant and truly homophobic. He hates and fears Jean-Claude just from seeing him in interviews and pictures online," Micah said.

"Sounds like a case of the lady protesting too much," I said.

"What do you mean?" Benito asked.

"That maybe he hates Jean-Claude, because he's attracted to him."

"Oh Jesus, do not say that where Nestor can hear you," Benito said, and he actually went a little pale.

Claudia was grinning. "I think Anita's right."

Benito turned to her. "Nestor can't fight Anita, but you, he could challenge you for his honor. *Por favor*, Claudia, do not tempt fate; the only thing Nestor hates more than pretty gay men is any woman who can fight."

"Oh, definitely closet gay," I said.

"Maybe even from himself," Nathaniel said. I looked at him, expecting to see him teasing with the rest of us, but his face was all serious. I might have asked why, but Rafael spoke up.

Rafael smiled and shook his head. "As amusing as it would be to see you accuse Nestor of hating women because he secretly likes men, Anita, *por favor*, please, as Benito says, do not tempt fate."

"Wait, are you saying that Nestor will be here tonight along with Hector?" I asked.

"No, but even if I defeat Hector tonight, Nestor will challenge me later."

"Luca will wait for a few years, but I agree that Nestor won't have the patience," Micah said.

"I am worried that Hector has challenged me now because his own leader, Victor, has put him up to it."

"What does Victor gain from Hector being king?" I asked.

"He would put Hector as king over the St. Louis clan, and then he would let the other clans fight among themselves until we were all small kingdoms again. Hector would be king, but he would do as Victor bid him."

"Hector is his sacrificial lamb, he's not a smart enough fighter to win tonight," Micah said.

"Perhaps," Rafael said.

Micah grabbed the other man's shoulder and spun him to look at him. "The only thing that can defeat you tonight is you, Rafael. I do not know why you think Hector is such great leadership material, because I don't see it."

"You told me as much."

"Luca will be the better leader someday."

"But he is not the better fighter," Rafael said.

"Luca is still learning how to fight, but nothing will make Hector a better thinker."

"Hector is not stupid," Rafael said, and he was more upset than I thought he should be over a stranger.

"I never said he was."

"Why do you defend Hector so much?" I asked.

There was another flash of looks between everyone, and this time it included Micah. "What aren't you telling us?" Nathaniel asked.

Rafael looked at me and there was such pain in his eyes. "You know the human mates that are allowed among us."

"Yeah, it's the way you're getting me in to watch tonight."

"Wait, what?" Nathaniel asked.

"When did you invite Anita to watch the fight tonight?" Micah asked.

"In the showers, and that can wait. I want to know why Hector is so special to you, Rafael. Why is he so special that you're almost ready to let him kill you, just so you don't have to kill him?"

"You know all those crazy exes I spoke of?"

"Yeah."

"Hector's mother was one of them."

"So, Hector is . . ." I didn't want to finish the sentence; it was too Greek myth, or maybe Greek tragedy?

"My son," Rafael finished for me.

8

"YOU DON'T KNOW that for certain," Benito said, while the rest of us just stared at Rafael.

"Suelita says he is mine, why would she shame her husband if it isn't true?"

"When did she tell you?" Micah asked.

"She called me after Hector made his challenge."

"Suelita fears for her only son's life," Claudia said. "She'd do anything to save Hector, even lie about you being his father."

"I do not think she lied," Rafael said.

"What did she want you to do?" I asked.

Rafael looked at me, but it was like he wasn't hearing me. He knew I was talking, but he wasn't following. "What did Suelita want you to do as his father?" I asked.

"She wanted me to promise I would not kill our son."

"Did she ask you to let him kill you?" I asked.

"No, she asked me to offer third blood instead of death."

"And that offer has made you seem weak," Benito said.

"Has she told Hector?" Micah asked.

Rafael shook his head. "Her husband is the only father Hector has ever known, and she wishes to keep it that way."

"So, she tells you, so that you don't want to hurt him, but she doesn't tell him, so he still wants to kill you?" I asked.

"She is trying to get inside your head, Rafael. If she truly meant you to treat the boy as a father should, then she would tell him you are his father," Benito said.

"I'm with Benito on this one," I said.

"Even I think it's a trick to mess with your head before the fight, and I just learned about it," Nathaniel said.

"Suelita is a mother terrified for her child, she will do and say anything," Claudia insisted.

"Does Hector look like his mother?" Micah asked.

"Why does that matter?" Rafael asked.

"Because he looks nothing like you."

"Not all children look like their parents," Rafael said.

"Does your son from your marriage look like you?" I asked.

"I have not seen my ex-wife or my son in so long I am not certain I would recognize him." He couldn't hide the pain in his face when he said it.

"I'm sorry, Rafael," I said.

"If Hector's mother is lying, then she's trying to set you up for her son, so he can kill you and take your throne," Micah said.

"And if she is telling the truth?"

"Then she is telling the truth to set you up for her son, so he can kill you and take your throne."

"You repeated yourself," Rafael said.

"No, I didn't. I just pointed out that if it's a lie, or if it's the truth, the result that Hector's mother is hoping for is the same, you dead and her son alive."

"Wise, as always, Micah." He said it, but not like it would change anything.

"You told me in the showers that you wanted me to seduce Hector if you die; are you seriously saying you'd want your lover to sleep with your son? That's a little too . . . I don't know . . . creepy."

"I didn't mean to tell you. I know it will make it harder for you to sleep with him."

I grabbed his arm and made him look at me. "Win the fight tonight and I sleep with only you."

He looked past me to Micah and Nathaniel. "Never just me, Anita."

I wanted to shake him so badly that I had to let go and step back. "You know what I meant, Rafael. Hector's mom is screwing with your head before the fight, and you're letting her do it."

"You may be right, but I cannot ignore that he could be mine, that I could have more than one son."

"You asked me to come watch you fight tonight; well, I won't come just to watch you give up and die."

"I am not giving up," he said.

"It sure sounds like it."

"You and I have fought together too long to lie to each other, Rafael," Micah said.

"What does that mean?" Rafael sounded angry now.

"We both know that if you don't believe you can win, then it's a self-fulfilling prophecy. If you go in there tonight thinking that you don't want to hurt Hector, while he's trying to kill you, then you have lost before the fight begins."

"You don't have children; you don't understand what it's like to have one and never be allowed to see him. To think I might have had a child that I watched grow up, that means something to me."

"Suelita knows how much it would mean to you," Claudia said.

"She has never forgiven you for not marrying her all those years ago," Benito said.

"She was not in love with me."

"She wanted to be queen, Rafael. She loves power and status," Benito said.

"How do you know that?"

"Because I keep track of the women that I think may be a problem."

"What did you think she would do?"

"You are right on the timing; I thought she would claim her baby was yours years ago, but then she married someone else, so I figured the baby must be his."

"Why didn't you tell me you thought Hector was mine?"

"If Suelita could have proven Hector was yours, she'd have offered a paternity test when he was a baby, but she didn't, because she knew the test would come back with a different father."

"She said she didn't want to trap me into a loveless marriage."

"That sounds like bullshit," Benito said.

"How dare you?"

"You pay me to keep you safe; well, part of that is looking at the women you date."

"Suelita never hurt me."

"Well, she's trying to kill you now," Claudia said.

"Enough!" Rafael yelled it, and both Benito and Claudia stopped arguing with him. He turned to me. "First I remind you of the Master of Beasts and his tortures and now this. If I were not walking the sands tonight, I would not try for sex with you, but time is running out, Gatito Negra." It was Spanish for *black kitten* and the honor name the local wererats had given me, acknowledging that I was small, but a predator that might eat them. For Rafael and me it had become his nickname for me. It rolled off his tongue sounding sexy and endearing like a lover's pet name should be. Just that sped my pulse, caught my breath in my throat and turned it shallow. I hadn't realized that he'd conditioned me so that just him saying the name a certain way was a turn-on. You never know what seemingly innocent things will become foreplay.

Micah hugged me and it was almost startlingly, as if I'd been paying too much attention to Rafael. I hugged him back and don't know what I would have said, because he spoke first. "You can use our room."

I held him tighter, memorizing the feel of him in my arms; the delicate strength of him always felt so right. I touched his curls with one hand and hugged him tighter with the other. "No, we'll use a guest room."

He drew back enough to meet my eyes. "Are you sure?"

I nodded. I didn't say out loud that I didn't want the scent of anyone on our sheets but the three of us. If Rafael had been someone that any of us was in love with, that would be different, but he wasn't one of our sweeties, so no.

I kissed him, and Nathaniel was there hugging both of us. Micah extracted himself and let us have a moment alone. Nathaniel smiled down at me, mischief shining in his lavender eyes. I knew that he was about to say something we might regret, or I might, but he didn't say it out loud, just looked deep into my eyes, and I suddenly knew what he was visualizing about Rafael and me and . . . him.

I laughed and pulled out of the hug. "You are incorrigible and that visual will stay with me."

"I meant for it to, and you still love me?" He meant it, but there was still that small part of him that wasn't as confident as he appeared. It was that part that asked, even if the tone was teasing.

"I am deeply, passionately, madly in love with you still and always."

"Still and always," he said softly, and kissed me as

gently as his voice sounded. I leaned into his body, my hands on either side of his shoulders as if I could hold on forever. I trailed my fingers through the thick straightness of his hair. I could run my hands through his hair and not mess it up. Micah's curls didn't recover from rough treatment.

"I love you," he said.

"I love you more," I said.

Micah came up beside us, putting an arm around each of our waists. "I love you most."

"I love you mostest," Nathaniel said, and kissed us each in turn. Then it was time to go with Rafael and find a guest room. Rafael's hand was warm in mine, but it seemed weird to leave the other men behind in the hallway to go with him. I had other lovers who made me feel less conflicted about being with them, and I finally realized that Rafael was the only one who never interacted with anyone else in our poly group. Maybe there was more than one reason that I'd offered him to sleep with some of the women in our polycule? Of course, Nathaniel's visual had let me know that he had felt left out when offers of doing threesomes with Rafael had been offered to our group. It's not that I forgot he was bisexual; it was just that I knew Rafael was so terribly heterosexual, and yes, I could now admit all the way in the front of my head that Nathaniel wasn't the only man in my life who would have taken a swing at Rafael if it was offered.

"You are thinking far too hard about Micah and Nathaniel now," Rafael said.

I squeezed his hand and looked up at him. I let him see in my face that I thought him handsome and yummy. It was enough that he smiled. "Thank you for that, Anita, but I think we need to find a way to make you think more of only me."

"What did you have in mind?" I asked.

"A little game of hide-and-seek."

I frowned at him. "You're a wererat; even in human form you'd smell me or hear my heartbeat from yards away. I can't hide from you."

"If I truly wanted you to hide, no, but I want to find you."

"I'm not sure I understand what you mean?"

"Hide under a bed and I will pull you out and ravish you." He wiggled his eyebrows at me.

I shook my head. "Nope, sorry, I've had too many real bad guys drag me out of hiding. It would be more trigger for me than foreplay."

He stopped so abruptly that it almost made me stumble with his hand in mine, pulling me up short. "I am so sorry, Anita, I forget for you some of the bondage games are too close to your reality."

"It's okay, you asked, I said no, we move on to a new idea."

He looked away and his face was serious again. If this kept up and short of releasing the *ardeur*, we weren't having sex today. I touched his face lightly and turned him back to look at me.

"Tell me what you want, Rafael. If it's a chase and takedown, we can figure it out."

"I feel the press of time, Anita. We are running out of it if we are to plan something elaborate between us."

"Then maybe we should go simple instead of elaborate," I said.

"What did you have in mind?" he asked.

I shook my head. "It's like I can almost see a question in your eyes, Rafael."

"What question," he said.

"Ask it, and I'll know."

He took in a big breath of air and it shook on the way out. He looked a little to the side as if he didn't want to watch my face while he asked. "I want to make love to you, Anita."

"I've already said yes to sex, Rafael."

He shook his head, and now he gave me the full weight of his dark brown eyes. "Let me make love to you tonight."

I fought not to frown at him. "Okay, I mean haven't I already agreed to that?"

"For this once, I don't want to tie you up, or play the bedroom games we usually do. I would like to simply have sex with you."

"I'm not really a straight missionary kind of girl," I said, still not understanding what he was asking.

"That is what I thought, we come up with something that will make us both happy." His voice was okay, but he looked away while he said it, hiding his eyes.

I squeezed his hand, trying to draw him into a hug, but he stayed turned away. I grabbed his suit jacket and pulled him around so that he had to look at me or over my head. There was pain in his eyes, as if I'd said something that hurt him, and I had no idea what had just happened to add to the weight of sorrow on him today.

"I feel like we're having two different conversations here, Rafael. Please, just talk clearly with me. We were friends years before we added the benefits, so please just for a few minutes talk to me like I'm your friend that you have sex with, not just another crazy woman that you date."

He smiled and then laughed. "You are not crazy, Anita, maybe you are not crazy enough for me to be comfortable."

"Hey, I offered to set some of your belongings on fire if you needed me to be crazy for you."

He hugged me. "No, please don't."

I hugged him back, my face pressed against his chest.

"Then talk to me, just talk to me, not around me, or about what you think is in my head, but just treat me like you used to treat me before we started having sex. Talk to me like I'm your friend and we'll go from there."

He rubbed his face against my hair. "If you were my friend, I would say I am dating a woman who is into hot bondage sex and at first that was amazing and exactly what I wanted, but now I would like to make love to her. I would like to have sex with her that didn't include tying her up, or chasing her, or even the delight of tearing her clothes off, though I would like to do that later."

I settled into his body as much as his gun and knives and mine would let us. Nathaniel wasn't wrong about the weapons getting in the way. "Deal on the clothes tearing for later, but we don't have to have rough or bondage sex every time we're together, Rafael. If you want to make love without it, we can try."

"Try," he said, and started to pull out of the hug.

I grabbed his jacket and kept him from going too far. "Damn it, Rafael, stop picking at every word choice I make and just listen to what I'm actually saying, not what negative shit is translating in your head."

"I don't know what that meant," he said.

I fought not to sigh out loud. "It means if you want to make love without any bondage, then let's do that."

"I thought you only did bondage."

"Not always."

"Or only with multiple people at once like the three-way you offered earlier."

"Look, we'll discuss that later, but right now if you want to make love to me, then the answer is yes."

"Yes, just like that," he said, studying my face.

"Just like that," I said, smiling up at his serious eyes.

"Is this where you tell me I should have asked sooner?"

I shook my head. "No, this is where I remind you that I said yes, make love to me, and you're still talking."

He smiled and then it blossomed into a full-out grin, which I don't think I'd ever seen before. "No more talking," he said, and took my hand in his and started leading me down the hallway.

9

RAFAEL GOT ME out of my clothes, so that I stood nude in front of him by the bed, but he was still wearing his dress slacks; even his belt was fastened. His feet were bare against the carpet, the hem of his slacks too long without the dress boots to hold them up. I traced my hands down the front of his chest; my skin looked even paler against the brown of his, and I liked the contrast. He took my hands in his.

"Your hands are so small, but you are the only woman that I have ever undressed whose pile of weapons beside the bed is larger than mine." He smiled at the end of the sentence and raised my hands up so that he could lay soft kisses on my palms.

"You knew I wasn't like all the other girls before you got me out of my clothes."

"I did," he said, and kissed first one of my wrists and then the other. His lips gentle, his breath warm. He began to kiss his way up my arms, first right, then left, until he came to my elbow. He kissed the bend of my arm, right, left. I expected him to keep kissing up my arms, but instead he went to his knees in front of me and laid a kiss on my stomach.

My voice was breathy as I said, "You're wearing too many clothes."

"This is the first time I have made love to you, not just sex, but lovemaking." He looked up at me and there was something in his face that was tender, or vulnerable, or something I had no words for. "I want to remember to pleasure you before I take my pleasure; the pants will remind me."

"Clever you," I said, and traced my fingers down the side of his face. He bent forward and kissed my stomach again a little lower than the first time, and then lower still. He kissed one gentle touch at a time down my stomach, his hands on my hips either to hold me in place or just to have someplace to put them. He laid gentle kisses over the mound of me, and the sensation was even more because I shaved and there was no hair between me and his lips. He kissed as deeply on me as he could without spreading my legs apart and then looked up at me. His breath came out in a sigh that felt almost hot as it spilled between my legs. It made me shiver and touch his shoulders to steady myself.

He moved to the side, kissing where my hip met my body, and then went to the other side and did the same. His hand cupped against the front of my body. His skin was warmer than mine, so that I pressed into his palm like my body was asking for him to touch me more. It was an involuntary movement like a flower turning toward the warmth of the sun.

"So eager," he said.

I opened my eyes and hadn't even realized I'd closed them until I looked down my body at Rafael. "Don't you want me eager?"

"Yes, yes I do," he said, pressing his hand more firmly against the front of my body, rubbing the bottom of his hand so that it began to press and tease without actually touching directly on the most sensitive parts of me.

He kissed the side of my hip and then slid both his hands up my body until he cupped my breasts in his hands. He started fondling them gently, and it wasn't enough sensation for me. I didn't always need bondage, but I needed more than this. I pressed my hands against his, and said, "Harder, please."

He raised his eyebrows at me and then began to dig his fingers in just a little bit more, squeezing my breasts in his hands, pulling on them. It brought a small involuntary sound from me. He stood up and cupped one breast, so that he could suck my nipple. He started out too soft again, and I felt like I needed to explain to him that lovemaking didn't have to mean everything was gentle, at least it didn't for me.

"Harder, please," and he did what I asked, until I told him that was enough. It wasn't hurting, but it was firm, and I could feel the pull of his mouth on me; that was what I wanted. He sucked until I made happy noises for him, and then he did the same on the other breast, until my legs were wobbly, and I was holding on to him for support.

He drew back and put his hands around my waist as he knelt on the floor again. This time he kissed and licked his way down my body until he could flick his tongue between my legs. I gasped for him, and he drew back and said, "Sit on the bed for me."

It wasn't what I'd expected him to ask, but I did it. He spread my knees and leaned down to lick me, which was fun, but not quite the angle either of us needed. I lay back on the bed with my knees trailing over the side, and he put his hands under my thighs and began to kiss softly, gently down first one thigh and then the other. He was so slow and so careful that I was making impatient, eager noises before he got to the center of things, but he didn't touch me there. He kissed in the little hollow where the leg and body meet, and then he kissed the other side deeply, using his tongue as if he were kissing my mouth or other things. It felt wonderful, but it was teasing by this point, so close, but not close enough.

He finally licked up the center of me, and it brought my upper body off the bed like he'd lifted me. "So sensitive," he said, licking around the very outer edges of me.

"Please," I said.

"Please what?" he asked.

"You know what."

He licked a little further on one side and it felt amazing, but not . . . and then the other side, and he began to mirror himself on one side and then the other, licking around and over everything and everywhere but the one spot I wanted him to touch. It felt so good and at the same time was making me want to scream with frustration.

"Please, Rafael, please."

"You mean this?" He flicked his tongue over the one spot he'd been avoiding, and just that caught my breath in my throat.

"Or this?" he asked, and slid his tongue underneath the spot, so he was touching just the edges of what I wanted. It was both exquisitely wonderful and exquisitely frustrating.

"Rafael!" I cried his name, but it wasn't in pleasure, more exasperation.

He laughed, a deeply masculine chuckle, and then he licked across me and it made me cry, "Rafael!" but in a good way. He began to lick, swirling his tongue over and around that spot, doing bigger circles farther away from time to time, and then he'd lick me exactly where I wanted him to until I was almost there, almost, almost, and then he'd move away.

I finally yelled at him, "Damn it, either do it, or don't."

He drew back with his face shining with how happy my body was with everything he'd done, and asked, "You don't like being teased?"

"Not this much, no."

"I have enjoyed doing it."

"Sadist," I said.

He gave that deep chuckle again, and then he put his

mouth between my legs and began to suck. After everything he'd already done it was almost too much sensation
and not enough, as if my body didn't know if it was coming or going. He figured out that it wasn't working and
began to lick swirls over that one spot, and finally he
used his fingers to spread everything else aside so he
could suck only on that one spot. I started screaming before I'd actually come, because it was almost too much
after all the foreplay and then suddenly I was going over
that edge of pleasure and it was like he held the center of
me in his mouth, pulling me through and into and over,
as if the world dissolved into the sensation of his mouth
on me. I screamed and writhed until the world was white-
edged, like seeing through mist. I lay twitching, unable to
move or focus my eyes as I felt him stand and move away
from me. The next thing I was sure of was him pushing
his way between my legs. It raised my body off the bed
and made me cry out for him. I saw his skin dark through
the paleness of the condom as he used one hand to help
guide him inside me. Normally he'd have had to work his
way in, but I was so wet that all that hard, eager length
just slid inside me.

He said something I think was a curse in Spanish.
"So wet."

"Make love to me." I sounded breathy and almost not
like me, but I managed to say it.

He did what I asked, pushing himself gently into me
and pulling out, until he found a rhythm that was gentler
than any we'd ever done together. He worked us farther
up on the bed and stayed on top, but kept his upper body
raised so I could move underneath him. We found a
rhythm together of his thrusts and my hips rising to meet
him, over and over, in and out. I couldn't see him gliding
in and out of me, but I could feel every inch of him as I
rose underneath him to meet his thrust with mine.

"I am close," he said.

"So am I." My voice was breathy, and I fought to keep my rhythm with his, and then I felt the edge of orgasm. "Almost," I told him.

"Feed when we go."

"Yes," I said, and then from one thrust to another he brought me screaming, neck bowed backward to shriek his name without deafening him.

He cried out above me and his body thrust one last time inside me and all the barriers came down. I fed on his strength as he held himself above me, I fed through his skin everywhere he touched me, and through him like a doorway I fed on all the rodere.

I'd learned to keep my touch light with people I knew so that I didn't intrude too far into them. I had accidentally gotten memories, thoughts, emotions before, and there were ones that enjoyed the energy orgasm. They had to welcome the energy in so it was their choice, though Jean-Claude had shared memories of Belle Morte being able to bring pleasure against people's will like metaphysical rape. I worked really hard not to do anything like that. Jean-Claude had taught me how to fly through them, skimming like wings above their energy, feeding but not too much, not too deep. Face after face, a hand raised as if to touch me, another raised as if to fend me off, but they couldn't keep me out completely, because Rafael had given them to me. Even as I rode the amazing wave of power buoying me up as if I could fly for real, and felt it spill out of me to spread like golden magic to everyone who had a cord plugged into my power, I still had enough of me left to understand why they feared us. There was a moment where I couldn't feed off someone, like a rock in the stream of power, so I did what water does and flowed around it and moved on to other faces, bodies, emotions from joy to happiness, fought to pull back so that emotions weren't touched, and then the faces turned upward with joy and welcome and that was the best feast of all,

because it was a sharing. I liked sharing better than taking. Thousands of people, thousands and then I was coming back, back like the ocean pulling back from the shore
to go home, and then there was that rock again that I could
engulf. It stopped me like the ocean noticing one pebble.
What was that? Who was that? I pushed at them, concentrated all that power on just that one . . . he was twenty-
something, handsome, smooth-featured, pale brown skin
with greenish-gray eyes. If I hadn't had Micah's eyes to
compare to, I'd have said they looked exotic. They were
arrogant, defiant, enraged, but under that was . . . fear,
and . . . something . . . something else. I dived deep into
those forest-green, gray-mist eyes, I flew straight into his
gaze and traced that something. Hector's energy pulsed,
because of course that was who it was; he tried to push me
out of him, tried to shield something from me, from us, I
wasn't even sure which us I was referring to, and I didn't
care. The energy was only warm on top, like icing on a
cake, but what was underneath was cold, so much colder
than a shapeshifter. He tried to push us out, and he was
able to shove us to the surface almost. We were back staring into Hector's face, his eyes like forests and mist, and
then they filled with brown light so dark it was almost
black, as if night fell on the forest and started to burn it
down. Hector was the *moitié bête* of a master vampire. A
vampire that didn't belong to Jean-Claude.

10

"HOW IS IT even possible for a master vampire to hide themselves this completely from us?" I asked as I paced at the foot of Jean-Claude's bed. I'd gone to him for sympathy and hugs while we discussed the nasty surprise waiting inside Hector. Instead I couldn't get up on the bed for comfort, because Asher was already there with him and he still wasn't on my cuddling list. Since Jean-Claude could feel most of my emotions unless we both shielded harder than we were currently shielding, he knew I wanted a hug, but he didn't come to me or tell Asher to move, which pissed me off. I was already scared; anger wasn't a good addition.

Jean-Claude was lounging on the huge, custom-made bed, watching me. He was wearing one of his favorite robes, the black one with black fur edging. It was also one of my favorite robes to see him in; there was just something about the utterly white skin of his chest framed by the black fur, his long black curls mingling with the fur until it was hard to tell which darkness was which, and he'd even opened the top enough so I could see the pale brownish cross-shaped burn scar on his chest. He'd opened the robe purposefully that far because he knew how much I enjoyed the view, which pissed me off even more.

"We have an emergency here, Jean-Claude, or didn't you sense the vampire master that's got its hooks in Hector?"

"You know I did."

"Then why aren't you more upset?"

"I have sent word for everyone to gather here, so we can plan our strategy for tonight, *ma petite*. Rafael is off telling his people in person, and then he will join us here. Until everyone arrives there is nothing more we can do, so why do you not join us on the bed for the cuddling and comfort?"

I stared at him, openmouthed, not sure what to say. I wasn't sure if I was more upset that he didn't seem to be taking the threat seriously, or that he was trying to encourage me to cuddle with him and Asher, when he knew I hadn't forgiven the other man for his years of terrible behavior.

"You have shocked her speechless," Asher said from the bed where he lay beside Jean-Claude. I was working so hard at ignoring him, because he was still on my shit list from the epic string of bad choices he'd made that had led all of us to dump him. Jean-Claude had taken him back recently, but with one other exception the rest of us were still pissed at him. At first being pissed at him had made him less attractive to me, but as he kept behaving better, it got harder to stay angry at him, and even harder not to see him as beautiful.

His hair was foamy golden waves around his face. They'd taken time to blow-dry their hair after cleaning up after sword practice; normally they would have sex in the big tub, but they'd cut it short because I was feeding on Rafael and Jean-Claude had needed his attention on that to make sure the energy went where we needed it to go, instead of like a flood that just washed over everything, which was what could happen if I didn't have help controlling it. The first time I'd fed on Rafael had been an emergency feed to save Jean-Claude's and Richard's lives; that time I'd known exactly where to send all that energy, but day to day—that wasn't my area of expertise.

Jean-Claude stroked his hand along Asher's hair where all that gold hair was hiding half his face like a veil. That was why they'd dried their hair instead of having sex, because if his hair had been wet, Asher couldn't have used it to hide the scars on the right side of his face. Holy water burns vampire flesh like acid. The Church had tried to burn the devil out of Asher centuries ago. Jean-Claude had saved his life, but the holy water scars went down the left side of his body. All of that was hidden now behind a brown brocade robe with golden and brown fur trim. Since there was black-on-black brocade on Jean-Claude's robe, they looked even more like a matched pair than normal. Belle Morte had collected beautiful men with blue eyes. Jean-Claude's had been the darkest, and Asher's were the palest blue I'd ever seen in a human. Jean-Claude's eyes reminded me that the sky was always blue no matter how dark the night, and Asher's eyes were winter skies, pale and cold, but glittering with humor right now. I didn't want him laughing at the fact that I was speechless with provincial shock, not when the thought that only me being angry with him was preventing me from crawling onto the bed and getting cuddles from both of them. The offer for more than just cuddles had been put back on the table once Jean-Claude made up with him. Normally it wasn't hard to keep saying no, but I hadn't seen them cuddled on the bed together like this, just the three of us, since the big fight that had been my last straw with Asher. I was remembering why I avoided seeing them together.

"*Ma petite*, are you listening to me?"

I blushed and looked away to try to hide it. "No, I mean yes, but please repeat it all."

Asher laughed, not that sex-on-a-stick thing that Jean-Claude could do, but just the sound of happiness. It made me want to smile, because I loved him, or Jean-Claude did. I would never really know how much of my love for Asher was mine alone and how much was bleed-over from Jean-Claude having been in love with him for centuries. They'd been on and off over that time, but they were still each other's love of several lifetimes.

"I am sorry, Anita, truly sorry for laughing, but this is the first time that I've known for certain that you miss me as I miss you."

I tried to frown at him, but it's hard to look tough when your skin hasn't faded from blushing. "Fine, you look scrumptious and the two of you together look more, but even if I forgive and forget and we all go back to being lovers, it won't fix the fact that I can't make Rafael my rat to call without Narcissus and his werehyenas declaring war."

"He will not start a war, *ma petite*, Narcissus has had time to cool down over the insult of Asher leaving him for Kane. He had to fight to regain the respect of his clan after that mess, it has occupied much of his time."

"But just yesterday you said I couldn't make Rafael my rat to call, because of Narcissus."

"*Oui*, but that was before we learned that a master vampire powerful enough to hide from all of us has made Rafael's latest challenger into a conduit for his power. If this Hector wins, then his master gains the energy that feeding on the rodere gives us. We cannot allow that to happen. Narcissus will understand the danger to our power structure."

"He will understand the danger, but I do not know if he will see reason," Asher said.

"Do you truly think that Narcissus will continue his

threats against Rafael and his wererats even after he learns of this new threat?" Jean-Claude asked, moving just his head against the pillows to look at the other man.

"Narcissus will have to do something to save face, though; he could kill Kane and risk killing me and risk your wrath," Asher answered.

"Or he could start something unfortunate with the wererats."

"War, you mean?" I said.

"Not so big a word as that, *ma petite*, but it is within shapeshifter culture when two different animal groups come into conflict to have a duel between chosen champions."

"Narcissus could challenge Rafael directly," said Asher.

"That is very rare," Jean-Claude said.

"But if Narcissus does issue a challenge to Rafael and he refuses, then it could be seen as weakness or even cowardice. My understanding of wererat culture is that it would open Rafael up to even more challenges from other ambitious wererats," Asher said.

"Unless Narcissus has a death wish, he should leave Rafael alone," I said.

Asher shook his head hard enough to have his hair shiver around his shoulders. The golden strands glinted in the lamplight, and just like that I was back to being distracted by his beauty. Damn it.

"You see what Narcissus wills you to see—the fop, the cross-dresser that can outqueen the most flamboyant gay queen, he makes a joke of himself partly to stop others from doing it for him. He is extremely sensitive about being born intersex."

"I've seen him nude and honestly it didn't look that much different to me."

"But it is not us that looks in the mirror every day."

I looked at the beautiful man with his hair hiding half his face, so that only the angelic beauty of the unscarred side showed, and I knew he wasn't just talking about Narcissus.

"I've felt how powerful Narcissus's inner beast is, but in a physical fight Rafael will kill him."

"It is not that simple, *ma petite*."

"What do you mean?"

Asher answered, "Female werehyenas are bigger than the males just like the real animals, but in werehyenas they are monstrously bigger, and they usually only have one form, bipedal, because they use their hands for more than fighting."

"So, because Narcissus is half woman and has girl parts, he's this really big powerful half man, woman, whichever he prefers. My money is still on Rafael."

"Female hyenas do magic; literally, they can do spells like out of fairy tales and legends."

"I've never heard this before."

"That's because they don't tell outsiders. I didn't realize how unusually the St. Louis hyenas were run until I was sent away to Dulcia's territory. She runs her hyenas in the traditional manner. The fact that their leaders can work magic is what has given the hyenas in this country an edge over other animal groups."

"Wait, hyena shapeshifters are rare in this country. The magic, or whatever, hasn't helped them gain the upper hand in most of the cities I visit," I said.

Asher sat up in the bed, letting the robe spill forward and show the edge of the hard scars on his chest. It wasn't comfort with me that had made him forget, but how strongly he felt about what he was telling me. That made me listen, because he hated showing his scars most of the time. "Most of the original werehyenas were slaves. Their own tribes sometimes turned against them, bound them with magic and sold them into slavery, because they feared to kill them since they believed their spirit would just take over another hyena or even another person.

They gave the spells to control them to the new masters.
The spells were forgotten or lost and after a few very
bloody rebellions being put down, the werehyenas went
underground. They hid what and who they were from
everyone. It is why it is so rare for a group of hyenas to
be prominent in an area. They do not want to call that
much attention to themselves if they are run in a traditional manner."

"Narcissus runs a very public bondage club over the
river in Illinois. He dresses to attract attention."

"Dulcia did not speak well of him."

"I'll bet, but wait a minute, werehyenas are contagious
just like all the shapeshifters, so how did they pass on the
magic, or is it more like a natural psychic gift?"

"It's natural and comes with the change once the person can control the violent part of the beast. If they wanted
to train the woman, they trained her; if they didn't think
she could be trusted with their secrets, they executed her
before she could come into her full power. For a long
time, they killed any white women who survived an attack, and all clans were led by women of color. The oldest
and most successful clans still are run that way. They
thought of Narcissus as a man until he changed for the
first time, and he's trained in their mystical arts. No one
has challenged him and survived."

"I always wondered about that, I mean he's not much
taller than me, and he's slender, delicate-looking even,
and he has these big muscle guys in his clan."

"The men are afraid of the females in the clan and
they should be."

"That's why he didn't want to let women into his clan,
he was afraid that a full female would beat him?" I said,
thinking about it as I said it.

Asher nodded. "But that hasn't happened, he's still the
biggest bitch around."

"Are you seriously saying that Narcissus would beat Rafael in a real fight?" I asked.

"I've seen Narcissus fight two of the females that came into his clan, and I have not seen Rafael fight, but unless Rafael can do magic while he's fighting hand to hand, then I do not see how he could win," Asher said.

I tried to wrap my head around the idea that fragile-looking Narcissus would win against the much tougher-looking Rafael. I mean, if they were professional fighters in boxing or mixed martial arts, Rafael would be cruiser-weight or heavyweight and Narcissus would be bantam-weight at best and maybe even flyweight. The only reason I even knew all the weight classes was that the new shape-shifter fight league had reached out to St. Louis to see if anyone wanted to come play. There was no way that the two men would ever be in the same match, no way.

"Asher has always had a good eye for male flesh, *ma petite*. If he bet on a fight, he usually won. When we were with Julianna, Asher's betting prowess helped us live comfortably on our own."

It was the first time I'd ever heard him use Julianna's name without the usual sinking of sorrow from either of them. She'd been Asher's human servant and the love of both their lives at the time. Twenty years of bliss before the Church burned her as a witch for consorting with vampires and poured holy water over Asher. Her death could have killed him, especially as injured as he was, but he'd survived. It made me wonder if he'd survive Kane's death. I didn't ask out loud, it was a little too cold-blooded even for me.

"So, you're saying if Asher thinks Narcissus will win, then he probably will?"

"*Oui.*"

"You know, before I realized Hector was the rat to call for another vampire, I'd have been worried about Narcissus killing Rafael and leaving a vacuum of power at the top of the wererat hierarchy," I said.

"Or for Narcissus to be king of both hyenas and rats," Jean-Claude said.

"Wait, that's not possible. They don't allow leadership to cross over like that."

"But that was before the Coalition began to draw all the many different animal groups under one leadership; our Micah has started to forge them into one voice for human politics. For many local problems they now reach out to him and the larger group, which is formed of many different wereanimals."

"Are you saying the Coalition may have set precedents for Narcissus to try to do a sideways coup?"

"He's threatened it," Asher said.

"Jesus, when were you going to tell me about all this?"

"I just heard about it myself. I told Jean-Claude because I saw him first, and now I am telling you. I will leave it up to the two of you who else needs to know."

"Micah needs to know," I said.

"We will tell everyone when they arrive," Jean-Claude said.

"We can't let Narcissus bully us like this, not with another vampire trying to move in on us," I said.

"We are all in agreement, *ma petite*. We will begin to discuss our options when our others arrive."

"I am sorry for my part in the problems with Narcissus," Asher said.

"Your part, your part? It's all your fault."

Asher took in a breath big enough that I could watch his chest rise and fall, which since he didn't have to breathe at all meant it was a very big sigh. "My anger wants to deny it, to find excuses to say that it was the vacuum of power after Raina and Marcus died when Richard took over the werewolves that allowed Narcissus to grow the hyenas into a force to rival both the werewolves and the wererats. That if Richard had policed them as tightly as Marcus had, Narcissus would not have the power to threaten us now."

Some of my own anger faded. "Fine, fine, you're right on that one. Richard has been working on his issues, but not in time to fix it all."

"Richard began working on his issues before I did. I made fun of him for it and I am ashamed that I, what is the phrase, threw him under the bus, to try to save myself."

"You weren't wrong," I said.

"No, but it doesn't lessen my larger part in the current crisis."

"Come join us, *ma petite*." Jean-Claude patted the bed between them.

"Why do you keep offering when I've already said no?" I asked.

"Because you are frightened and want comfort."

"I'm not frightened," I said automatically as if Jean-Claude couldn't sense my feelings.

"*Ma petite*, once I would have let the lie go, but as others in our life have learned to control their issues, I have learned to reach out and ask of you what I need rather than taking crumbs from the table of your love." He patted the bed again.

"What does that even mean right now?"

"Can you not feel what I am feeling?"

"No, you're shielding too tight."

"And you are not," he said.

"If I shield hard enough to keep you out that far, I cut off everyone and I risk cutting Nathaniel and Damian off so much that they start to die."

"Then trust me, *ma petite*, when I say that it would make me incredibly happy if you would give this inch and join us."

I crossed my arms as much as the shoulder holster would let me and scowled at him.

"I am not asking you to have sex with us here and now, *ma petite*, just let us hold you. Let us offer you the comfort that you crave, that we crave to give you, while we wait for the others. When they arrive, we will have our war council, but until then we may hold each other and gain comfort before the war begins."

"You don't mean Narcissus starting a war, do you?"

"*Non, ma petite*, a master vampire has crept into this country when I am supposed to be the king of us all. My power is supposed to be absolute; even if we weather this threat and keep the wererats, the other vampires will learn that one of them found a chink in my armor, and just as Rafael cannot appear weak without bringing more challengers to his throne, so with my own. If I do not make an example of this vampire, then others will search for weakness and they will find it, because no one is unassailable."

"You're afraid, too," I said.

"Yes, very much."

"Why very much? What have I missed?"

"I know that there is a master vampire near us. I know who his *moitié bête* is, and I know where that person is, and yet knowing all of this, I still cannot sense the vampire. Do you understand the implications of that, *ma petite*?"

I suddenly had trouble swallowing past my pulse, and yet my skin felt cold. "Shit, they have to be incredibly powerful."

"And very old, perhaps far older than I am."

I stared at him, my pulse still racing into my throat, so it was like choking, and just like that I realized I wasn't choking on my fear, but on his. He sat there cool and calm like a smooth sea, but underneath he wasn't just paddling as fast as he could, he was starting to drown.

Jean-Claude held his hand out to me. "Please, *ma petite*, let us hold each other and be comforted by the touch of each other before we have to put one or all of us in harm's way."

I looked at his hand still held out and then I looked at his face. If it wasn't the face that launched a thousand ships, it was the one that opened my heart up to the possibility of love again. I looked from him to Asher. He was staring at his lap, his hair down like a curtain hiding his entire face as if he couldn't bear to see me, or maybe couldn't bear me to see him. If he'd been staring at me all bold and gorgeous, I might have hesitated, but he'd been saner and explained things well, and he was trying. Isn't that all any of us can do?

I went to the bed and climbed up on the foot of it. It was still big enough that I had a ways to crawl to reach them. Jean-Claude smiled at me, his face alight with happiness in a way that he would never show in public because the older vampires thought showing soft emotions was a weakness. I started crawling toward them, still in all the weapons and the clothes, because the war council would start any minute. I didn't even try to make the long crawl over the big bed sexy, I just moved toward them, but maybe that was enough, because Asher raised his head enough to look at me with one pale blue eye like a star lost in the golden cloud of his hair. I knew what the scars near that eye looked like, I'd kissed them often enough.

I took Jean-Claude's hand and he pulled me the rest of the way between them. Asher stayed stiff and awkward beside me, keeping the hair like a shield between us. Jean-Claude put his arm across my shoulders and across Asher's, but the other man didn't look at either of us or try to hold us back. He sat with his hands in the lap of his brocade robe and wouldn't look at me.

I cuddled in against Jean-Claude and just looked at all that golden hair and didn't know what to do. I finally said, "You asked me up here, remember, Asher?"

"I'm so ashamed of how I behaved."

I reached out and let myself touch the thick, shining hair until I could sweep it back and see the unscarred side of his face. I tried to sweep all the hair back so I could see all of him, but he grabbed my wrist and said, "Not yet, please."

"Okay," I said, and dropped my hand away from his hair. We ended up holding hands and looking at each other from inches away. The first tear slid down his face, and it was pink with the blood of whatever willing donor he'd fed from tonight.

I caught the tear on my finger before it could travel down his face. "Don't cry," I said.

He started to cry harder, and then suddenly Jean-Claude and I were holding him, and he was saying over and over again, "I'm sorry, I'm sorry, I'm sorry."

I said the only thing I could say. "It's all right, Asher, I forgive you."

And that was how the rest of the "war council" found us. There was a time in my life when I'd have been embarrassed to be found in tears holding on to anyone, but there wasn't anyone in the room who didn't know the history between us all. They would either understand, or they could go to hell.

11

WE DRIED OUR tears and made our battle plan, but Narcissus surprised us by agreeing that the mystery vampire was a danger to us all. "I will step aside and let you make Rafael your rat to call, if I have your word that you will feed the *ardeur* on me later."

"We've been through this before, Narcissus; you're a gay man and I'm a woman—sex isn't going to work for us."

"If Jean-Claude is with us to distract me, I'll do my best to close my eyes and think of England."

The comment made me laugh. "Think of England, you mean close your eyes and it will be all over soon?"

"Yes," he said, and he wasn't laughing.

"I know you have both parts, but it's the guy part we'll need for me; won't not liking lady parts mess with your concentration?"

"To bring more power to my hyenas and to me, I'm willing to try."

Jean-Claude said, "To be very clear between us: for one feeding of the *ardeur* you will step aside and bring no reprisals when Anita and I bring Rafael over as her *moitié bête*?"

"I'm not stupid, Jean-Claude, any vampire that could hide from you and Anita has to be incredibly powerful.

For them to come to St. Louis in the heart of your power and expect to go unnoticed by not just you but all of us in the supernatural community, they are either insane, insanely arrogant, or so powerful they aren't afraid of any of us. That means they're ancient, Jean-Claude; I don't want an ancient vampire to be in charge of St. Louis. Unlike Rafael and you, this is my only territory. I can't leave the city to some new master vampire and regroup—if I'm taken out here, my clan and I are gone, dead, or enslaved. My clan and I lived through Chimera taking us over, but only because Anita and the wererats came to our aid. I know I have not behaved as if I remember that debt, but I do. I will try to be the leader my clan needs and not some love-crazed fool."

I looked into his eyes and there was the serious man to go with the power I felt rolling off him. We agreed to feed the *ardeur* on him later, after we took out the threat that was hovering just out of sight over all that we loved, or even over those we hated.

12

"ANITA CAN'T GO to the fighting pits without body-guards," Micah said.

"You are one of the few we have ever allowed inside our inner sanctum that was not one of us, but that does not mean you can dictate to us," Rafael said.

"I would never have agreed for Anita to go tonight if I had thought you meant to hold her to the usual rules."

"Guys, guys, I feel like I've missed something," I said.

"The leaders of the rodere are not allowed bodyguards inside the warehouse where the fighting pits are located," Micah said.

"So? I go around all the time without bodyguards," I said.

Micah shook his head. "You don't understand, Anita; from the moment you step outside the car you are sur-rounded by wererats, and if one of them picks a fight with you, then it's your fight. No one can interfere. No one can help you."

"If you are not strong enough to fight your way through the crowd, then you are not worthy to lead," Rafael said.

"But Anita isn't a real shapeshifter, she doesn't have all our speed and strength and she absolutely doesn't heal as well as we do," Micah said.

"Rafael, I would not have agreed or formed a plan around this much risk to Anita," Jean-Claude said.

"And I would not have suggested it if I did not think she could do it."

"I appreciate the vote of confidence, Rafael, but Micah is right. I'm good, but I'm not in the same league as you guys. I'm still too human."

Jean-Claude asked Micah, "*Mon chat*, did you fight your way through the rodere to attend the fights?"

"Yes, but I am a shapeshifter and I can bring out claws without shifting, which is allowed for fighting through the crowd. I was also allowed Bram. He couldn't guard me, but he was there in case everything went to shit. If it had gotten out of hand, we'd have done what we had to do to get out."

"Is Anita allowed someone with her like Bram?" Nathaniel asked.

"Micah was a visiting leader. We only let him in at all so he could understand the rodere well enough to represent us in Coalition business," Rafael explained.

"Anita is Nimir-ra for the leopards, that makes her a leader," Nathaniel said.

"Very true, *mon minou*."

"It cannot be another leader and they cannot fight her battles for her. If they interfere, then they will both be escorted outside. If they were rodere, they could be forced into the fighting pit to finish the interrupted fight with death as a possibility," Rafael said.

"How bad was it when you went?" Nathaniel asked Micah.

Micah shrugged. "Not that bad after I made an example of one of the bullies."

"What kind of bullies?" I asked.

"Big guy who sees a little guy and thinks, why is he leader, he's not so tough."

"You showed him the error of his ways, I assume, *mon chat*," Jean-Claude said.

"Yes, but Anita can't call claws like I did to make that point."

"She will be allowed blades, because she is still technically human," Rafael said.

"Everyone who's proven themselves worthy in training has blades, Rafael," Micah protested.

"Yes, but only two blades apiece; Anita can take in what she likes."

"Can I take in whatever weapons I want?" I asked.

"No guns," he said.

I looked at Claudia and Benito, who had been very quiet. "You were both encouraging me to go tonight. You want to chime in now?"

They exchanged a look, and then Claudia made a gesture like *you go first*. "I honestly thought you'd be allowed guards," Benito said.

"So why don't I have guards?"

"We all thought you would be allowed bodyguards as of old, Anita, but the last time a queen sat with the king of the rodere was when women weren't allowed to fight the men, so to keep the queen safe she had warriors that would fight for her. I would not have asked you to join me tonight had I realized that the old rule no longer applied," Rafael said.

"It's sort of my fault," Claudia said.

"How so?" I asked.

"Look at me. I can beat the men and I've done it. I'm not the only one either."

"I know you're not the only female wererat guard we have," I said.

"Yes, and because they're guards, they're expected to go into tonight with the same rules as the men."

Benito said, "But not all the wives will be forced or expected to fight tonight."

"If Anita were my wife, then I could claim to be her protector, but she is very publicly with other people, so we can't lie," Rafael said.

"Older women do not have to fight," Benito said.

"Because they come from a time when it was not expected, they are literally grandmothered in to be non-combatants," Rafael explained.

"I am sorry, Anita," Benito said. "If I had realized that you would be expected to fight your way to the stands, I would not have pushed for you to come tonight."

"The apology is appreciated, but what do I do now? The whole plan to keep Rafael safe from the big bad vampire that has its hooks in Hector is predicated on me being there with my necromancy and Jean-Claude able to see and act through me."

"I did not expect the vote to be so strongly against you. It surprised me and as their king, it is my job to know what they are thinking and feeling. I failed you tonight, Anita."

"What do you mean, vote?" I asked.

"They've got an online voting system set up so that rodere across the country can vote on policy and things that impact them all," Micah said.

"It was Micah's idea to stop the complaints that I favored St. Louis since it was my home territory."

"What was the vote exactly for?" I asked.

"I let it be known that I would sit you beside me tonight, that I wanted you to watch me fight."

"They couldn't vote that you not come," Claudia said, "but with Micah they voted that he be allowed one other leopard, but that he had to be one of them, to get through the crowd."

"I was okay with it, because in theory I agree with the idea that if you're not good enough to get through a crowd that is just trying to bully and intimidate you, then you aren't strong enough to be a leader of any group," Micah said.

"Is this because Anita is technically Nimir-ra?" Nathaniel asked.

"Or the lions' Regina to Nicky's Rex?" Micah asked.

"I said I wanted Anita to sit beside me in the queen's throne, that it had been too long since it was used. I thought it would be nostalgia and . . . I don't know what I thought, but I opened the way for them to say if she is our queen, then she must abide by our rules, which means she might have to fight her way to the stands."

"What do you mean, might?" I asked.

"A lot of the wererats like you, Anita. They remember that you saved us from Nikolaos and the Master of Beasts. They may say hi, or thank you, but they won't attack you," Claudia said.

"But others fear you," Rafael said, "they fear how it feels when you feed on them through me. They think it is evil. They may take this opportunity to hurt you if they can."

"Define *hurt*," I said.

"No, Anita," Micah said.

I looked at him because he didn't tell me no very often. "You think I can't do it?"

He took a deep breath and then held it and let it out slowly. I could almost see him counting as he did it. Trying to center and calm himself before he answered. "I want to say no, but honestly if you have blades and are allowed to use them as ruthlessly as you would as a preternatural marshal, then I think you could."

"If I can do it, why are you so worried?" I asked.

"They can't kill you, but you can't kill them either, Anita. You're small like me, but on top of it, you're a woman and no matter how much you hate it, that does make a difference. You don't train to wound, you only train to kill. I'm worried that your training will take over and you'll kill someone."

"What happens if I accidentally do?"

"Then the rules change," Claudia replied.

"Change how?" I asked.

"If you kill one of us in the melee, then they can kill you," Claudia answered.

"That's why I'm worried," Micah said.

"I'll be acting as your guide tonight since it's your first time; if it happens, I'll fight with you," Claudia said.

"I will be at Rafael's side, so I cannot be with you, but I will send help if it happens," Benito added.

"So you're not afraid that I can't defend myself, you're afraid that I'll be overzealous and kill someone else?"

"You don't train to save lives, Anita, just to take them," Micah said.

"You train to kill rivals, how is it different?"

"I also train to discipline people when I don't have to kill them. Your version of that is to stab them with blades that have no silver content or use lead bullets and let them heal."

"Do I take in non-silver blades?" I asked.

"Do you own any?"

I blinked at him. "Not really."

"And that's my point," he said grimly.

"You bought non-silver blades for Fredo's classes," Claudia said.

"I think of them as practice blades for class, and in regular kali, *practice blade* means aluminum or plastic with no edge and lighter weight than real blades," I said.

"But for the invitation-only classes, *practice blade* means non-silver with an edge," she said.

"It would be a live blade anywhere else," I said.

"But for tonight, it will cut and wound, but they will heal, and it's almost impossible to kill one of us without silver."

I nodded, but added, "I'm going to take a few blades with enough silver content to cause wounds that won't heal instantly, just in case people need the reminder."

"I agree," Claudia said.

"I would like you to dress as my queen tonight, Anita," Rafael said.

"Define *dress*?"

"Sexy dress, heels," he said with the vague answer that so many totally straight men give when pressed for clothes suggestions.

I shook my head. "You know I can't dress like that and carry blades. Hell, I can't fight in heels, or at least not as well. If you want me all dressed up, you need to give me enough bodyguards to make me feel secure." In my head I thought I still wouldn't have wanted to dress for anything but the fight, but that could just be my nerves talking.

"Would it be too much to ask for you to wear makeup and leave your hair down?" he asked.

"Makeup, sure; we'll negotiate on the hair. It gets in my way in a fight."

"You're angry with me," he said.

"Angry, no; upset, hell yes."

Micah raised his hand. "I'm upset with you, too. If you knew it was a possibility that she would have to fight through the crowd like I did, you should have mentioned it while we were making our plans."

"I told you, if I had dreamed that they would vote to force Anita to fight her way to my side, I would not have suggested her coming tonight," Rafael said, and there was just an edge of warmth like a breath of power to dance warm over my skin.

"Apologies are lovely, Rafael, but if anything happens to Anita between the moment she enters your world and sits down beside you, then we will revisit your oversight," Jean-Claude said.

"Are you threatening me?"

"Oh yes."

"We're allies here," I reminded them.

Micah said, "No, in this moment we are men engaged to marry the woman we love, and we all trusted Rafael to know his people well enough to risk you."

"What he said," Nathaniel added, and his energy trailed hot to meet with Rafael's so that suddenly I could see black fur in the darkness inside me where the beasts waited. The leopard flashed yellow eyes upward, but the rat's black eyes were like a glint of darkness within a moonless night.

The rat started to ease into the light, and the leopard followed it as if it were hunting. One great black shape hunting the smaller and then the next moment the rat was huge, as big as the leopard.

I blinked and tore my attention away from inside me to the room and found that Rafael had moved beside me. It was like being plugged into a wall socket—a jolt of energy that shot through me to the rat inside. So much power it almost hurt, and just like that the rat jumped the leopard hard enough that it staggered me. Rafael grabbed my arm to help steady me, but the rat got bigger and the beasts were tearing me up.

I jerked away from him, and Nathaniel was there, holding me. The moment he did the panther roared inside me and the rat was getting the worst of it, but they were still tearing me up inside. I knew the damage wasn't literal, I knew they weren't tearing up internal organs, it just felt like it.

I didn't need to see Rafael to know he was kneeling with us and the rat grew again, sending the leopard rolling. Nathaniel rolled himself around me, and the leopard fought back, but I needed it to stop.

"Rafael, back off!" I yelled.

"What's happening?" Micah asked.

"I can feel the rat inside her now," Rafael said, and he didn't sound upset about causing me pain, more like he felt wonderment as if something about it felt good.

Nathaniel said, "It's not supposed to work this way."

His voice sounded like he hurt, too. They should have both been hurting; that was part of what a *moitié bête* could do, take some of your pain.

"I'm a king," Rafael said, as if that made sense of it all.

"You're not her king, I am," Micah said, and he touched my face, still standing above us all. His leopard rose in a wave of warmth and power that went directly from the skin of his hand to where he touched my face. His leopard poured down into that darkness and pulled my leopard to it. He didn't try to fight the rat, he just called my leopard like a black shadow to meet his, and there was no more room for anything else, especially not with Nathaniel beside us.

"Her eyes," Claudia said.

Nathaniel's skin ran warmer and he looked at me with the gray eyes of his leopard. He was the only shapeshifter I'd ever met whose natural eye color was more exotic than his beast's.

Micah said, "Look at me." Still on our knees, we looked up at him, and I knew that for the first time all three of us were looking at each other with leopard eyes.

13

WHEN THINGS HAD calmed down enough that my eyes weren't the bright yellow of my leopard, I turned on Rafael. "What the fuck was that about?"

"I didn't know your eyes could change like that," Rafael said. He looked shaken and he had apologized, but it was too late for that, at least to me.

"It's just started happening," Micah said.

"What? Why, Rafael? Why did you keep pushing at it when you knew you were hurting me?" It was all I could do not to touch him physically, and I didn't mean in a romantic way. I wanted to at least shove him, but I knew better. If I shoved him and he did anything aggressive at all, I'd do more. I wanted to do more. I was pissed, and I was about to risk life, limb, and maybe more with him as my closest animal to call. No one else would get to me in time if he pulled something like this again.

"The power, Anita, I'm so sorry, but the power was incredible. It felt so good and I could feel that there was more, that if we just touched more, the power between us would be even more." He reached out as if to touch my hair, and I hissed at him like a cat does. That sort of scared me, so I just walked farther away from him.

"Could he bring her rat for real if we weren't with her?" Nathaniel asked.

That stopped the fight. We all looked around at each other. Jean-Claude cut to the heart of it. "If *ma petite* is to choose a beast form at last, then we need to discover if she can choose which one it will be."

"She might get more than one form like I did," Micah said.

"We can't take that chance," Nathaniel said, shaking his head.

"What would be so wrong with her being a wererat?" Rafael asked.

"I thought you were our friend," Nathaniel said.

"I am."

"Then you know for our happiness she needs to be a wereleopard."

"We all date between species here in St. Louis," Rafael said.

"Don't get cute, Rafael," I said. "If I change, it needs to be leopard."

"I will not argue the point, you are far better at relationships than I am, but I honestly did not know that your eyes had started to turn so easily."

"It doesn't happen all the time," I said.

"But it's happening more often," Micah observed.

I nodded and agreed.

"Why was the connection so much stronger right off the bat?" I asked.

Nathaniel said, "Since Damian and I became a triumvirate with Anita, none of the other animals to call have a stronger connection than I do, until just now."

"Has anyone else been a leader of their group?" Benito asked.

"Micah is," Claudia said.

"No, Micah is not her *moitié bête*, he is her Nimir-raj; it is a different connection," Jean-Claude said.

"How can he be her leopard king when she is not truly a wereleopard?" Rafael asked.

"Much of what *ma petite* does metaphysically is impossible, it is one mystery among many."

"But Rafael is the first animal to call who ruled his animal group," Micah said, and he drew me into the circle of his arms. I tried to let the lingering anger go and ease into it, but I couldn't do it. I let him hold me, but I couldn't relax against his body.

"Why should that matter this much?" Nathaniel asked.

"I don't know," Micah said.

I willed myself to melt into his arms, his body, and let go of the terrible tension and the ache in my gut from what my inner beasts had done. I had a thought that made the relaxing even harder.

"What do I do if this happens again tonight?"

"I was allowed one other wereleopard with me. We need to pick someone for you that isn't a wererat," Micah said.

"I'll go," Nathaniel said.

"No, Nathaniel, and you know why," I said.

"I can't fight well enough," he said.

"It's not your strong suit," I said.

Micah kissed the side of my neck, and I snuggled in against the side of his face. We both reached for Nathaniel at the same time, and he came to us and wrapped his arms around us both. We held each other in a three-way hug, and the rising level of leopard was like some vibrating purr of energy. It felt so right. It felt like home. They were home. If any animal energy was home, this was it.

"Do you have any animals to call that can fight well enough to go in with you tonight?" Benito asked.

"It doesn't matter, she is my queen, so only wererats can stay at her side," Rafael said.

"You can feel some of this energy, I know you can," I

said. "Do you really want me to lose this with them tonight by accident?"

Rafael took in a big breath of air and let it out slow.
"No, of course not." But I didn't have to be a full-on
shapeshifter to know he'd just lied.

"You want her to be your queen for real," Micah said,
not accusing, just as a statement.

"After the power I just felt, who would not?"

"You son of a bitch," I said, and started to go forward,
but Micah and Nathaniel held me closer. I sank into the
warm, vibrating energy, but the edge of my own anger
started adding to it, and it wasn't as relaxing.

"You didn't want me to lie, and now you do not want
the truth. What do you want from me, Anita?"

"King or no king, Rafael, don't think you will ride
roughshod over me now that you're my rat to call."

"If I were a human or vampire servant, there would
have been sacred words and an exchange of body fluids,
but because I am only a beast, your power just called out
to me and I answered, because I chose to answer; all your
other beasts have been accidental or had no choice in the
joining."

"What's your point, Rafael?" Micah asked.

"Anita's power called me like you would call a dog,
but I am king of the rodere and no one's dog to call to
heel."

"We did this to keep you alive tonight, don't make it
about egos now," I said.

"I am saying that your power may work the same on
me, but I had to want the connection; perhaps that is not
the only difference in our joining compared to all your
other animals to call."

Jean-Claude finally spoke from where he had been
watching us all, and probably feeling the energy like a
disinterested metaphysical observer. That he did that used

to bug me, but I understood now that he couldn't sense as much if he was tangled up in it sometimes. I wanted his insight more than I wanted him in our group hug.

"*Ma petite* will not go with you tonight if she cannot bring one of her other *moitié bêtes* with her."

"You said this was the best way to stop the vampire that's trying to take over the rats," I said.

"It is," he said.

"If they kill Rafael, they could possess us all," Claudia said.

"They could turn us against all of you," Benito said.

"We will find another way to defeat the vampire that is trying to test our powers," Jean-Claude said, his face blank and empty of emotion.

"But you will have lost the rodere as your food and as your military arm," Rafael said.

"If you win tonight, we lose nothing."

"Weren't you telling me all afternoon how dangerous a *moitié bête* could be?"

"You are one now as well, Rafael. You have extra powers even if *ma petite* is not beside you. We have done our part."

"Please, Jean-Claude, don't do this," Claudia said.

"We do not beg the vampires for anything," Rafael growled at her.

"If the vampire is there tonight and can call rats, then you being my beast half without me there with you isn't going to be as strong as if I were a real vampire," I reminded him.

"With you by my side, how much stronger would it be?"

"A lot," Nathaniel and I said in unison.

"Let her bring one extra person with her," Claudia said.

"It will undermine her claim as queen."

"Not as much as her not being there at all," Benito said.

Rafael looked at the two wererats. "You, too, Benito?"

"I don't understand all the metaphysics, my king, but I know that changing her into one of us and losing the closeness I feel between her and the leopards is poor repayment for her risking her life for us tonight."

"She risks her life to save all that Jean-Claude and Micah have built," Rafael said.

"My king," Benito said, and just that, but Rafael's face softened out of that arrogant handsomeness that he hid behind sometimes, usually when he knew he wasn't going to win an argument.

"I give you my word, Jean-Claude, Micah, Nathaniel, Anita, that I will not do anything tonight to call your rat above the others. I was drunk the way you can be when a power first manifests itself, but I am a king and I am better than that. I will not betray the trust you have in me."

"How do I trust you with my gut still aching from what you did?" I asked.

"I have given you my word, Anita. In all the years we've known each other, have I ever broken my vow?"

I stared at him and finally said, "No, you haven't."

"Your word is good," Micah said.

Nathaniel said, "Your word is good, but I felt your power and your force of will. I knew you were king, but I didn't understand what that meant, until now."

"All kings are powerful, or we would not be kings of our animal groups," Rafael said.

Nathaniel shook his head, hard enough for his hair to fly around his face. "I don't mean that. I mean I could literally feel your will, your willpower pressing on me when we were . . . inside Anita just now. Your strength of purpose is frightening, Rafael."

"Is that a complaint or a compliment?" he asked.

"Neither, both."

"I must go and change for the fight, and prepare myself mentally, so if you have a point, make it." There was a touch of irritation, almost anger, which was unusual for him. Shit, I hoped he didn't get any of my anger issues.

"Let Anita have one person with her like Micah did."

"Claudia will stay with her."

"Someone not rat."

"I gave you my word."

"I'm not worried about your honor; I'm worried about the energy of that many wererats in that close a proximity to Anita just after she's made you her rat to call."

"No one mentioned that was a problem before," Rafael said.

"I hadn't felt her rat be stronger than I've ever felt it inside her. Now I have."

"What do you mean?" Micah asked.

"We've helped Anita stay human because we play her beasts off each other. One of us will let her smell our skin and different beasts, it's kept her from choosing or changing form for real."

"We know all that," Rafael said, and again there was that note of impatience that wasn't typical of him.

"When Anita goes to our pard, she has Micah and me with her. When she goes to the lupanar she has Richard with her, or sometimes it's the leopards and the wolves together. She's never had to walk into one of the big group meetings without one of us at her side."

"Are you saying, *mon minou*, that she needs Rafael to stay near her tonight?"

"No, I know that's not possible, but I do believe Anita needs at least one other beast with her so that she plays the energies off each other if she needs to."

"None of the other beasts to call may come, it would undermine me almost as much as if one of her other kings came at her side."

"Pierette can stay with Anita and Claudia."

"No, no leopard, it will be seen as Micah's token."

"Not if you introduce her as a potential lover."

"What is it with all of you pressuring me into a three-way?"

"Rafael has already turned it down, turned her down," I said.

Nathaniel stared at the other man. His face said it all, astonished. Rafael actually looked uncomfortable and started explaining like a guy who thinks himself macho and cool and turned down something cooler-than-thou. "I'm sure she is lovely, but I have never had a woman suggest a three-way without it going terribly wrong."

"I tried to convince him the offer was legit and not some deep-seated girl trick to see if he'd cheat on me, but in his defense one ex stabbed him and another burned his stuff over three-ways," I said.

"You are dating the wrong people," Nathaniel said.

"As I explained to Anita earlier, I have dated the wrong people for many years."

"We've all been with Anita and Pierette, and nobody stabbed anyone or set anyone on fire," Micah said, as if he couldn't quite believe the last part.

Nathaniel literally waved his hand in the air as if erasing the whole thing, then said, "You don't have to sleep with Pierette if you don't want to, though why you wouldn't want to—no, never mind. My point, Rafael, is just let Pierette be with Anita as her girlfriend and potentially yours. She can hang on both of you in sight of the crowd."

"It will start the women fighting over me again."

"But the other women aren't Anita's lover and Pierette is," Nathaniel said.

"You mean the old idea that Rafael would be free to sleep with women that I'm already sleeping with, but no one else?"

"Yes, and taking her in there as both your guard and your girlfriend means that she can touch you. If you need to smell her leopard, she can put bare skin near your face, and it will look like flirting."

"*Mon minou*, you have become devious."

Nathaniel smiled. "I've always been devious; I was just really bad at it."

"It is a way for Anita to have extra protection to fight her way through the crowd where you can't help her, and energetic help to hold human shape after you go down to the pit," Micah said.

"And no man's reputation has ever been harmed by having two beautiful women on his arm," Jean-Claude said.

"It depends on the man," Rafael said, "but your point is made." He looked at Claudia and Benito. "What do the two of you think?"

"I am relieved that Anita and Claudia would have an extra pair of blades with them," Benito said.

"Pierette got an invitation from Fredo, too. She's good with a blade and incredibly fast," Claudia said.

"How is she empty hand?" Rafael asked.

"Still good," Claudia said.

Rafael nodded. "All right, I agree."

"Thank you for agreeing," Nathaniel said.

"You have become far more determined than I remember you being, Nathaniel."

"You remember the anger issues Richard had for so long that turned out to be Anita's anger in him?"

"I remember, we were all relieved when she discovered how to take back her anger."

"I think I've gained some of her resolve."

"Anita is one of the most resolute people I know," Rafael said.

"Yes, she is."

The two men looked at each other for longer than seemed necessary, and then Rafael said, "I will have to watch you more closely from now on then, won't I?"

"More like you should stop discounting me when you negotiate with us."

"I do not discount you."

Nathaniel gave a small smile. "It's okay, most people do, or did."

"Then my apologies, Nathaniel, I will do better in the future."

"Thank you."

"In the spirit of honor, if we feel that *ma petite* is in danger, then we will come to her aid, even if we must fight our way through all the wererats to do it."

"I would expect nothing less, and if I die, then do whatever you have to do to get Anita out and safe."

"Don't worry, we will," Micah said.

With my stomach aching from the game of metaphysical keep-away that Rafael had just forced Nathaniel to help me play, I wasn't feeling as friendly as I had before, but . . . "I'd rather the plan is you don't die and instead kill the son of a bitch."

"That is my preferred plan, too," Rafael said with a smile.

Benito said, "We must go if you are to prepare."

His smile faded and he nodded. "Do I deserve a kiss, or are you too upset with me?"

"Are you reading my face or my emotions?" I asked.

"Your face, I think."

I nodded. "Since I'm going to be friendly with you at the fight, sure, why not."

"That's not very enthusiastic," he said, frowning.

"You just hurt me in a nonconsensual way because the power was a rush; sorry, but I expected better of you."

"I am sorry, Anita."

"You keep saying that today."

"I am off my game, I admit that." His face was suddenly the seriousness of earlier. I needed him better behaved toward me, not depressed, and then I realized that there was still part of him that believed Hector might be his son. Jesus.

It cut him slack, so I went to him. I gazed up into that solemn face and said the only thing I could think to say that might help. "I'm sorry about all the conflicts. I honestly believe that Hector's mother is gaslighting you so that you will hesitate tonight."

"Logically I know you are right, but I would like to look at him so strong and promising and think he might be mine."

"And now you have to kill him," I said.

"There is a faint chance that neither of us has to die tonight. I did offer, but it is doubtful that they will accept defeat that does not end in death, because that means if he wins, then I'm still king."

"He's probably not going to agree to that," I said.

"No."

"Then fight to win, because I'll be there tonight and if you lose, he'll try to take me."

"Take you where?"

"Rafael, if the vampire could take over the wererats and kill me, Jean-Claude's power base would be destroyed."

"I did not think. You cannot come tonight." He grabbed my upper arms and his fear for me was real.

"If she is there, then so am I," Jean-Claude said.

"It's a way to have his power there without the other vampire understanding that me being a necromancer makes me a much better conduit for vampiric powers than most human servants."

He stared down at me, face almost pained, then hugged me close to him as he turned to look at Jean-Claude. "I told Anita she should seduce Hector if I die. I did not think that she might be the next target."

"Even if he wins and slays you, he cannot just go into the crowd and start killing people," Benito said.

"If he does, then he will not be our king for long," Claudia added.

"What do you mean?" I asked.

"If a challenger kills a king, but we hate him, then we kill him then and there while he's still wounded," Claudia explained.

"Wow, you guys really are harsh," Nathaniel said.

"We have the most complete culture of all the animal groups in St. Louis, and one way we stayed strong and whole when others were torn apart by the power of the werewolves' and the wereleopards' old leaders was by being so ruthless that no one wanted to push us past a certain point."

I hugged him one-armed around his waist. "Then I'm not in as much danger as I thought, which is good, but I'd rather have you alive than help kill Hector after you're dead."

"Good to know," he said, looking down at me with almost a smile.

"Now kiss me like you meant it, and then I'll see you at the fight later."

That did make him smile. He leaned over and I went up to meet his kiss. He kissed me with his hands strong and searching on my body, so I returned the favor and his mouth was suddenly so eager at mine that it took my breath away. I forgot where we were and what was happening and it was just him in my arms, just us kissing and exploring each other's bodies. It was only when he pulled my shirt out of my belt even with the gun holster that I broke the kiss laughing, a little nervous and breathless and happy.

He was breathless and laughing, too. "For such a kiss, I will fight harder."

"Good, because I'm still hoping to talk you into that three-way."

That made him laugh even more, and he left with laughter still lightening his features. Benito gave me a nod just before he closed the door behind them both.

The rest of us were quiet for a moment, and then Jean-Claude said, "*Ma petite*, that was well done. He left with fighting spirit."

I turned and looked at him. "I have too many of your memories now. I've seen a thousand women and a few men undermine you or someone else with a pissy attitude on the eve before the big duel or battle. Hell, Richard used to do it to me all the time. I won't do that to somebody else."

"Where is the Ulfric? Shouldn't he have been here during some of this?" Claudia asked.

"He's out of state on a big extended family vacation," I said. "And the dominants of the werelions are all off on a leadership-building camping trip."

"I asked them to check out the new company that's specializing in supernatural executive retreats," Micah said.

"Nicky and Mephistopheles are going to go apeshit when they find out all this happened and they missed it," Nathaniel said.

"Magda won't be too happy either," I added.

"Why don't the lions have more of a whole culture like Rafael was saying? They weren't taken over by Raina and Marcus, or someone like Chimera," Nathaniel said.

"The old Rex wasn't strong enough to run them like regular prides run," Micah said.

I added, "He'd have been killed and taken over years ago if there'd been more werelions in this country."

"Werelions tend to kill each other on sight if they aren't part of the same pride," Micah said.

"Only because they're afraid that's exactly what the new group has planned," Claudia said.

"But the Coalition has given them another way to contact each other and explain that someone got a new job and needs to move to a new city, a new pride territory," Micah said.

"You've made a lot of really good changes, Micah."

"Thank you, Claudia, I do my best."

"Now, you and I need to change for tonight and pick out your weapons," Claudia said, and she was looking at me.

"We also need to help Pierette dress and arm herself," I said.

"Yes." And then Claudia suddenly grinned in a way I almost never saw.

"What?" I asked, smiling just from the look on her face.

"If we all live through tonight, it may be the best girls' night out I've ever had."

I laughed and said, "After tonight, let's plan a girls' night out that's a little less death-defying."

"Deal," she said, and offered me a fist bump.

I touched her bigger fist, and we went off to find Pierette and tell her what she'd been voluntold for.

14

THE THREE OF us were dressed almost identically and it wasn't on purpose, as if we'd looked in the same closet except for size and placement of weapons. I was in black tactical pants, black T-shirt, with black cross-trainers; Claudia in black tactical pants, white T-shirt, and black cross-trainers; and Pierette in black pants, white T-shirt, and white cross-trainers. My custom wrist sheaths with their high silver content were easy. They could go where they'd gone for years. It got trickier after that. I'd been practicing with the swords, but I'd never tried to carry them. I was learning kali, which is a Filipino martial art, stick and blade. I had a bag to carry the blades and sticks in, but no sheaths. I had a waist-sheath Spyderco knife that I'd bought for class. Most people wore a waist knife with the hilt up along the ribs, but I was too short-waisted to wear it that way and had to wear it horizontally, hilt forward for a cross draw. I added a couple of Emerson assisted-opening folding blades into the pockets along the legs of the tactical pants, though I'd go for the waist blade first. I also had two karambits, which were curved knives, though that didn't do them justice. They were supposed to mimic the shape of a tiger or leopard claw, and they did just what claws do, tear and gut. The smaller

one was a necklace sheath, and the bigger one hooked
over one of the many pockets in my black tactical pants.
If I drew either of the karambits, then things had gotten
serious and I was being forced to do major damage.

Claudia was carrying just a knife at her waist, hilt up
because she had waist for days, and a sword on her back
in a custom shoulder harness. Her long black hair was in
a braid nicely out of the way. I was wearing it long for
Rafael and yes, I'd put on makeup. I had hair ties in one
of my pockets in case I decided that I didn't want to be
blinded by my hair in a fight. I could always take it down
before Rafael saw me, or maybe by the time I got to him
I wouldn't give a damn what he thought of me. I automatically grabbed a pair of tourniquets that were both
rubber-banded to combat gauze that would help slow
bleeding. I'd started carrying them shoved in my tactical
pants pockets since I'd started going out with more humans, both fellow marshals and SWAT, for delivering
warrants on preternatural citizens. There wouldn't be any
humans there tonight and shapeshifters could heal anything that either would help with, so I almost put them
back, but that still, small voice in my head that had kept
me safe in so many dark places gave that little push. I
didn't argue with it, I just put the tourniquets and combat
gauze in the pockets of the tac pants. I had to remove one
of the folding knives, but in the end that little voice said
it was a good trade. Besides, five knives were probably
enough. I really missed having a gun tonight.

Pierette had a custom-made back harness that held
two swords with the hilts coming off the same side. I'd
asked if it wouldn't be easier for there to be a hilt over
each shoulder. She'd replied that it's easier to do a shoulder roll if you've got one shoulder that's clear. I was really going to have to get one of the sword-sheath
harnesses. She had a waist knife with the hilt forward
like mine, for the same reason. She was only a little taller

than I was, and her hair was so short that she didn't have to worry about it getting in the way. She'd put on makeup when she realized I was wearing it, and then she suggested makeup to Claudia. I'd never seen her wear any, so I'd just assumed she didn't like to wear it, not that she didn't know how. But she surprised me by letting Pierette put mascara and eyeliner on her with just a little neutral color to the eyelids. It was both neutral and eye-catching, which was a trick I'd never mastered with makeup. I went for bold eyes and bright lipstick, because it looked good and I honestly didn't know how to do anything else. Maybe we could have a sleepover and Pierette could give us makeup tips. I almost wasn't kidding.

The three of us rode in the back of a big SUV with two of the wererat bodyguards in front. I knew that there would be other vehicles out of sight, scent, and hearing range waiting in case I gave the signal. They were full of bodyguards that weren't wererats, because all of them that we'd want to fight on our side would be at the fight tonight.

I also knew that there were Harlequin guards scattered in the shadows doing what they'd done for thousands of years: be the best spies and assassins the vampire world had to offer, though half of them were wereanimals like Pierette. Her vampire master, Pierrot, was out there hearing and seeing what she did. They had one of the smoothest and closest connections of any master and *moitié bête* I'd ever met.

The fighting pits were in a warehouse by the Mississippi River, but I felt the energy of the rodere blocks before we got close to the river. It reminded me of the energy of the lupanar when all the werewolves were there waiting in the woods around their throne of carved rock, the only thing that had survived the destruction of their culture under the last leaders. I'd never thought before that a group of shapeshifters that had a throne carved of solid stone must have a story behind it. Damn thing was too heavy to move, so how did it come to be sitting in the middle of the Missouri woods? It was like I was suddenly wondering, What were the cultures that all the other animal groups had lost? Could we get them back? Did we want them back?

Pierette said, "You are very quiet, my queen."

"I can feel the energy."

"Of what?"

"The rodere."

"Already?" Claudia asked from the other side of me. I looked at her. "Yeah, can't you?"

She shook her head.

"Why should I feel it more than you do?"

"I don't know," she said.

"Do you feel the werewolves this way?" Pierette asked.

"Yes, but not this strong. It's like the leopard, but more, so much more energy." I rubbed my arms and realized I was already goose-bumped.

"Should we tell Jean-Claude she's feeling it like this?" Claudia asked.

"He knows," Pierette said.

"Micah, then?"

"Jean-Claude will tell him if he thinks he needs to know," I said.

"Why are you feeling it this far out?" Claudia asked.

"Not sure, but I think it's because I made Rafael my *moitié bête* and he's king in a way that Richard isn't for the wolves."

"Micah would be this for the leopards if you weren't all so . . ." She stopped.

"What? Just say it, Pierette."

"Broken."

"Broken how?"

"There are rituals and ways for our kind, too, my queen."

"We'll talk about some of the leopard culture we're missing after this is over."

"If you wish."

"I wish," I said, and took her hand in mine and squeezed it. "I want to be the best queen I can be for everyone. Help me do that, Pierette."

She smiled in her red lipstick that not only matched mine but was mine. We were sharing a tube of it tonight as if we were on a date at a club and had only a tiny purse to hold everything, so consolidating lipstick was just practical. It wasn't her usual color, but if we wanted to be able to kiss tonight and not ruin each other's color, it had to match, or at least complement.

"I would help you set the moon in the sky, my queen, if you but ask."

That made me smile and lean in for a careful kiss. It was as I drew back from the kiss that I realized the skin-thrumming energy of the wererats was less the moment I touched her hand. I told her and Claudia, and we spent the last few minutes of the drive experimenting. A finger on her skin wasn't enough, but a hand against her skin, or hers on mine, was enough to dim it. Holding hands or kissing or hugging calmed it so that I could feel it like an echo.

"I think with more people who aren't rat I might be able to shut it out completely."

"I'm even happier that you have Pierette with you tonight then, because if you are this attuned to our energy now, wait until you're surrounded by us."

"I'm a little worried about that now," I said.

"Maybe the energy won't bring your beast, my queen; maybe it is just the energy that Rafael feels and through him you feel it, too."

"Maybe," I said, and then I felt it like a great beating heart that just happened to not be inside my chest, but it was still my heart. It still pulsed and beat for me. I touched my hand to my chest as if I could feel my heart start to beat in time to it.

Pierette still had my other hand in hers. She squeezed it tight and put her other hand around my arm. "My queen, what is wrong?"

My voice came out low because I was listening to the pulse of that power. "I'm not sure anything is wrong. If this is what Rafael feels, then no wonder he's arrogant."

"Does it still help for us to touch?" Pierette asked.

"Not as much, let's see what happens when we stop touching."

"I can feel the power of so many of us in one place now," Claudia said.

"It's not just that," I said as I drew my hand away from Pierette. The moment I didn't have her skin against mine the power swept over me like a giant ocean wave. So. Much. Power. I stopped breathing for a second, as if I were holding my breath, waiting for the wave to pass over my head so I could surface.

"Anita," Claudia said, voice sharp.

It startled me and I took a gasping breath as if I had really been underwater and just surfaced. "What else is in there beside the fighting arenas?" I asked.

"What do you mean?"

"You don't get power like this just from fighting."

"Spilled blood is sacred, my queen, and lives sacrificed even more so."

It felt like I was fighting to lift my chest enough to get a deep breath. I had to figure out how to navigate this power level before we got out of the car. I just called inside my mind, "Jean-Claude, are you feeling this?"

"I am." His voice came like an echo.

"How do I deal with it?"

"I can tell you how to harness it, or block it, but swimming through it is harder. It is so very alive, *ma petite*, and that is not my area of expertise."

"Power is power—help me navigate?" I said.

"We will try, my queen."

"Sorry, I didn't mean to say that last part out loud."

"Are you doing that mind-to-mind thing?" Claudia asked.

"Yeah."

"Jean-Claude?"

"Yeah."

"We're pulling into the gate," Claudia said. It was a tall fence with razor wire at the top.

"We're out of time, Jean-Claude; if you have any advice, now is the time." I said it out loud and I didn't care.

Jean-Claude didn't bother with words, he just shared knowledge and skill at working with supernatural powers. Centuries of practice that he thought might help me now. I got glimpses of memories that went with some of it, but it was like shuffling and then cutting cards, you got hints of images instead of the full card, but it was like I could suddenly count cards and keep it all in my head. If anything that he knew would help me tonight, I had it just like that. Let's hear it for practice, because we'd started training in the metaphysical the same way we did in the physical. It wasn't as formal and the groups were smaller and more personal, but we'd never been better at this part of things, except for Richard, who was like a missing piece of our puzzle. I pushed the thought away and realized that it hadn't been my thought, it was Jean-Claude's; he felt the loss of Richard more than I did, because I'd found people to fill Richard's place in my heart and my bed, but Jean-Claude was still looking to fill all the holes that our absent werewolf left for him. Jean-Claude pulled the emotion and thought back and shielded more carefully from me. He was a lot better at cherry-picking what he shared with me; I still had a tendency to do an info dump that included a lot more than I needed to share.

"I will be here if you need me, *ma petite*, and if the need is great, I will be there in the flesh."

"Don't endanger yourself," I said.

"I will be discretion itself, *ma petite*."

The guards at the gate opened them for us, and the SUV glided between them and the energy stole my breath again. "Remember what you have learned, *ma petite. Je t'aime*."

"*Je t'aime*," I thought, and then I swallowed hard as if I'd changed altitudes. We'd come through a magic circle like my friends that were Wiccan, witches, cast when they were working magic, and just like their circles it was meant to raise power and contain it. It felt like I was inside that giant beating heart; the power was all around me so that it felt like the car was vibrating with it, but I knew it wasn't real. Magic was like emotions, they both felt real, until you tried to explain them to other people and then they didn't make any sense.

"Why is there a permanent magic circle here?" Pierette asked; she was looking through the tinted windows of the SUV as if looking for threats, or for who was casting circles.

I answered her question in a voice breathless as if I'd been running. "To keep the power in."

"We told you this was our seat of power, Anita," Claudia said.

"The lupanar doesn't feel like this at all."

"The wolves are powerful here in this city, but they are not us. The rodere have never been conquered. Never been broken so that we forgot who we are—we are an unbroken line going back thousands of years." Claudia said it with such pride and with the beating, roaring pulse of their power all around me; she should have been proud.

I felt tears start to build in my eyes, I wasn't even sure why. I turned to Pierette and clung to her hand. It helped anchor me a little in the pounding surf of magic. "This is what you meant when you said we were all broken here in St. Louis, isn't it?"

"Yes," she said.

"The rodere are not broken," I said, and felt the first tear trail hot and unwelcome down my cheek.

"No, they are powerful and whole."

"Is this what we're all supposed to feel like?"

"I do not know about all, but yes, this is what we are meant to be."

"Can the leopards be this?"

"Only if we can find our wizards again."

"Wizards?"

Claudia said, "Without our brujas we would not be rodere."

"I've never met one of your witches," I said.

"Why would you? You've never been here before and they are not bodyguards."

I felt diminished in the face of the power all around me, or as if I should have power to answer it and I didn't. The beasts inside me stirred not to rise, but as if they felt my thought. *Where is our magic?*

It was the hyena who stared up at me with brown eyes and slit pupils. I looked into her eyes and realized that I'd learned earlier today that the hyenas had never lost their magic either. What the hell had happened to the rest of us?

15

I GOT OUT of the SUV with Claudia on one side of me and Pierette on the other. The driver and his wingman weren't allowed to hang around with us, or more particularly me. They had to drive off and put the SUV out of sight of the main road with the other vehicles. We didn't want a police officer to do a casual drive-by and wonder about too many cars parked after dark in a warehouse district.

The three of us stood alone with huge warehouses surrounding us except for the gate just behind us and the fence. I wasn't going over the razor wire. I looked past the few people still outside the warehouses to the river. St. Louis is too large a city for it to be truly dark, but even without the illumination I would have sensed the river. The Mississippi is just too damn big to be ignored this close to it. The energy and flow of it, the sound of it faint and persistent, and water, you knew a big body of water was close by like a big lake, or even the ocean. The river had that kind of aliveness to it.

I realized that the rush and beat of the energy was tied to the river somehow. Had the rodere's witches, their brujas, used the river as part of their circle of protection, or had the river just been here and they'd worked with it, because they had no choice? Some things are just too vast and too powerful to be ignored. I guess it was a chicken/egg question that didn't matter. The heartbeat of power used the river like blood to keep it pumping. It was like a huge mystical battery.

"Anita, are you all right?" Claudia asked.

I nodded. "The magic is . . . loud."

Pierette took my hand in hers, though since we were both right-handed, she had to compromise her gun hand, because she knew I wouldn't compromise mine. Not here and now with strange magic everywhere and the first few people looking our way.

"It beats through your body like a second heartbeat," Pierette said.

"You touching me isn't making it quieter," I said.

"I felt the energy, but now it's much more," she said.

I squeezed her hand and let it go. "If it's making it worse for you and not helping me, then I'd rather have you with a clearer head."

Pierette accepted that without question. We were lovers, but she was my bodyguard first and she never forgot that, which was one reason we could date. There were a handful of people looking at us from the door of the nearest warehouse. I should have been able to sense their energy, tell if they were human or shapeshifter, but I couldn't. The magic all around me was so overwhelming that I was head-blind to anything smaller.

Claudia walked confidently past the group by the first warehouse and we did our best to exude the same air of *I have places to go and no time to chat*, but one of the men called out, "Claudia, whatcha doing bringing a cat into our house?"

It took me a second to realize he meant Pierette, or maybe he meant me and her; no, that would be plural, *cats*. Claudia answered him without stopping, "Rafael knows she's coming."

I felt the energy react like water that had been disturbed. I knew that one of them was moving toward us. He was like a bad swimmer floundering and making too many waves or like someone trying to be sneaky in the woods but who crashed through the underbrush like a herd of noisy elephants. I didn't question it, just moved, and I was there before the man could touch Pierette. She was facing him, too. He hadn't snuck up on her, but it was like the energy all around us made him move slow, or me fast.

He thought he was fast, because he was startled when he found us both looking at him and ready. He was about our size, delicate-looking for a man, and he didn't look as strongly Hispanic as Rafael, more Asian-ish.

"No fighting in sight of the road, Danny, you know that," Claudia said, looming over all of us.

"I didn't draw a blade," he said.

"You draw a blade within sight of the road, and you go into the pit as warmup. Those are the rules," she said.

I hadn't known that rule, but I waited until Danny walked back to join his group of friends before I spoke low to Claudia. "Any other rules that will get us thrown to the wolves, or rats, or whatever?" I asked.

"The punishments aren't for first-timers, only for the people that should know better."

"Good to know," I said, as Pierette said, "Reassuring." We looked at each other and smiled. It was more than a friend smile, but then we were more than friends.

We were in a dark space between two warehouses now, and I felt the waves of power move smoothly, but it was still a lot of energy getting displaced. Something big was "swimming" toward us.

I moved up beside Claudia and whispered, "Something powerful ahead."

"Neva," Claudia called out, "we are honored by your presence."

"I knew you would know I was here, Claudia, but how

did you know, Anita Blake?" The woman stepped out of
the shadows, or maybe the shadows thinned out and let
us see her, but either way she was taller than Pierette, but
still well under six feet, so I guess average height. Her
skin was very brown and showed her age as if she'd spent
all her life in too much sunshine and not enough sun-
screen. Her hair was still thick and black, unbound
around her thin shoulders. She stood very upright, no
stoop at all, but her body had begun to wear down anyway. Her bones were strong, but her muscles were thin-
ning down the way that comes only after seventy.

"I don't know." And that was the truth.

"Why have you brought a leopard among us?" she
asked, and I wasn't sure if she was addressing me or
Claudia.

"She's with me," I said, not really answering her question.

The woman smiled and it was like the shadows thick-
ened around her, so that her eyes gleamed like black diamonds, but her face was almost obscured as if her eyes
glittered bodiless. I called my own power, just a pulse of
it, and felt Jean-Claude down that metaphysical cord,
helping me. The darkness thinned, so I could see the out-
line of her face more clearly, but her eyes still glittered
with more than just her inner beast.

Pierette moved a little uneasily and was looking behind us as if there was a threat there, too. I wanted to ask
what but kept my attention on the woman. Claudia was
just standing beside me, trying for neutral but not quite
hiding the tension in her body.

I felt that sense of something swimming through the
power again. It was both as big as the woman and not, or
bigger, it was as if whatever it was ebbed and flowed and . . .

"Neva, they are guests of our king, not intruders,"
Claudia said.

"Blades will not be enough for this, my queen," Pierette said from behind me.

"Not enough for what?" I asked. I could feel it, but I didn't understand what I was sensing.

"Can't you smell them?"

"No." But the moment she said *them*, I understood that it was a group of things moving through the magic, so many of them that their shape changed like starlings forming shapes in the air because there were so many of them, and then I knew even before I heard the first claws clicking against the bricks of the pavement.

I did that slow horror-movie turn because I was almost sure what was behind us and I didn't want to be right. Rats, thousands of them.

16

I EXPECTED THEM to rush us, but they stopped a few yards away as if they'd come to some invisible barrier I couldn't see. Some of them stood up on their hind legs and sniffed the air, but most of them waited in silence, barely moving like a frozen dark river of furred bodies. Only the glittering of their eyes as it reflected the dim light here and there proved that they weren't all asleep like some magic Pied Piper lullaby. They should have been squeaky, or squabbling, or grooming, or something. The unnatural stillness of them was almost more unnerving to me than anything else.

I had to swallow past my pulse, which was trying to choke me, or maybe that was my heart trying to climb up and out. Pierette asked, "If I draw a blade, what will they do?"

"Whatever Neva wishes them to do," Claudia said; her voice was low and careful as if she didn't want to make any sudden moves or noises. Good to know that I wasn't the only one who felt like we were on the edge of battle and all we needed was the first person to make a move, any move, and then bad things would happen.

"Is this some weird initiation that no one told me

about?" I asked, trying to make a joke of it, but my voice held the panicked beat of my heart, breathless and thin.

"No," Claudia said, as if she thought I'd asked a serious question.

"Why does our magic know you, Anita Blake?" Neva asked.

"What do you want me to say?" I asked.

"The truth."

"I told you the truth already, so just tell me what you want me to say and I'll say it."

"Are you afraid of our small brethren?" she asked.

"You can hear how fast my heart is beating, you know I'm afraid."

"Look at me, Anita Blake."

It was a little too much like a command for my taste, but I'd worry about who was the toughest later, so I looked at her. I trusted that Pierette and Claudia would keep an eye on the furry horde, for what little good it would do us. We needed heavy firepower to have a hope of keeping the rats from engulfing us, things like shotguns and fully automatic machine guns and flamethrowers. Since we didn't have any of that, I looked at Neva. Honestly, she was a much better view than the waiting rats. Funny how you don't realize you're scared of something until it's staring you in the face. I'd forgotten how much I didn't like rats.

Her eyes were like black diamonds except they weren't just reflecting the dim light like the real rats, her eyes had their own light as if she were a vampire. The only shapeshifters that I'd ever seen with eyes like that had a vampire they called master. Holy shit, did she belong to the same vampire that Hector did? I wasn't the only "vampire" who had multiple animals to call. If Hector's master was the same, then we were in serious freaking trouble here.

"Anita Blake." She said my name like it tasted bitter.

"Neva," I said, for something to say while I screamed down my metaphysical connections, hoping that Jean-Claude was getting all this.

She turned her head to look at me out of one eye the way a bird will, and I caught a glint of light in her eyes that wasn't black. I blinked and took a step toward her, then thought to ask, "May I come closer to see your eyes better?"

"A step, or two, no more; I do not want you tempted to go for a blade. I would hate to explain to our king what happened to his concubine."

I didn't really like being called a concubine, but she had several thousand rats waiting to swarm over us, so until that changed, she could call me any damn thing she wanted. I moved slowly and deliberately the two steps she'd given me; I didn't want a misunderstanding.

She stared at me aggressively, both eyes forward, and there it was, starshine in her black eyes. They were the darkness of space with stars scattered and shining in the permanent night between the worlds.

"I've seen eyes like yours before," I said, keeping my voice low and careful, just in case.

"You have never been to the heart of our people, so you have never seen eyes like mine."

"I think I know why your power and I are getting along so well."

"Tell me."

"How about if I show you?"

"Show me what?"

"I'm going to call a little of the magic in me, so you can feel how similar it is to yours."

"We are not necromancers here."

"This isn't necromancy. I just don't want you to freak out when I open myself to the power, okay?"

"Show me something worth seeing, Anita Blake."

I took that for reassurance that she wouldn't freak out and I called an ability that hadn't come through Jean-Claude, or any of the shapeshifters I was tied to, but a self-professed goddess. My skin ran with the energy she had shared with me. The magic around us pulsed and then hesitated like a heart skipping a beat.

"Your eyes," Neva said, "this can't be."

The beat of magic around us caught up with that lost beat, and it was as if my body were a gong and it had hit me solidly in the chest. It stole my breath and staggered me backward.

Claudia caught me or I might have fallen. "Neva, you are not allowed to harm her."

"I did nothing," she said.

I fought to have enough air to say, "Not her . . . fault." I looked up at her as I said it and watched her face pale.

"Neva, what have you done!" She turned back to the other woman, and her anger and fear raised her beast enough that I jerked back from the heat of it.

Pierette said, "Anita's eyes are not the witch's doing."

"I can see them for myself. Neva, what did you do?"

"It is you and our king who should have told me that she carries our magic inside her." Her anger and fear translated to heat like I'd opened a blast furnace. I stumbled back from them both, and it was Pierette who caught my arm so I didn't hit a wall.

"Control your little beasts, witch," Pierette said.

I looked and saw that the rats were beginning to creep forward, still unnaturally silent and well behaved. I looked at them with eyes made of black space and starlight, and their energy wasn't right. They weren't ordinary animals of any kind. They watched everything with a weight of intelligence and thought that wasn't very rat-like. Rats are smart, very smart, but they're animals and no matter how intelligent they can't look at you with that sense of a personhood in their eyes, their bodies.

"Wererats don't come this small," I whispered.

Pierette said, "They are just rats that the witch is controlling."

"No, they're not just rats." I didn't know what they were, so I had no word to substitute, but I knew what they were not, and that was a normal animal of any kind.

"What do you see, Anita?" Neva asked; it took me a second to realize she'd used just my first name.

"I'm not sure, but something's wrong with them, or right with them, but right or wrong, they're different." I glanced back at her and physically she looked the same, though now I could "see" where the tip of the short sword on her back poked out of the line of her shirt. Her thick, unbound hair hid the hilt that came out above the opposite shoulder. How was she carrying it? Just thinking about it gave me the hint of straps under the short-sleeved blouse. I looked at Claudia and I knew where she'd hidden a small blade on her calf, because now I could see the slightest difference from one leg to the other. It had been like this the first time when Obsidian Butterfly had put her power inside me, but never again. I'd gained other powers, but this hypervision for weapons and dangers had never come back. If Neva could see what I saw, then she knew where every weapon was hidden on Pierette and me. Nothing could hide from this.

Neva and Claudia were arguing. Claudia demanding what she'd done to me, and Neva angry that no one warned her I had a piece of their magic inside me already. I glanced back at the rats and realized they were listening. I don't mean the way a dog does, but the way people do. They were hearing and understanding what the two women were saying back and forth.

"Obsidian Butterfly," I said. I had to say it a little louder for them to hear me enough to stop bickering.

"What did you say?" Claudia asked.

"Itzpapalotl." Neva used the original Aztec name.

"Yeah, that's her," I said.

"What of her?"

"She's the master vampire of Albuquerque, New Mexico. When I visited her a few years back, she shared power with me. That's where the eyes came from for me. Where'd you get yours, Neva?"

"The gods of the people were not vampires."

"I can't speak to all the Aztec pantheon, but I can tell you that Obsidian Butterfly is a vampire, but if you ever meet her in person, don't tell her that. She thinks she's a goddess; no harm letting her keep thinking that and a hell of a lot safer for you."

"Why would Itzpapalotl share power with you?" Neva asked.

"She wanted me to help her get rid of some mutual enemies. Who shared energy with you?" I asked.

"Our ancestors."

"What does that mean?" I asked.

"Our magic comes from our ancestors and the gods they walked with," she said, as if that cleared everything up.

"Were the gods they walked with Aztec by any chance?" I asked.

"Some, our people have been touched by the gods of all the lands we have passed through."

"And the rats?" I asked.

Neva looked at me and there was a moment of staring into the starlit darkness of her eyes. The first time I'd looked into eyes like that I'd been rolled so completely that the vampire could have done anything to me, but now I stared into them and did not fall into them, because I had an answering power in my own eyes. I might owe one would-be goddess in New Mexico a thank-you note.

"What of our small brethren?" she asked.

"I thought your magic was controlling normal rats, but whatever they are, they aren't normal."

"They have always been here," Neva said.

"The rats are part of the power here," Claudia said.

"The magic has changed them as it changed me," Neva said.

"Just to be clear, Claudia, you're saying that Neva's eyes have always glowed like this, it's not new?"

"Since I first joined the rodere at eighteen."

"And all the witches of the rodere have eyes like this?" I asked.

"When the power rides them."

"Good to know," I said out loud; in my head I thought, *Good to know she's not possessed by the same vampire that's got Hector.*

"It is getting late, we need to get Anita inside," Claudia said.

"Yeah, if I have to fight my way through the crowd, we best get started," I said.

"The fighting has already begun, Anita Blake," Neva said. She walked past us, and the rats made room for her, spilling wide around her so she could walk and not worry about stepping on them. She walked away without glancing back at us, but one of the rats stood on its haunches and looked back for her. Could she see through its eyes? I looked at the rat and it looked back at me. We stared at each other. Its fur was black, darker than most of the others'. It stretched up tall, showing a small spot of white on its chest and a white paw. Its nose wiggled as it sniffed the air; did my magic smell different to it, or did Obsidian Butterfly's power smell just like home? It settled back on all fours and looked at me. Again, there was that sense of too much mind staring back at me from the small body.

"The rat is looking at you," Pierette said.

Claudia came to stand beside me. "We need to go inside," she said.

I nodded at the profoundly serious-looking rat. "Is this normal for the rats here?"

"No, they never pay this much attention to anyone but the brujas."

"What do you want?" I asked.

"I want you to come inside with me," Claudia said.

"I'm asking him," I said.

"You mean the rat?"

"Yes," I said, still staring at the small pointed face.

It made a noise that I think that was supposed to be a squeak but sounded lower-pitched, like it would sing bass in rat choir. It turned and walked away, body longer and sleeker, as if it had lost some mass in the last few seconds.

"Bye," I said, as if it could understand me.

The rat stopped and turned its upper body to look back and squeaked at me before racing away into the shadows.

"Did that sound like he said *bye*?" I asked.

"No," Pierette said.

"They don't talk," Claudia said.

"If you say so," I said.

"Your eyes are back to normal," Pierette said.

"Then let's go."

"Can you call the eyes back at will?" Claudia asked.

I thought about it, then nodded.

"Good, because all the rodere respect the magic of our brujas."

"Respect or fear?" I asked.

"Both."

"You want me to flash the eyes as we go inside?"

"Save them in case we're losing," she suggested.

"What would happen if I accidentally drained the energy out of one of them?"

"Would it just weaken them?"

"No, they'd start to dry out like mummies."

"Like what you did to Chimera?" Claudia asked.

"Yeah."

"Don't do that," she said.

17

AFTER NEVA AND the rats outside, I thought I was ready for anything inside, but I was wrong. They wanted to touch me, not to hurt me—women, men, young, old, they touched my arms, squeezed my shoulder, shook my hands. The first one who tried to hug me nearly got punched, but Claudia touched my hand in time so that they hugged me without getting hurt.

"It's so good to see you in person," a woman said, and hugged me like I was her long-lost friend. I smiled and nodded and said, "I'm glad I could be here tonight."

A man grabbed me in the fiercest hug yet and tried to kiss me. I turned my head to the side so he got my cheek, and Claudia pulled him off me before I could decide how violent to be about a stolen kiss.

"I'm sorry," he said, "I'm sorry."

It was a woman with half her head shaved and more tattoos and piercings than I'd seen in a while who took my hand in hers and said, "When you feed the *ardeur* on us, it's amazing."

"Thanks," I said, not sure what else to say.

She stepped a little closer, both hands holding mine. I thought her eyes were black, but they were just the darkest charcoal gray I'd ever seen. "My name is Mariposa, it means *butterfly*."

I looked at the butterfly tattooed on her left shoulder and smiled. I think the smile encouraged her a little too much, because she leaned in even closer and said, "I would love for you to feed on me in person."

My face must have shown that I didn't know what to say, because she laughed and said, "Don't tell me I'm the first one who's asked."

I nodded.

She laughed again, lips parted enough that I could see her tongue was pierced.

Pierette pulled me back with an arm across my shoulders and drew me into a hug. Mariposa grinned and just moved back to let the next person take my hand. She was the first one to proposition me, but not the last. I'd known the *ardeur* could be addictive, but I'd trusted Rafael to be strong enough to resist. I hadn't even thought about what might have been happening to the other wererats. I felt careless that I hadn't thought about it; Jean-Claude breathed through my head, letting me know that it hadn't occurred to him either, and that did make me feel a little less slow on the uptake.

A man grabbed my arm and I'd had so many people touching me by then that I just turned to him with a smile, trying to be friendly, or at least diplomatic. I felt his body lunge forward before I even saw the blade in his hand. I didn't have time to go for one of my own knives; all I could do was use my free hand to sweep his arm past me. He'd committed too much energy to stabbing me, so when I swept his arm, he stumbled past me even more than I'd planned. I put my hand over his where he was still gripping my arm and used it like a handle to help his stumble become a fall that put him on his knees.

He tried to twist back toward me with the blade in his hand, but I still had his other arm. I went from using it like a handle to turning it into a joint lock on his elbow. I put enough pressure on it to let him know I'd break it if he kept moving.

He kept turning toward me with the knife, so I broke his elbow. It made a nice meaty pop. Normal people scream and stop fighting after that, but he didn't even bother to scream. He just kept turning toward me, and with his elbow broken the arm was no longer stiff enough to act as a barrier. He let me tear his arm up and didn't even hesitate as he slashed for my thigh, and I tried to switch one hand to his shoulder to keep him away from me.

18

I FELT THE hit of his blade on the outside of my thigh, because I'd turned my leg so he missed the femoral artery on the inside of the thigh, and the moment I felt the knife bite into me I used his arm and shoulder to try to put him flat on the ground and keep his other arm and the knife away from me. I'd done similar moves in practice and in real life, but I forgot one thing—I was stronger now, a lot stronger.

His arm tore away from his body, gushing blood everywhere, and it was so fresh and there was so much of it that it was hot on my skin. I screamed and he was already screaming, and all I could think was *Where's the knife?* The blood was so thick and fast that I couldn't see what the bad guy was doing, and with his arm barely held to his body by skin, I couldn't use it to feel his movements. My fingertips found his back and that was something I could understand. I let go of his useless arm and rode his back down to the floor. I drove my knee into his back because I wasn't big enough to keep him down with just my weight, and pinned his remaining shoulder to the ground to keep the knife that was still in his hand away from me. I drew the knife at my waist with my other hand and plunged it into the side of the man's neck and gave it a twist on the way out. Almost no blood came out; that wasn't right. I'd seen enough throat wounds to know they bleed like a son of a bitch.

I heard someone yelling my name, but I kept staring at the knife in my hand and the barely bleeding neck wound. What was happening? Why wasn't it bleeding more?

"Anita!" Claudia was kneeling on the floor, balanced on the balls of her feet, shouting at me.

I blinked at her and wanted to ask her, *Why isn't his throat bleeding more?* Even though it was just steel he should have bled before he healed it.

"Anita, can you hear me?" Claudia asked.

I blinked at her again and then nodded.

"Are you hurt?"

"My leg, he cut my leg." My voice sounded beyond calm, there was no emotion to it at all. I felt dull and distant. I wasn't hurt bad enough to be in shock; what the hell was wrong with me?

"How bad?" she asked.

I shook my head, not sure how to answer the question. "He was going for my femoral, but I turned so he only got the outside of my thigh," I said in that dull, emotionless voice.

"Take his blade, and then I'll look at your wound."

I looked down his arm where his hand was still wrapped around the knife. It was as if his arm had gotten longer and everything was farther away than I knew it was; distortion like that wasn't good. Maybe I was more hurt than I thought.

I looked at Claudia and her expression softened for a second. "You must finish the kill by taking his blade."

I wanted to say, I hadn't meant to kill him, I hadn't even drawn one of the blades with high silver content. How could he be dead? I moved the knee that I was driving into his back, but he never reacted to the pressure change, but until the head and heart were gone, death wasn't a sure thing, so I kept one knee on his remaining shoulder so I'd feel if he tried to move, and then I reached down his arm for the blade he was still gripping.

Somewhere between reaching for it and getting to his hand, that unnatural stretching of reality stopped happening. Maybe it was just shock? I took the knife out of his soft, unresisting hand, and that was when I knew he was dead. I hadn't meant to kill him, and if the blade I'd just taken from him didn't have a high silver content, he hadn't meant to kill me either. God.

19

THE KNIFE I'D taken off the dead man had been silver. He'd meant to kill me; good, that made me feel just a teensy bit better about what I'd just done. If there'd been more fighting to do, I could have rallied and kept going, but strangely, no one wanted to fight me now. Of course, no one wanted to hug or flirt with me now either; since I was drenched in fresh blood, I couldn't really blame them. Going from a violent, life-and-death fight to nothing meant that all the adrenaline just washed away, which left me feeling weak, faint, nauseous, and really needing a few minutes out of sight of strangers to get my shit together.

I had cleaned my blade on the dead man's shirt and put it back in its sheath. I didn't have a sheath for the silver blade I'd taken off him, so it was still naked in my hand. I held it out wordlessly to Claudia.

"You're entitled to the sheath and any other weapons or equipment that he's carrying," she said.

I glanced down at the body lying there in the huge pool of blood. I understood now why the throat wound hadn't bled much; the hydraulics had lost too much fluid by the time I got to his neck. The blood was still shiny; it's almost cheerful red when there's enough blood in the right light. It would start to darken soon.

"Is there some place I can clean up?" I asked in that detached voice that people who don't understand violence think means you don't care, but that's not it at all. It means you care too damn much, so much that your mind is trying to shut down so that you won't feel all the emotional fallout all at once, because if you do, then you're going to fall apart right here, right now.

"There's an area where the fighters get ready and there's a bathroom," Claudia said.

"Which gives me the most privacy?"

"Bathroom," she said.

"That," I said.

She started guiding me away from the curtain opening that was the way into the main fighting pit. That was fine with me; I'd had enough fighting for the moment. Pierette moved up beside me and took my left hand in hers. I squeezed her hand to let her know I appreciated the gesture, but I took my hand back. If anyone was too nice to me in that moment, I was going to lose my shit, and I couldn't afford that in front of all the wererats here.

They looked at us as we passed, some not wanting to make eye contact, but others stared, and some even nodded. I didn't know if I was supposed to nod back or ignore them, so I pretended I didn't see and did nothing but follow Claudia's tall figure. She was walking ahead of me like a good bodyguard, clearing the crowd, but we moved in an oval of emptiness; people were staying away from us, from me. They weren't all horrified, but they were all being careful of the crazy woman who had just torn a man's arm off.

The numbness was starting to wear off, the nausea was getting worse, and I was having to concentrate on not letting my hands shake. The cut on my leg was stinging. I didn't have a limp, but it hurt. "Is there a doctor on site?" I asked.

Claudia looked back at me. "Leg hurting?"

"Starting to," I said.

She stopped and turned to me. "There are doctors in the fighters' area."

I sighed and fought a serious urge to rest the top of my head against her as if I were a tired five-year-old, but I fought it off. I'd just torn a man's arm off; surely I could not break down for a few minutes longer.

"Sure."

She looked at me for a second, as if she knew I wasn't sure at all, but she didn't question it, just turned around and started leading us back toward the curtained area and the fighting. I should have known better than to try to leave the fighting early; that never really worked out for me. Onward, motherfuckers, onward.

20

CLAUDIA HELD THE curtain to a narrow hallway, but it was like a wall at a sports stadium. It curved around to either side, and I could hear the movement of a lot of people just out of sight. The noise was murmurous like an ocean made up of the movement and sounds that people make even when they think they're not making any noise at all. She led us to the left, and we passed more curtained doorways leading into the stadium, or I guess the fighting pit.

We came to the first door, but it didn't lead toward the sound of the crowd, it was on the wall opposite all the curtained entrances. There was also a tall, muscular guard standing by the closed door. He looked impressively big until Claudia got close enough and then you realized he was at least six inches shorter than her. Hard to be the biggest dog in the room when you're not.

"Claudia," he said, giving that little nod I'd seen people give me in the crowd after the fight. Among the rodere it seemed to mean more than just an acknowledgment of *I see you.*

Claudia didn't nod back, which was my first clue that maybe it was like a salute in the military. You had to salute officers, but it was up the higher rank if they saluted back. She just said, "Franco," but that was all. Apparently, she didn't think he rated a return salute.

He opened the door for her, but when I tried to follow her in, he put an arm in my way. I stared at the arm and thought about my options. "Franco, why is your arm blocking my way?" My voice sounded normal, almost pleasant. I recognized the tone; it meant I was ready for a fight, but I was going to try to talk my way out of it first. Conservation of energy and all that.

Pierette said from behind me, "Shall I move him for you?"

"You should not be in here at all, cat," Franco said.

Claudia was on the other side of his arm now. "Franco, she needs a doctor."

"Anyone who lets themselves get that cut up just coming through the rats outside the pit doesn't get to use our doctors tonight. Those are the rules, Claudia, you know that."

"It's not her blood," Claudia said, stepping out of the doorway, so that I had to back up and Franco had to move his arm. Pierette stayed a little behind and to one side of me. I stepped back far enough to give myself room in case I actually had to fight my way through Franco to get medical care. Pierette moved wide and to the side of me so we could flank him if it was allowed. I admired the wererats' having so much culture and tradition, but I was getting tired of being on the wrong side of it all.

I was hoping a dramatic gesture could cut through the bullshit, so I pulled the front of my T-shirt away from my body. It clung to my skin, soaked, and I fought the urge to start screaming *Get it off me*, because up to that point I'd been ignoring the sensation of so much blood in my clothes that it was like I'd been dumped in a pool fully clothed. I knew logically that I had to have been this messy before; I mean I was a vampire executioner and had spent years beheading chickens or slitting the throats of bigger livestock to raise zombies. I had to have had this much blood on me at some point, right? But if I had ever been more blood-soaked than I was right that second, I couldn't remember it.

I pulled enough of the T-shirt out of the front of my pants so that I could squeeze it out like you'd wring a wet washcloth, but instead of water I wrung blood out on the floor.

I looked up at Franco as I held my newly bloody hands out from my body. "Not my blood."

"You are really unpopular to have that many of us challenge you," he said.

"Only one person tried to kill me outside, just one," I said.

He looked even more disdainful and arrogant. "One person hurt you this badly, you so aren't getting in to see the doctors. They're here for the fighters."

I could feel my temper start to rise like it usually did if I wasn't working at staying calm, but standing there covered in the blood of a man that I'd torn apart by accident, because I didn't understand how strong I was, I didn't want to stay calm. I'd wanted to find a private corner to fall apart and scream and maybe cry, and shower and change into something clean, but no one was going to give me room to cry, so if I couldn't deal with my real emotions right now, I'd pick a different emotion.

"You have to explain it to him, or make him move, Anita. I'm sorry, it's just how it works," Claudia said.

"Fine," I said, and I glared up at the big man. He was at least seven inches taller than me. I looked into his dark brown eyes for a second and then moved my gaze down to the center of his body. If he made a move, that was where it would start. Whether it was a punch, or a kick, or going for a blade, or even just taking a step forward, he had to move the center of his body first. Eye contact was great, but the eyes could lie, the middle of his chest couldn't. Funny, it was almost the same spot where the heart was, so that even in violence we led with our hearts.

My anger was warm and washed away the need to cry or be hysterical. Rage had been my shield against the world for so long that it was like putting on a favorite sweatshirt all comfy and worn in all the right places, so that you could cuddle into it and feel safe.

"I'm covered in the blood of my enemy, who tried to kill me with a silver blade."

"Silver, how long did the fight last for someone to go for silver?" he asked.

"He started with it, out of the gate."

"Show him the knife," Claudia said.

I'd forgotten I had it, sheathed and tucked in at the back of my pants. The fact that I'd forgotten it meant I was more shocky than I'd thought. I pulled the knife out, sheath and all.

He looked at the blade. "You killed Tony?"

"If this is his blade, yeah."

"How can you be good enough with a blade to have killed Tony? You're not even a real shapeshifter."

"I didn't kill him with a blade," I said, and the anger was starting to seep away on a wave of weariness that just washed over me and made me almost sway.

"What, did you kill him with your bare hands?" He made it derisive, a very *I'm the big strong man and you're a weak little girl* tone. I'd heard that tone all my life and I was so fucking tired of it.

"Yes," I said.

"How?" Again, with that disbelieving tone.

"I tore his arm off at the shoulder and he bled to death."

"A human couldn't do that."

"No, a human couldn't do that," I said, and my voice was soft; the anger that had kept me safe was just gone.

"Rafael gave you what the rest of us fought to earn. Now you have our strength without changing form. What else did he just give you that the rest of us bled for?"

My inner beasts stirred, but only rat looked up from the darkness, black eyes gleaming dark on dark inside me. I was surrounded by too much matching energy for any of my other beasts. The magic that had thinned down once we stepped into the warehouse pulsed through me like my body was a gong to be struck and made to vibrate. It wasn't just sound that vibrated, that thrummed inside and on every side of me, it was power.

Franco staggered back against the wall as if he might have fallen without it. Claudia hadn't moved. Whatever this magic was, it could be aimed, or maybe it just went in the direction of my emotions. Franco was standing between me and someplace I wanted to go. He was standing between me and medical care. He was standing between me and getting out of all this blood.

My rage came back not like a comfy sweatshirt this time but like a suit of armor, and what good is armor without a sword? And then I thought, *I don't know how this magic works. If I aim it at him, will I be able to control it? Will it kill him by accident like the man outside?* I suddenly knew every blade Franco was wearing. The only place I couldn't see was his back, so he might be carrying there, but otherwise I knew them all.

"Your eyes, your eyes, no one told me you were a bruja." He pressed himself against that wall where the power had thrown him, but it wasn't the magic keeping him there, it was his fear.

"Are you going to try to stop us from going through the door?" I asked.

He shook his head, pressing himself a little harder against the wall. "Brujas can go where they like."

"Good to know," I said.

Claudia held the door for us. Pierette and I walked

through, and Franco kept cowering against the wall. He was a wererat, he shouldn't be afraid of little rats, so what the hell did the brujas do to put that level of fear in him, and why hadn't Rafael mentioned that the wererats had their own flavor of magic? If he'd just assumed it didn't matter to me, we needed to talk. If he'd left it out deliberately, we really needed to talk, but later, after he'd defeated Hector and we'd chased down the vampire that was trying to make a move on the rodere. But first—first I'd let a doctor look at my leg and see if I could borrow some clean clothes. I'd have liked to think a shower was possible, but I wasn't feeling that optimistic.

21

I DON'T KNOW if it was the magic or interacting with Franco, but I was calmer until I saw myself in the mirror that covered half of one wall. It wasn't Carrie-at-the-prom bad, I only had a little bit of blood on the ends of my hair on one side, and black hair hides it better than strawberry blond does; so does black clothing. If you hadn't been around a lot of violence, you might not even have known my clothes were covered with blood, but I'd been around a lot of violence and I knew exactly what I was looking at. I could feel the blood starting to dry on my skin and the cloth of my shirt starting to stick wherever the bra didn't keep it at a distance. It had never occurred to me that sports bras were meant for wicking up sweat and that meant blood was just another liquid to them. Good to know for later.

Claudia waved her hand in front of my face. I blinked and looked at her; it was as if I was experiencing everything in slow motion. "You're in shock," she said.

I thought about nodding and finally said, "Yes."

"I can't tell how much of the blood I'm smelling is hers," Pierette said from the other side of me. Had she been there a moment before, or just walked up from somewhere else? Was this just shock?

Claudia called out to someone and Dr. Lillian was there. She'd cut her thick gray hair very short so that the delicate bones of her face were more noticeable. She looked older, but not old, if that made sense, but knowing how much older Rafael was than I'd assumed, I realized for this much to show on her she had to be eighty, or even older. Could she be over a hundred?

She smiled, her gray-blue eyes full of that no-nonsense warmth that the best doctors and nurses seem to have. "How are you feeling, Anita?"

"Fine," I said, automatically.

The smile faded and she shined a little light in my eyes, made me follow her finger as she moved it. "You are not fine. You are in shock." She looked up at Claudia. "You said this blood wasn't hers."

"Most of it isn't."

Doc Lillian sighed. "The curtained areas are full, but we need to see her wound."

They had three curtained-off areas in the locker room area, like a makeshift version of an emergency room. Someone was screaming and someone else was cursing in Spanish loudly enough to be heard over the screaming. The third curtained area had blood flowing out from under the curtains like the blood of . . . I looked away from the blood. I'd seen enough for one night. The rest of the room looked like a nice locker room at most MMA gyms, except for the big mirror in the one wall, which was usually something you saw more often in a gym that catered to mostly women.

"I need to see your wound, Anita," Doc Lillian said.

"Okay," I said.

"That means I need you to undress enough for me to see it."

I nodded. "Sure."

"I need you to take your pants down enough for me to see, Anita."

I nodded.

"Can you do it now?" she asked.

I reached for my belt and started undoing it. I vaguely knew that I'd normally not want to be standing in plain sight for dropping trou, but it just didn't seem like a big deal now.

Doc Lillian knelt beside me. A man I didn't know appeared with a tray of medical supplies. Once it would have bothered me for a strange man to be in the circle with my pants halfway down my legs, but he was wearing scrubs and it was all very medical professional; besides, Pierette was my lover so the days when I was embarrassed by just men were long past, and if anyone got that big a thrill out of just seeing a little underwear and naked thigh, they could go fuck themselves.

My leg didn't even hurt anymore until Lillian squeezed antiseptic cleaner all over it. The sharp sting of it cut through the fog in my head, and when she wiped the wound with a piece of gauze, the edges of the wound caught on the gauze. The sensation made my stomach roll.

"It's not bad," Lillian said, "but it will need stitches."

I had to swallow past the nausea before I could say, "Can you numb me first?"

"Does your body react to drugs like you're still human?" she asked.

I had to think about it. "If it's an ordinary wound, it heals too fast for regular medical care, but this doesn't seem to be healing that fast, so maybe?"

"It was a silver blade," Claudia said.

"Had they tried with a regular blade first?" Lillian asked.

"No," Claudia said, "I believe Tony meant to kill her."

"He was trying for my inner thigh, but I turned so he couldn't get my femoral," I said.

"You turned so the cut would be to your outer thigh," Lillian said.

"Yeah."

"I believe we can numb the area before I stitch you up."

"Great," I said, and I meant it, because I really hated getting stitches without painkillers.

"We can wait for one of the private rooms to open up," she said.

I shook my head. I'd decided to grit my teeth and just do it, so . . . "I'm short, I can stretch out on a bench by the lockers."

She smiled at me as if she was proud of how brave I was being. Dr. Lillian had worked on me before and she knew what a terrible patient I usually was, but there wasn't time for that today. I needed to get to Rafael. I don't know if it was seeing the blood on the floor or what, but I suddenly felt an urgency to be with him. Then I realized he was worried about me, wondering where I was. I was feeling his urgency, not mine. I could control some of the connection between us, but he was powerful enough to be able to push against that control. Either way, he wasn't wrong.

"How many more fights until the main one?" I asked as Doc Lillian ordered how she wanted me to hold the leg while I half leaned, half lay on the narrow bench.

Pierette sat down on the bench and said, "I'll be your pillow, my queen."

"If I'm laying my head in your lap, can you at least call me Anita, instead of *my queen*?"

"For tonight, you mean?"

"Sure," I said, and I laid my head on Pierette's thigh. I'd never laid my head in her lap before, so there was a moment like kissing for the first time when you don't know where the noses go, and then my cheek found that sweet point where my head rested just right on the curve of her thigh.

She offered me her hand to hold while Doc Lillian got the syringe ready. I didn't try to be tough, just took the offered hand. I tried to find something to stare at while the doc injected the local. Did I mention that I really don't like needles? The curtains on one of the ER "rooms" were moving as if there was a quiet fight going on inside it. I stared at the curtains and tried to piece together what was happening behind them. It gave me something to think about while the needle went in and Lillian started asking me if I could still feel when she touched my skin.

A man in scrubs came stumbling out of the curtains. I started to say "Look out" to the nurse holding the tray, but he moved smoothly out of the way without so much as moving any of the instruments. It also meant that the other nurse fell backward into Pierette and me, or would have except that she put up an arm and that was all the man needed to regain his balance.

"Did he hurt you?" Lillian asked.

The nurse raised his arm up. It was bleeding.

"Knife or claws?" she asked.

The man made a disdainful face. "He's not powerful enough for claws."

"Is he allowed to cut up the medical staff?" I asked.

"No," she said.

The man who'd gotten cut said, "Yes."

I looked at Lillian.

"My rule is that if you harm my staff, then we don't work on you."

The bleeding man said, "The rule here is if you can't protect yourself, then you deserve to be hurt."

She touched my leg. "Can you still feel this?"

"Pressure only," I replied, then asked, "How do you guys get anything done if everything is a fight?"

"I'm going to start stitching you up."

"Just tell me when you start, I don't want to startle and make you drop a stitch," I said. I tried to concentrate on the curtain that the nurse had just come out of, and then I looked at his arm. "Why aren't you healing?"

"Silver," the nurse said, and he didn't seem offended by it. I'd have been pissed.

"Why did he cut you?" I asked.

"I'm starting now, Anita," Lillian said.

"Do it, doc," I said.

I felt the pressure of the needle and then that unsettling sensation of it starting to pull through the skin. It wasn't sharp, so it didn't technically hurt, which I was grateful for, but just feeling the needle go through my skin made my stomach roll a little. I held tighter to Pierette's hand and it helped.

"Why did he cut you?" I asked again.

"Diego," Claudia said from where she was standing over us. Apparently, she didn't plan on any more stumbling nurses getting past her to Pierette.

I said, "Diego, why did he cut you?"

"He's an asshole."

"Besides that," I said, and smiled before Lillian started tightening the stitches in my thigh. My stomach rolled again.

"Big baby can't take a few stitches, says I hurt him on purpose."

Claudia said, "Painkiller doesn't work on us."

"I've had stitches with no drugs, it hurts a lot." I tried to focus on how much better this was than that. It really was better.

"Did you hurt him on purpose?" Pierette asked.

"Not yet," Diego said.

Lillian was tugging on the stitches, which made me too aware of the hard thread going through my skin. My stomach clenched and tried to do a flip-flop at the same time. I squeezed Pierette's hand tighter.

Diego drew a knife out from under his scrubs and moved toward the curtain. He moved just enough of the curtain to slide back through and said, "Let's try that again, Pedro."

Claudia said, "Pedro is an asshole."

"He's a bully," Lillian said as she finished tugging my skin back together. My stomach did another roll and I squeezed harder on Pierette's hand. She leaned down and whispered, "You're going to break bones, my . . . Anita."

I stopped squeezing and would have let go of her hand, but she held on. "It's okay, Anita, you'll get used to your new abilities."

"I pulled a man's arm off; how do I get used to that?"

"Time," Claudia said. She knelt so that I wouldn't have to crane my head up at her. Her face was all sympathy and something more, shared grief I think, as if me struggling with my issues had raised old ghosts for her. Had she torn someone apart like that, by accident? I wanted to ask, but staring into her brown eyes, seeing the pain in them made me hesitate. Bad memories shared isn't always better; sometimes it just spreads the misery around but doesn't lighten it for anyone.

"There, all done," Lillian said. Her voice made me look at her smiling, aged face. I looked at the peacefulness in her eyes and envied her. Would I ever feel as peaceful inside as she looked?

"Thanks, doc," I said. "Anyone have a T-shirt I can borrow? I'd rather not wear this much blood all night."

"We might have some scrubs."

"I'd really prefer a shirt, but if nothing else, I'd really prefer to be less bloody."

"I'll go see what I can find." She went with the male

nurse and his tray of instruments in tow like his only job was to follow her around and be helpful. Maybe that was his job, or maybe he just had that much respect for the doc.

I sat up on the bench and started pulling my pants up. I'd have loved to borrow pants, too, but the tac pants had too many weapons attached to them. I'd let the blood dry to me before I'd give up the easy carry of that many of my weapons for the night. I realized that this was the first time I'd been around this many shapeshifters while wearing this much blood and not had anyone get weird about the fact that I smelled like food. I stood up and Claudia stood with me; I realized she was there in case I needed to be steadied. She was in full bodyguard mode. Pierette was still sitting on the bench, looking up at us, and I realized that she was there in case she needed to give me a hand, too. They were both taking such good care of me, but if a fight started, it was against the rules for them to interfere unless it was to save my life.

Pierette reacted to me staring at her by laying her hand on my hip and smiling up at me. I couldn't help it, I smiled back. I had a moment of thinking it felt wrong to be fastening my pants instead of taking them off with her right there. When you start thinking things like that about someone, they've crossed from casual lover to something else; exactly what that *else* was we were still figuring out, but it was nice to realize there was an *else* to figure out with her.

It must have shown in my face, or maybe my skin smelled different, because her smile widened and filled her eyes with an eagerness that made me smile back and let an answering eagerness fill my own eyes. I started to lean over for a kiss but felt the change in the air as the outer door opened. It made me stop what I was doing and finish fastening my belt.

I felt Claudia stiffen before she turned more solidly toward the door. "Hector, what are you doing here?"

"Is that any way to talk to your soon-to-be king, *mi cariño*?"

"I am not your *cariño*."

"Once Rafael is dead, you will be."

I hadn't even seen Hector in person, and already I hated him. Perfect.

22

PIERETTE AND I moved a little back and to the side of Claudia so we could see him and the room's only entrance. Funny how that hadn't bothered me until now. Hector was at least six feet tall, but that was still six inches shorter than Claudia, so he didn't look nearly as impressive as he seemed to think he looked. He was wearing only fightwear shorts that hit him upper midthigh. They were even slit up the side and bright orange and black, which was a good color against the brown of his skin. The shorts left most of his muscled body bare to view. His long black hair was done back in a braid. If he hadn't swaggered into the room like he owned it and everyone in it, I might even have said he was handsome. If this was Hector without a crown, God help us if he won tonight. It wasn't just the loss of Rafael, it was just a bad idea for the tall, dark, and arrogant stranger to be in charge of anything. Maybe I was prejudiced against him, but I didn't think I was wrong.

"I believe that Rafael will kill you tonight, but either way it doesn't change the fact that I will never be your girlfriend," Claudia said.

"I don't want to be your boyfriend, Claudia. I just want to fuck you." He was close enough now that I realized his eyes were even greener hazel than they'd looked when I fed on him. The eyes were pretty, and if I was totally honest, he was in good shape with pale brown skin so even and smooth over all that muscle that he looked pettable, but pretty is as pretty does. The nice package couldn't make up for the way his gaze went up and down Claudia's body so that it was very clear he was doing a lot more than just picturing her nude.

Her hands curled into fists at her sides.

"Now, Claudia, you know you can't challenge me until after I kill Rafael."

"He's baiting you, Claudia, don't allow him to manipulate you," Pierette said.

Hector's lascivious gaze moved to her, but in the second it took for it to change targets it went from sex to hatred. I wasn't exaggerating either, he looked at Pierette as if he hated her. It was way too personal a look for just having met.

"What are you doing here, kitty-cat? You have no business here among us."

"She's with me," I said.

His gaze stayed on hatred as he looked at me. "Anita Blake, you have no business here either."

"Rafael says otherwise."

"When he dies, your safe passage dies with him."

"I didn't get a safe passage through the rats outside. I fought my way through just like everyone else."

"So, you really did tear one of us into pieces with your bare hands? Such dainty hands, I don't believe the story now. Did you go for your silver blade as soon as you got scared?"

"I never went for silver."

"Lies."

"No lies," Claudia said.

He looked at her and this time there was intelligence and something else, calculating his chances, debating something. I couldn't read the expression. "If she is not one of us, then she could not have done what they are saying she did."

"She bled Tony out with her bare hands, I swear it."

"You smell of truth, but I knew Tony. A human couldn't have killed him unarmed."

"I never claimed to be human," I said, but even my tone wasn't happy. I still hated the idea that I wasn't human; no, I hated that I had never been human, not if that meant normal.

"You aren't one of us, and you aren't a vampire, so you're human," he said.

"I saw my first ghost when I was ten, I raised my first dead at fourteen, I'm not sure human was ever what I was."

Hector studied me out of those green-brown eyes. It wasn't a teasing look, or arrogant, it was thoughtful. If the arrogant asshole was just the icing that hid an intelligent, deep thinker, Rafael was in more trouble than I'd thought, but then maybe he'd seen this part of Hector before, maybe it was what made him think the guy could be king someday. As a future leader smart was good; as an enemy to defeat, not so much.

"Point taken, Anita," and he said my name the way it's meant to be pronounced, *A-nee-ta*. He tried to walk around Claudia to get closer to me, but she moved so that he couldn't circle around us.

He looked at her again. "I thought you didn't like me, Claudia."

"I don't."

"Then why do you keep attracting my attention every time I look at another woman?"

"I'm supposed to take Anita to Rafael."

"Take? Are you her bodyguard here, where everyone must fight for themselves?"

"I did not guard her outside in the open."

"But you guard her now?"

She hesitated but said the only thing she could say. "No."

"Then I am going to move around you to talk directly to Anita; if you move between us again, I will take it as a challenge."

Lillian came back from the depths of the lockers with a white T-shirt in her hands. "You are not allowed to challenge anyone but Rafael tonight, Hector, you know the rules."

"Just as no one else can fight me before I kill Rafael."

"You keep using that word. I do not think it means what you think it means," I said. I kept my face blank, wondering if he'd get the movie reference.

He scowled at me. "That made no sense."

"I should have known you weren't a *Princess Bride* fan."

"What are you talking about?"

"We think Rafael will kill you tonight," Pierette said.

"I do not have to talk to you, cat."

"Fine," I said, "we all think that Rafael is going to kick your ass tonight. Is that better? Did your little prejudiced feelings get hurt because the big, bad wereleopard talked to you?" Yes, I did the baby-talk voice to go with the teasing.

It was his turn for his fists to curl at his sides. "I will be king tonight, Anita, and then everything that is Rafael's will be mine, including his lovers."

I shook my head. "I don't belong to Rafael and you know it."

"You belong to your vampire master, Jean-Claude, we all know that, but here you are in our holy of holies. You should not be here, Anita Blake."

"Tony agreed with you," I said.

Hector blinked at me, frowning a little, and then his eyes narrowed. "Are you threatening me?"

"Would I do that?"

"She's not threatening you; go change in the back, Anita," Lillian said, thrusting the T-shirt at me.

"We wear the blood of our enemies with pride here," Hector said.

"Have you ever been covered in someone's blood and had to walk around all night still fighting while it dries on your body?"

"Of course," he said.

"Liar, our fights are fast and over with. They never last all night," Claudia said.

"You're so hot when you're being a pain in my ass, Claudia. I used to want to fuck you because you were hot, now I just want to shut you the fuck up."

"With your dick?" I asked.

Lillian said, "Go change." She even gave me a little push in the direction she wanted me to go, which was away from Hector.

"What did you say?" he asked.

"Nothing, she's going to go change now, aren't you, Anita?" Lillian said.

I'd have argued with most people, but she'd just sewn me up and healed me too many times to count; that gained her something. I actually tried to leave to go change, but I caught movement out of the corner of my eye, and I was just out of reach of Hector's hand. He hadn't even swung at me, just tried to grab me. Insult to injury, he'd treated me like a potential victim and not a potential opponent.

"No human could have seen that."

"You're the one who keeps calling me human, Hector. I'm not claiming to be something I'm not."

"I will be king, Anita, and if you do not want to be part of the spoils of my victory, leave before the fight begins."

"Rafael wants me at his side, so that's where I'll be."

"This is your last chance, Anita."

"I think you're full of shit, Hector."

Anger ran through his face, tightened the muscles in his shoulders and upper chest and one arm. His body was getting ready to take a swing at me. I half hoped he would do it, because I was within my rights to defend myself. I might not be able to win a full-blown fight, but I knew I could hurt him before anyone could separate us. If he hurt me first, then me hurting him too badly for the fight to go on tonight would be within the rules, or I was almost sure it would be. Hector having to bow out would give us more time to find his master. I wanted that time.

"If you hit her, she's within her rights to defend herself," Claudia said.

"Are you saying I can't win against a little girl?"

"Tony attacked her with a silver blade, and she killed him without drawing a weapon."

He glanced at Claudia, then back to me, considering. "You smell like the truth, but I still don't believe it."

"Take a swing at me and I'll prove it to you," I said, and that little smile curled the edges of my mouth. It wasn't a voluntary smile. It was the one that I got just before I hurt someone. My BFF Edward called it my *I'm going to fuck you up* smile. I'd have hidden the smile if I could have, because if you knew me, it was a serious tell. Of course, Hector didn't know me.

"What the hell are you smiling at, little girl?"

I wanted him to go for me first; he had to start the fight. "Is that the best insult you got, that I'm little and a girl? Because neither one is an insult, just true. Now I mean is it an insult if I say . . ."

"Anita." Claudia said my name with that caution that my friends learn after a while.

". . . you're a little boy who's totally out of his league?"

His upper chest tensed more, the one arm stiffening. If that was the arm he swung with, then Rafael would see him coming a mile away. His voice came low and careful the way mine did when I knew if I lost control of it, I'd do something violent that I wasn't ready to do yet. "I am not a boy and I am not out of my league with Rafael."

"I wasn't talking about Rafael, Hector baby."

He frowned as if my teasing was too hard for him to follow. Who was the real Hector, the confused boy or the intelligent man that kept peeking out? "What are you talking about, Anita Blake?"

"Us, me, Pierette, Claudia—you're out of your league with us."

His body relaxed; damn. The arrogance was back, so sure of himself. "None of you are out of my league for dating."

I smiled and this time it was a happy smile. "I wasn't talking about dating us, Hector, I was talking about fighting, but now that you mention it, all three of us are out of your league for both."

He laughed; it was that sound of a big, athletic, handsome man who has been bigger, faster, stronger, and better than all the other men for most of his life. It can make a man be incredibly arrogant and have a sense of entitlement because no one ever tells him no.

"Have you seen my fiancés?" I asked. "You're cute enough, but you so aren't as gorgeous as they are."

He frowned again, as if I was making him think too hard. I wondered if he was like some of the inner-city athletes who were great on the court or field, but all the rest of their lives had been skipped over so that they were undersocialized and couldn't read well. "After the were-rats are mine, your vampire master's beauty won't save him, and once he dies all that survive will be ours."

I blinked at him, because that was a little too much truth in advertising for this early in the game. "So you're just going to tell us your dastardly plan for citywide domination now and not wait for the villain speech later?"

"Would you rather I pretend that you and Jean-Claude are stupid?"

"I guess not," I said, but my pulse was a little faster than it should have been.

Hector took a deep breath of the air. "I like smelling your fear, Anita. I like it better that you're afraid of me now." He smiled, but it was more a snarl than a smile, showing teeth to remind the other person that even in human form teeth can still tear flesh.

Pierette said, "So you declare that you will use the wererats to attack Jean-Claude and his vampires?"

"I do not answer to cats."

I repeated the question.

"The wererats are the majority of Jean-Claude's foot soldiers; take them and the numbers are on our side. He knows that. We all know that. Why pretend?"

"What will you do if you take the wererats and the vampires, then what?" I asked.

"Then I truly will be king."

"You shouldn't be this confident," Claudia said.

"Perhaps Jean-Claude and all your pretty boys should be watching their backs tonight," Hector said. He leaned in as he said it and I let him, because I was watching his eyes and not the rest of him. His eyes were a solid dark brown, no green at all, and down in the depths of that darkness was power that tried to pull at me.

I felt my eyes fill with my own power and I said, "You can't roll me with your eyes, whoever you are."

I felt Hector move a second before his elbow tried to connect with the side of my head. I moved my head away and my arm up to sweep his elbow away from me and let his own momentum carry him past me. I drove my foot into his leg at the same time. If he'd been human, it would have broken, but he just went to his knees and I was coming in at his back for a throat shot with a blade in each hand as he tumbled out of reach across the floor, coming up on one knee and foot, hands up and ready for me.

We faced each other, both of us breathing a little hard not from exertion but from the emotion of it. I'd have killed him if he hadn't moved and he knew it. "Your speed and skill of arms is much improved."

"Improved over what? We've never met before," I asked, still in a fighting stance with naked blades in hand.

He blinked and his eyes were back to the greenish brown of Hector, all the vampire powers locked away. "Over what I was told." He held his hands out, palms toward me, in the universal gesture of *I mean no harm*, or at least *I'm done for now.* "I think maybe it's too dangerous to play with you, Anita Blake." He stood slowly, carefully with his hands up so I wouldn't have any excuse to rush him.

I came out of the fighting crouch and backed up slowly but kept the knives out. He'd just threatened everyone I loved. If I could kill him here and now without starting a war between the wererats and vampires, I'd so do it.

"I will go back to watch the lesser fights now, and you can decide if you want to watch me fight Rafael more than you want to be at the side of the men you love most in the world while they fight for their lives."

My heart started thudding too fast, adrenaline pumping through me like champagne shaken too hard. I whispered through my head just enough to see if Jean-Claude was listening in, and he was there like a cool line of calm. I didn't have to get to a phone; he'd warn everyone.

"Liar," Claudia said, "everything was true, but not that last. Jean-Claude and the others aren't fighting for their lives, you're bluffing on that."

"Am I?" Hector said, and again there was that feel of another older, less cocky personality.

"We can smell the lie," Lillian said.

Pierette moved closer to him, hands out to her sides, showing that she didn't mean any harm, but Hector moved so that he could keep an eye on both of us. He ignored the other wererats more than the two of us; that seemed wrong. They were a fighting culture, everyone was dangerous.

"It was worth a try," Hector said, "but now I'll leave so you can change. I can be a gentleman when I must." He backed toward the door, hands out, so he gave us no excuse.

Jean-Claude breathed through my mind, "Thrust power into him, now, before he leaves."

"Why?" I whispered.

"Trust me, *ma petite*."

I did, so I thrust power toward Hector. Jean-Claude hadn't specified which power, so I went to my default—necromancy. I thrust it into that tall, handsome body, but I wasn't looking for wererat. There it was like a cool, underground stream hidden away, vampire hiding under all that hot shapeshifter energy, and then I was thrust out so hard I staggered backward into the lockers.

Hector's eyes burned with dark brown fire like sunlight through brown glass. "Naughty necromancer, you've made Rafael your rat to call, or you couldn't have pushed past Hector like that, but it won't matter once Rafael is dead." He turned and went for the door with a confident swagger, Hector in charge of the body again.

One of the nurses said, "What was wrong with his eyes?"

"Vampire, he's a vampire's animal to call," I said.

"You've met the vampire before," Pierette said.

"Yeah, I got that feeling, too," I muttered.

"No, I mean I know you've met him before."

I looked at her and her eyes were a dark charcoal gray. Her master Pierrot's eyes in her face. "I hoped your power would force a mistake, and it did."

"What mistake?" I asked, looking into a face that I

was beginning to hold dear and seeing someone else looking out of it. I wasn't sure I'd ever get used to it.

"He overreacted to your necromancy and revealed too much of himself."

"I didn't get a sense of who it was holding Hector's leash," I said.

"I smelled something that wasn't Hector, but I couldn't tell much else," Claudia said.

"Pierette could, couldn't you, my darling?"

"Yes, master," she said, and that they were both still using the same mouth to have the conversation was just weird enough that I almost missed my cue to ask, "What did you smell, Pierette?"

"It was a who," Pierrot said, and it was him, because he liked to milk a reveal. Pierette was much more straightforward—it was one reason she was part of our poly group and he wasn't.

"Who?"

"Padma, Master of Beasts."

"The vampire council member who almost took us over once before?" Lillian asked.

"Yes," they said.

"Motherfucking son of a bitch," I said, and I went for the door. I was going to kill Hector and now. The were-rats could get mad at me later.

23

CLAUDIA CAUGHT ME at the door, putting her hand against it so I couldn't open it. I knew how much she bench-pressed; if she wanted to hold the door shut, there wasn't anything I could do about it. "You can't kill him, not before he fights Rafael."

"The hell I can't."

"If our laws allowed us to kill him now, like this, I'd help you. I'd love to tear his arrogant ass to pieces, but until he fights for the crown, we cannot touch him."

Lillian spoke from behind us. "We are allowed to defend ourselves, but nothing more until he fights our king."

I could see Pierette behind Lillian, still just standing there as if she were listening to things we couldn't hear, which I guess was Pierrot in her head. "Tell them how dangerous he is, Pierrot, or Pierette, or whichever, tell them."

Pierette turned to me and between one blink and the next her eyes went from solid brown to dark gray. Did my eyes ever do the change that smoothly? Did I want to know?

"He is one of the old council members, but we have no way of knowing if our dead queen made him more powerful with her magic, or if she kept him powerless. If the first, then we will slay him, but if the second, we are all in terrible danger."

"He's the son of a bitch that skinned Rafael alive as torture because he wouldn't give the rest of you up," I said. I'd have tugged on the door handle if I'd had a hand free, but I still had a knife in each hand, which raised the question of how I had planned to open the door in the first place. I realized I'd gone for the wrist knives. I sheathed the one in my left hand in the right wrist sheath, which was on top of the wrist; the left sheath carried the knife on the underside of the wrist so I could draw them simultaneously. I'd carried them almost longer than any other weapon I owned. They'd been the first silver I'd bought after bullets. I tried to feel bad about the fact that I'd gone for a killing weapon first thing, but all I could think was if we killed Hector, it might kill Padma and then we'd all be safer.

"I know who he is and what he did, Anita," Claudia said. She looked somewhere between sad and in pain, but she still kept her hands on the door so I couldn't go after him.

"Then let's finish this," I said.

"If you kill Hector before he fights Rafael, then the rest of the rodere will turn against him. They will not see it as his victory, as some of the vampires see the defeat of the Earthmover and the Mother of All Darkness as your kills and not Jean-Claude's, but vampire culture is not based on duels, and ours is, Anita. If they lose faith in Rafael, they will challenge him constantly, they will challenge all of us in his inner circle until we are dead, and then someone else will rule what is left and they will not be friendly to you and Jean-Claude."

I was suddenly tired, all the adrenaline of the last few minutes draining into my feet and into the floor. There's a cost to ramping up for a life-and-death struggle, but if you keep going up without fighting, it can exhaust you almost as much as a real battle.

"You smell defeated," Lillian said from behind us.

"Why can't any of this be simple?"

"That is a child's question, Anita," Lillian chided.

My anger roared up from that pit it lived in and filled up all my tired empty cup. I looked at the doc, and knew I looked angrier than she deserved, but anger would keep me going tonight, good behavior wouldn't.

"Such rage, luckily I know you now, and I know it is not really aimed at me," she said.

The anger started to fade, but the tiredness was there waiting to engulf me. I had miles to go before I could sleep, so I fed my rage on the thought that one way or another Hector would die tonight. If he killed Rafael, then the rest of us would finish it immediately, no games, no rules. I told myself that and made myself believe it, and it kept me going out the door. It was only when we were about to enter the stadium that I realized I was still wearing the bloody clothes. I'd forgotten to change shirts, but I didn't go back. It was too late for going back. I'd go forward covered in the blood of my enemy; let it be a warning to others, so I didn't have to kill anyone else by accident tonight. No, if I killed again, I wanted it to be on purpose.

24

MY THIGH DIDN'T hurt until I started following Claudia up the stairs toward Rafael. She'd called it a stadium and it was, just smaller than one meant for baseball or football. It wasn't even that the painkiller was wearing off so much as the stitches let me know they were there both holding the skin together and sort of pulling as I moved up the steps. Stitches on the arms never seemed to bother me as much as stitches on parts of the body that moved me forward.

There were hundreds of wererats packed into a space that fit inside a large warehouse. I had to shield hard and even then, the air around us vibrated and hummed with their energy. How had I not felt it earlier? It was like the magic outside had dimmed as we stepped into the warehouse; this was contained at the entrances to the stadium. I didn't know how they'd done it, but I knew really good magic containment when I walked through it.

A hand reached out from the bleachers and Pierette moved up closer to me, not like a bodyguard block, but like she was just hurrying to keep up with me. The hand fell away, and we kept following Claudia upward while my new stitches pulled. I glanced at the crowd for threats and just because the energy made me want to look. There were

people in rat form scattered in among the human audience.
I wondered if the energy had overwhelmed them and
forced the turn, or if they'd come here and slipped their
skins on purpose.

Pierette and I were small enough that she was able to
take my hand on the steps without touching the crowd.
She leaned in and whispered against my ear, "Nathaniel
says that you are shielding too hard. You're close to cutting him and Damian off." Her eyes were back to gray, so
a message from Pierrot and my homeboys.

I let out a long breath and let my shields shift. I was
good at shielding; I wasn't so good at selective shielding.
I stumbled on the step and only her hand in mine kept me
from falling. I pulled her hand hard enough to stop us
where we were, and leaned close to whisper, "I can't do
something this delicate to my shields while I'm moving."

Pierette rubbed her cheek against mine like a cat
scent-marking, but that was okay, her touching me helped
steady me. It felt good to touch the type of animal you
could call, and leopard had been my first. It helped me
think of Nathaniel, and that helped me think of Damian.
I visualized my shields not as metal walls, but as stone,
and they were vines that were allowed through the stone
to touch me. Nathaniel's energy breathed through me, and
the vines were thorns and roses because he loved pain
and pretty things. It made me smile.

I opened my eyes to find that Claudia had come back
down the steps to stand two steps above us. She was
watching the crowd on either side of us, which made me
look to my side of the aisle; Pierette was already watching her side.

There was a ratman very close to me. His fur was soft
gray and white, not like a spotted animal, but like a man's
hair had gone from dark to gray and now white. His black
button eyes were almost as big as my palm. You don't
think about animals having bigger eyes for their head

size until you see them in larger-than-normal-life form. It looked almost anime, like he was a special effect. The fur looked softer, maybe it was the color, but I wanted to reach out and pet him to see if it was as soft as it looked.

I moved back a fraction to touch my hip to Pierette's, and even that helped shake me out of the urge. I hadn't been that attracted to wererats the last time I'd seen people in their furry birthday suits, not even Rafael, but then wererat hadn't been one of my animals to call until he and I made it happen.

I looked farther into the crowd and found a lot of them watching me. Some were hostile, but most were just too intense. I didn't remember having this effect on the leopards or wolves the first time I'd seen them in a group after they were my animals, but then maybe it was just volume. The wereleopard pard was tiny compared to this, less than fifty, but the werewolves were around this same size, so why was this different?

There was movement above us; I turned my hand going to a knife before I had time to stop myself. It was a tall, slender woman with her hair back in a loose braid; one strand was white not like age, but like it had always been there. She stared down at me with large black eyes, not rat eyes, but just brown eyes so dark they looked black until I realized I could see the difference between her pupils and her irises. Her hands were loose and empty at her sides, but the energy coming off her prickled along my skin and threatened to close my throat down. The moment I thought it, I cleared the energy around my throat, and I could swallow again. I pushed her magic, or whatever it was, outside my shields. I didn't even have to visualize my wall with its thorny rose vine, all I had to do was flex my will, but she was using magic against me; was that allowed in a challenge?

I asked Claudia, "Is she allowed to use magic against me?"

"If you want to be queen over all of the rodere, you must face all the powers at our disposal," the woman answered for Claudia.

There were two more women on the steps behind her. They had knives naked in their hands just like I did. Nice they weren't being sneaky about it. Maybe me getting out a knife had made it possible for them to do it? Damn it, I did not know enough rules here.

"Claudia, tell me the rules here."

"They want to sit at Rafael's side and have a chance to be his queen."

"No one told me that I'd have to compete just to sit down tonight."

"We didn't expect them to challenge you since you are not a wererat," she said.

"What's your name?" I asked the woman whose energy was still pushing against my shields.

"Rosa."

"Well, Rosa, you know I'm just here for tonight, so if you and your friends want to fight over Rafael some other time, knock yourselves out, but I'm not a wererat so I can't be queen here."

"If you leave, then we will not hurt you," she said. She tried to use her height to loom over me, but with Claudia beside me it wasn't that impressive. Her two friends behind her crowded a little closer on their steps, emboldened by me offering an olive branch instead of a fight, I guess.

"She used magic first, can I use magic, or a blade, or what? Tell me the rules, Claudia."

"Show her your eyes, Anita; let Rosa understand what you could do to her."

It took me a blink or two to realize what she meant by eyes, and then I called up the power that Obsidian Butterfly had shared with me. I knew my eyes had gone black with the glimmer of starlight, because I could see the knife at Rosa's belt. She might not have drawn it, but she still had a blade. I'd assumed she was armed, but now I knew for certain.

The other two were better armed, and that was just what I could see under their clothes around Rosa, so at least three blades apiece for them, counting the ones in their hands. I realized that Rosa's magic had been pushing at me the whole time I was looking for weapons on them. There had been a time when she'd have been a problem for me magically, one I would have solved with weapons, but that was then, and this was very much now.

I looked up at her, instead of at her center body mass like I would for a physical fight. The moment she saw my eyes she went pale and stumbled back into the women behind her. They saw my eyes then, and the one in the very back held her hands up like *I'm sorry* and backed away.

The second woman said something rapid in Spanish. I think it was a spell of protection or a prayer. It wouldn't save her, because I wasn't evil. Common sense would save her from me if she just went back to her seat, no deity intervention needed.

"Go back to your seats," I said.

"You cannot be one of our brujas," Rosa said.

I looked at her with the eyes that a would-be goddess had given me, and I saw her magic as a faint glow like a flashlight with a fading battery.

"Don't try your magic against mine, Rosa, just go back to your seat."

"You're afraid to fight me," she said, but her voice wasn't as certain as her words wanted to be.

"You know that's not true, Rosa, don't make me prove that you're the one who's afraid."

"I am not afraid of you!" Her glow was red now, like fire burning underwater.

"We can smell your fear, Rosa," Claudia said, and her voice held derision.

"No!" she yelled, and she pushed her red energy at me.

I reached through it like it wasn't there and felt it shred like mist against the rock of my shields. I had her wrist in my bare hand and my blade pressed against her sternum before she could move. Had I been that fast, or was she just that slow when she did magic, the way I'd had to stand still to redo my shields for Nathaniel and Damian?

I drew her life out through her skin where it touched mine. Her glow faded first as if it had been erased.

"No!" she cried out.

"Tap out," I said, but even as I gave her an out, I started to get that high from eating her life's essence.

Claudia said, "Tell her you give up. Say you give up your right to fight for Rafael's attentions tonight."

Rosa's skin was starting to cling to the bones of her body; her face looked skeletal, skin starting to dry out as I fed. She collapsed so suddenly to her knees that if I hadn't moved my knife out of the way in time, she'd have driven it into herself. She didn't try for her knife; it was too late for that. I kept my grip on her one wrist and held the knife out away from her so she wouldn't hurt herself on it. "Say you give up, while you can still talk," I said.

"Give up, give up, I give . . . up." She whispered that last as her eyes started to flutter. If she could pass out, she was lucky; I'd never seen anyone who lost consciousness during it, no matter if it was me or Obsidian Butterfly doing it. If I didn't stop, the woman would be reduced to a dried husk like a desert-dried mummy, but she'd still be able to scream.

"Anita," Claudia said, "she tapped out."

I realized I hadn't stopped, and I was still drinking her down skin to skin. I took a deep breath, let it out slow, and I began to reverse the energy. It was a rush to take the energy, but it was also one to give it back. Death and life, the two great energies that make the world go round.

Rosa's skin began to smooth out, her body becoming young and beautiful again, but when her nearly black eyes could stare up at me from where she'd collapsed to the steps, the arrogance was gone, replaced by terror. I never liked seeing that I'd done something that made people terrified of me, but in this case maybe that was what it took to stop more people from throwing their lives away trying to attack me tonight? If scaring the hell out of a few people saved their lives, or the lives of others, it was a fair trade.

"Go back to your seat, Rosa," I said, and my voice was gentle, as if she were sick and I were trying to send her back to bed to rest.

"Don't ever touch me again," she said in a voice squeezed down by fear.

I let go of her wrist and moved down a step to stand up. She still had a knife and she was supposed to be trained in its use. Pity and guilt for what I'd just done to her wasn't worth getting killed for, or even injured. I was so done with the wererats and their constant fighting.

I felt the witches behind me before I turned and saw them. Neva's power went before her like a marching band at halftime announcing *something scary this way comes*.

Claudia stepped between me and Rosa. "I have this one," she said, which meant either she was bodyguarding me after all or she didn't want to deal with the witches; me either, but Claudia had already called dibs.

Neva had two younger witches with her, both trailing on either side of her on the steps. One had short wavy black hair with pale tan skin, the other had long wavy black hair with deep brown skin; with Neva's complexion in the middle it was like a color wheel showing possible variations.

"Necromancers do not give life back," Neva said.

"It's how the spell works," I said.

"No, it is not," she said.

We looked at each other. It was the younger woman with long hair who broke the silence. "You enjoyed the rush of energy. It fills your aura with power."

"Just because it felt good doesn't mean I liked doing it."

"Isn't that the definition of feeling good?"

"Not for magic like this," I said.

"Why did you use the spell if you hate it so?" the short-haired woman asked.

"I asked her to," Claudia said.

That wasn't strictly true, but it wasn't strictly untrue either. The older I get, the more I realize that lies and truths aren't black and white, but so dependent on how you look at them, or how you hear them.

"And why did you ask her to use that spell on someone as harmless as Rosa?" Neva said.

"Because Anita and I are both tired of her having to prove herself every few minutes; she needed something frightening enough to stop the challenges."

Neva looked at the wererats around us who had seen what I'd done. "Then you have accomplished your goal, just as the wererats who saw Anita tear Antonio's arm off will not lightly attack her in the future."

It took me a second to realize that she meant Tony. "I'm really tired of having to prove myself tonight."

Neva looked at me and I sort of wished I'd kept my mouth shut. "Did Rafael not explain what would happen?"

"I was told no silver in the warehouse outside the fighting pit."

"It is not typical to pull a silver blade outside of a duel," she said.

"And he didn't mention anything about fighting other women to just sit down beside him."

"Rafael has never been a good judge of women, not even as a child."

I knew that Rafael was over fifty, so how old did that make Neva to have known him as a little boy? I wanted to ask, but vampires consider it rude if you ask them, so I figured all long-lived supernaturals would feel the same.

"He could simply come to you and escort you safely to your seat," she said, and she looked past me at Rafael. It was the look your parents give you as a child when you're out of reach, but they want you to be more polite and better behaved than you are being.

Rafael got up and started walking down the steps toward us. I could finally see all of him in his fightgear. He looked taller, leaner, and even more fiercely in shape than I knew he was wearing just the black compression shorts. They came down almost to his knees and there were no slits for movement in them like Hector had had, but they were more form-fitting. He looked sexy and fierce and I didn't care. I wanted to go home to the men waiting for me. I'd killed a man for no good damn reason.

Claudia moved aside so that Rafael could stand above me and Pierette, who had moved down a step to be between me and the trio of witches, or brujas, or whatever they wanted to call themselves.

"You killed tonight to defend your life, that is a very good reason," he said.

"You read my mind," I said.

"Yes."

"You were very subtle about it; I didn't know you were inside my head."

"I do not want to cause you pain as I did earlier with Nathaniel."

"Thanks." I realized he'd probably heard me think I wanted to go home and be with the men I was in love with, because if I was going to kill people, it should be for people that I actually loved. I blinked at him and didn't try to apologize; it was the truth, and if I couldn't keep Rafael from "hearing" my thoughts, then truth was all that was left between us tonight.

"May I take your hand?" he asked, no editorializing about how I didn't love him. Smart man.

"Sure, thanks for asking first."

"Underneath the shock you are angry with me. I do not want to presume anything with you right now."

The anger fountained up and then back down behind the numbness of the shock. "You can feel what I'm feeling and most of what I'm thinking."

"Yes."

"I can't feel anything from you, except caution. I didn't even think that was an emotion, but for you, it is."

He took my hand carefully in his and raised it up so that he could lay a kiss across my knuckles. "I am so sorry that your introduction to our world has been one of pain and death."

"Yeah, we will be talking about the whole *no they won't try to kill you tonight* thing."

"I heard that Tony used a silver blade on you."

"Yeah, but he'll never do it again." I still wasn't sure how I felt about what I'd done to the man, so I pushed it down with all the other things I wasn't sure about. The place wasn't as full as it had once been, because I'd accepted more of myself, but killing Tony was going to go in the box with the other things that made me feel like a monster.

Rafael started to hug me but stopped with a look at the knife still naked in my right hand. "I would hold you, comfort you, if you will allow it."

"It's not silver, you'll live," I said.

He gave me a startled look, because even inside my head I had felt nothing when I said it, nothing, just the emptiness where some of my emotions should have been, used to be, but some things are so awful you can't feel too much about them, not if you want to keep moving forward.

"I did not set you up, Anita. I swear I thought you would be safer than this here among us."

I studied his face, those dark brown eyes, and then I let down my shields, opened a brick for him in the wall so I could know that he meant it. He was telling the truth, but that was only a little better. It meant that he hadn't understood how afraid his people were of me and the vampires. Kings should know shit like that; Jean-Claude would have known, or would have known to admit he wasn't sure.

Rafael studied my face; felt my emotions, or lack of them; heard my thoughts, at least some of them. He was very carefully trying not to think or feel anything much. "What can I do to make this up to you?"

"Kill Hector, help us kill his master."

"And that will make up for the fact that you trust me less now?"

"It'll help." And still I felt nothing. I realized I thought I'd have to kill more people tonight. I no longer trusted Rafael to be a good judge of what would happen, so I was shoving my emotions deep so I wouldn't feel bad when the violence happened. I even acknowledged in the front of my head that I would not hesitate to use my new supernatural strength again, not if it would save my life, our lives, Rafael's life, Claudia's life. If it would keep the rodere free of the Master of Beasts, I would wade through a sea of blood and tear a dozen enemies apart with my bare hands. I would do what it took, whatever it took, to win, because if we lost . . . The Master of Beasts had had a rape fetish, the kind that wasn't safe, sane, or consensual. I'd forced him to give up his only son to be executed; he would make me and all those I loved pay for that. It was a price I was not willing to pay, so I decided to pay another price, the cost of victory, because no matter how many people I killed, no matter how bloodily and inhumanly I did it, it would still be better than watching Padma torture, rape, and kill everyone I loved.

Sometimes being the monster scared the shit out of me, and then there were moments like these when I realized I'd rather be the monster a thousand times over than be at the mercy of one.

25

NEVA AND HER backup witches surprised all of us by saying they would stay. Rafael hadn't been able to hide how unusual that was; the surprise and confusion of it ran through his body almost like fear. That was interesting and I filed it away to ask about later when the three witches couldn't overhear us. They stood behind us book-ended by Claudia and Benito on Rafael's side and Pier-ette on mine.

The two of us sat in the carved wooden thrones, though Rafael's truly looked like a throne with high carved spires on the back of it like something out of a European royal family except the carvings were rats, writhing in masses, crawling over flowers, chewing on human bones. There was even at least one plague doctor carved small, com-plete with the pointed mask, hat, and robes. The chair was beautiful and macabre. It was a chair for a movie wizard, or an evil king dressed all in black with jewels, not gym clothes. Of course, I didn't match my chair either. It was much smaller, less impressive, dainty even, but the slen-der wooden rods were carved entirely of rats, and the headpiece had two carved rats holding a huge round cab-ochon of bloodred ruby. It was bigger than my thumb and that pigeon bloodred that almost doesn't exist in modern rubies. It was only when the light hit it that I realized it was a six-pointed star sparkling in the depths of it. I'd seen star sapphires and rubies this big only in museum collections. Even knowing that rubies were a nine on the hardness scale, just down from diamonds, I worried about scratching it. Worrying about damaging the jewel and the carving was so mundane in the scale of things that it broke through the shock and made me more present looking down at the fighting pit. It looked like a small stadium had married a bullfighting ring, with the sand and some of the partial walls around the circle of it, as if sometimes there were things on the sand that people wanted to hide from. I had no idea why you'd needs walls for hiding from bulls in a fighting arena that was supposed to be for humans and wererats. They didn't shift into anything that big, and they climbed well enough that the small barriers would be useless. I might have asked questions, but movement on the left-hand side of the arena drew my attention.

I recognized Hector; part of it was he was the only other one in the crowd dressed in fight shorts, but his energy stood out to me now. If he hadn't come to visit in the locker room, maybe he would have blended into the hum and rush of all the other wererats, but now there was a taste to his power that couldn't hide from me. *Vampire*, my magic whispered, *there's a vampire near us*. It was the same little voice that had helped me stay alive for all these years while I hunted vampires. I'd have been dead a thousand times over if I hadn't listened to that warning voice.

"You seat a vampire's human servant above all the women in the rodere. How can you humiliate them like this?" It took me a second to realize that Hector was speaking over a microphone.

Benito handed Rafael one with a snake of cord attached to it. Rafael stood and said, "Anita has earned her way tonight with blood and death. She has honored the power of the rodere that I put inside her."

"But the leopard that stands beside Anita did not earn her way, yet she stands above the women of the rodere. You put a cat above your rats, Rafael; what kind of king does that?" Hector said.

There were mutterings in the crowd that said they agreed with him. The energy changed, as if the air were a little thicker with their outrage.

"It is rare for other leaders to visit us here, but when it happens, they are allowed one of their people to accompany them so that there are no accidental assassinations that would cause war between us and another animal group."

"First you let Anita sit in the queen's throne for our people, and now you say she is a visiting queen, someone else's queen. Wererats, tell me whose queen is she? Who does she belong to?"

Most of the crowd nearest to Hector yelled, "Jean-Claude!" In fact, there were a lot of voices from all over shouting "Jean-Claude," but there were enough yelling "Micah!" that it rose above the other voices. Someone nearer to us yelled, "Nicky!"

Hector said, "She is not Nicky's queen, she is his master, as she and Jean-Claude would be master over all of us!"

Boos from the crowd, cries of "No, never!" Even I had a second of feeling the pull to be angry. "His voice has power in it," Pierette said.

Rafael stood tall and proud, and for the first time I felt the power inherent in him. The energy that came from being connected to every wererat in the country and a few outside of it. It wasn't just power for Jean-Claude and me to feed on, but magic, the magic of command because most people don't know how to follow without giving up some of their own personal power, but in this case it was more than that. Literally to be part of the rodere you had to give Rafael the keys to your energy, to yourself. Until that moment I hadn't really understood how close the connection was to the one that Jean-Claude had with his vampires. I'd never heard of anyone saying that the ties to the leader of a shapeshifter group were a similar dynamic, but power doesn't lie.

"I am the only master here," Rafael said.

"We feel the vampires drain our lives away when you let her feed on you!"

When he said *drain*, I felt weaker; when he said *feed*, I felt pain like the memory of something trying to take a bite out of me. I started to shield harder, but Jean-Claude whispered through me, "*Non, ma petite*, we need to know what he is capable of."

I let the power flow over me without blocking it out, but it didn't cling either, but then I knew how to let things go, or to keep them from holding on to me; most people didn't, as in most of the crowd.

"I have hidden nothing from you when I am with Anita. I have shared the power we raise with all of you." But Rafael's voice was just a voice. It could not carry the crowd the way that Hector's magic could.

Neva leaned in between the two thrones and said, "Bring the power to your eyes, Anita, and tell me what you see?"

It sounded too much like an order, but I wanted all the information I could get tonight, so I did it. There was a black nimbus around Hector, and it wasn't his aura, because that was squeezed down tight to his body, a dark, red brick color. I'd been told my aura could spike red in places, which most psychics don't like being around, but the dirty red of Hector's meant illness. The aura is supposed to be clean and bright whatever color it happens to be, or a mix of colors for that matter; anytime it's dim or muddy something is wrong. It didn't feel like physical illness, more like mental or emotional, but whatever it was, it was serious.

"What is that black shine around his aura?" I asked.

"Good, you see as we do," Neva said.

"Padma never had the power of voice before," Pierette said.

"Hector is not a brujo," Benito said.

"The power is not his," Neva replied.

"Then where is the power coming from?" Claudia asked.

Pierette said, "Padma," at the same time I said, "The Master of Beasts."

"The darkness in him is not vampire," the younger witch with the short hair said.

"It is unlike any vampire you have ever seen, *mija*, but it is still one of them," Neva said.

"You've seen this darkness before," I said, looking at Neva. She seemed to glow just under her skin as if parts of her nerves ran with golden light. It was faint but seemed to remind me that stars are just distant suns.

"Yes, she came to us pretending to be Santa Muerte many years ago, but she was not Her, nor was she any goddess she claimed, but she was powerful. We called her Madre de la Oscuridad."

"I don't know what *oscuridad* means," I said.

"It means *darkness*," Claudia said.

"Madre de la Oscuridad, you mean Mother of the Darkness, do you mean *the* Mother of All Darkness, the first vampire?"

"So she claimed," Neva said.

I almost asked her if she'd been the actual bruja that told Mommie Darkest she wasn't a saint or a goddess, but it was probably an ancestor, because when vampires decide to play at being gods, they don't like being told they're wrong. Best just to go along with the delusion and kill them as quickly as possible. Of course, I'd killed her once already, but like all really good monsters once might not be enough.

I was suddenly so afraid that my skin ran cold with it, and I could no longer see the black energy around Hector or the glowing power under Neva's skin. I knew my eyes were back to normal. I'd drunk her power down, and I'd thought, we'd thought, it had killed her, but apparently we'd missed some, and the messy leftovers were inside the Master of Beasts, who had his metaphysical hand up Hector's ass. Fuck.

26

PIERETTE TOUCHED MY face and turned my eyes to hers, they were charcoal gray again, like storm clouds. Pierrot spoke with her lipsticked mouth: "It is not her, Anita; we would know if our evil queen were alive, for we would still be loyal to her."

What he said made perfect sense in my head, but the back part of my brain that had gone to some ancestral cave where the darkness was all too real and solid wasn't convinced by logic. Especially not with Hector's voice working its magic on me and the audience. Jean-Claude had wanted to feel through me how powerful Hector was, or Padma was, and he was feeling it, but I wasn't the one being touched by the words directly. When Hector said, "Rafael gives us to the vampires to be raped," it felt awful in ways that I couldn't or didn't want to understand completely. When he said, "He will give us away," it was like every time you'd ever been left out, abandoned, unwanted.

"We must distract the Master using Hector," Pierette/Pierrot said.

I looked up into his storm-cloud eyes set in her face and missed her brown. "How?" I asked.

Benito asked, "How do we distract him without attacking him?"

Pierrot smiled with her lips and then slid into my lap, one arm around my neck and the other hanging loose for weapons, though he/she wasn't obvious about it. It was natural for my arm to slide around her waist and my other hand to cup the side of her thigh to hold her more securely in place as she wiggled in my lap to find just the right spot. It would have been a lot more titillating if I'd been a man, but she still managed to be distracting. Maybe that was the point, because all the touching and adjusting helped calm me down. I could think again, and Hector's voice wasn't getting through. Pierette wasn't even one of my *moitié bêtes*, so was it just her being a leopard, which was my first animal to call? It always felt good to touch your animal of choice.

Jean-Claude whispered through my mind, "She is our lover, *ma petite*; for our bloodline that is power."

Pierette glanced at Benito, who was bending over us as Claudia kept an eye on the crowd around us and Rafael tried to refute Hector's accusations. "Hector's master has always had an eye for the ladies," Pierette said.

I said, "He has a rape fetish."

Pierette said, eyes still gray, "No bad thoughts, Anita. We need to tempt him and you frowning will not do that."

"He likes unwilling partners," I said.

"That is true, but he loves most of all to see a woman happy with someone else, in love with someone else, and then steal her away from them. If he can force her lover to watch the abuse, so much the better."

The anger was just there, as if it had been only minutes ago instead of years. I could still see Hannah with her face bloody, her dress torn, and Fernando laughing as she begged Jean-Claude to help her. Willie McCoy, the love of her undead life, standing there in one of his bright suits and ugly ties that he'd loved to wear even when he was still human. Jean-Claude had had to hold him back or he would have tried to save her, and he would have died trying. I'd had a gun and had used it to threaten and buy us time, but in the end we'd gotten lucky because a little inner council squabbling played out in our favor, but Padma had chosen Hannah because she and Willie loved each other so much. It had amused him and his son that Willie and Hannah loved each other so much that hurting her was torturing them both. We'd been able to prevent Padma and his equally awful son, Fernando, from actually raping Hannah, but I hadn't been able to save Sylvie, the second in line to the werewolves' throne, or Vivian, one of our wereleopards. I'd rescued them after the damage had been done, and we'd been able to kill the son, who had been the primary rapist in Sylvie's torture, but even revenge doesn't undo the damage.

Rafael handed the microphone to Claudia and leaned over us. "Your rage feeds mine. I was forced to watch some of the torture to the women before they started cutting me up. I want him dead."

"That's the plan," I said, smiling up at him so that only he could see that my eyes were nearly black with anger.

He smiled then and it was such a close echo of mine that I wasn't sure if it was his smile, or mine. It usually took longer to intermingle than this, but maybe it was the shared hatred?

Pierette raised her face up toward his anger. I wondered if he saw that her eyes were the wrong color or if he just saw a pretty woman gazing up at him. He moved past her offered kiss to me, though, saying, "One should always dance first with the woman you brought to the ball." He kissed me soft, and I leaned into it, my hands tightening around Pierette, so I didn't accidentally dump her off my lap.

"What are you doing, Rafael?" Hector asked, and I realized that Rafael's body might be blocking the view.

Rafael rose up from me to look deep into Pierette's

eyes. I couldn't see their color as she rose up to meet his lips in their very first kiss.

"How dare you insult all the beautiful women of the rodere by favoriting a wereleopard and a vampire's whore!"

There were mutterings of agreement from the crowd, but I didn't care, because I was watching Rafael and Pierette kiss inches above my head. I liked watching my lovers kiss over me, usually one on either side of me in a bed, but this was good, too. It helped bring me back to my center and chase all the ugliness of the death and blood away, which was no mean trick since the blood was starting to dry on me. Maybe the three of us could catch a shower later?

Rafael drew back from the kiss and looked at me. "I can feel how much you enjoyed seeing us together."

"Told you so," I said, and the look on his face made me smile.

"How you must hate what you are to turn your back on your true queens." The word *hate* seemed to burn and hiss along the skin.

Rafael turned from us with a last parting smile, then took the microphone again. "I love being rodere. I love my people and all that we have built together." He didn't have the magical voice, but his sincerity seemed to reach people without any extra vampy power.

"How can you turn to us with their mouths still hot on your skin and claim to love being a wererat?"

"Your words sound far too poetic to be just your words tonight, Hector."

"My words are my own!"

"I do not think so, I think you smell like someone else is in your skin."

"You are babbling, old man."

"Then let us stop babbling and start fighting," Rafael said. The change was so abrupt, it was startling, and judging from Hector's body language, I wasn't the only one surprised.

Pierette leaned in against my neck as if she were nuzzling me, but she hid her whisper against my skin. "It is too soon to fight. We must delay."

"We do not fight for kings in front of outsiders," Hector said, but his voice didn't have the oomph to it.

Pierette whispered, "That will do," as if she'd had something to do with Hector not wanting to jump straight to fighting.

"You threatened Anita in the locker room; if she did not leave when you killed me, you would have her, and you would destroy the vampires, kill all those she loved with the wererats doing your dirty work."

"I did not say that."

"Did you threaten to rape Anita after you killed me?"

"She should not be here."

"Answer the question, Hector, let us smell the truth on you."

"You're the one who brought her here tonight. You almost got her killed in the outer room."

Rafael asked a different question. "Did you threaten to rape Claudia after you were king?"

"It is within my rights as king to ask for any woman I want."

"Ask, but never to take," Rafael said.

"A king does not beg for what is already his by right."

Rafael yelled, pulling the microphone back so the echoes were perfect, "Did you tell Claudia that you would rape her?"

The crowd started saying, "Answer him" and "Why won't you answer?" and "Why won't he answer?" A woman near us said, "If he'd rape Claudia, none of us are safe." She was so right.

The crowd was chanting, "Answer, answer, answer, answer . . ."

Hector yelled, too, but he didn't move his microphone and it whined through his answer, "Yes! I will kill you, and then I will fuck Claudia and Anita, and the cat you dragged in tonight!"

It was such an ambitious brag that I wasn't even angry or afraid, because I absolutely knew Hector wasn't up to all three of us in one night, especially if we were unwilling to cooperate.

Pierette sat up straighter in my lap. "Padma should know better than to threaten me, let alone both of you."

Rafael laughed at him, and he wasn't the only one. People in the audience joined him, not a lot, but enough.

Hector snarled at him, and said, "I will kill you tonight, Rafael, and when I am king, no one will laugh."

"Even if you kill me tonight, Hector, you will never be king now."

"Enough talk, old man, time to die."

"Hector, you speak like someone who does not know our laws."

"All I have to do to be king is to kill you, old man, that's all I need to know."

Rafael said, "Let Claudia explain your mistake," and handed the microphone to her.

"You have challenged the three of us publicly in the fighting pits, Hector. By your own words, if you manage to kill Rafael tonight, then you will face all three of us together."

Pierette stood and drew me to my feet with her hand in mine so we could go stand closer to Claudia. She slid her arm around my waist, and I did the same. I trusted her to have a reason for the unusually bold public display, because normally she was much more circumspect outside the bedroom.

"I will have my way with all of you. I will rape the cat until her master fills her eyes and then I will slay them both," he said.

"You talk like a vampire, not a rat," Claudia said.

"And you talk like someone who is afraid to face me alone."

"You didn't challenge me alone, you challenged me along with Anita and Pierette, so that's how we'll fight: three against one."

"That is not what I meant."

"Words have weight in the fighting pit," she said, and it had the ring of an old saying.

Some of the people near him moved toward him and then he shoved one of them away. "Get away from me, you crazy old woman."

"We do not hurt our elders," Claudia said, and this time I had a bit of knowledge that must have come from Rafael. If any member of the rodere survived to true old age, they were revered and no longer had to fight to survive in the clan. It was such a rare thing to happen that it was considered sacred to be truly ancient among them.

Rafael took the microphone back from her. "Is she hurt?" he asked.

The crowd around the white-haired woman he'd pushed took the microphone from him after the group around Hector closed in with a silent threat of *share the microphone, or else.*

An older man with hair almost as white said, "She is not injured, but she says this one smells like a stranger to her."

"He is possessed by a vampire whose animal to call is rat like Nikolaos, but a hundred times more powerful than she was," Rafael said. Again, the statement was too abrupt for any of the supernatural groups I'd been involved with from vampires to werewolves. I didn't like the constant fighting, but I liked cutting to the chase.

There were some gasps, but mostly a heavy silence from the crowd. I expected them to move back from him even at the possibility of it, but I'd underestimated the wererats. They crowded closer to him, even though they had to know that touch made all vampire powers stronger. "What are you doing? Rafael is trying to poison your mind against me. He seeks to escape our battle because he knows he cannot win!" Hector yelled.

I thought the crowd was going to grab him and it would be over, but they never touched him. In fact, they kept their hands down close to their sides, in a clear attempt to appear harmless as they leaned in toward him. I realized suddenly that they were trying to smell his skin. Rats have one of the best senses of smell in the animal kingdom; apparently that still applied in human form for them.

Rafael said, "Did you forget the laws of the fighting pit, Hector, as you forgot to respect your elders?"

"I forget nothing, old man! What are you all doing? Get away from me!" He was shouting at the people around him.

Neva leaned in to speak low to me and Pierette, because she couldn't talk to me alone while we were standing so intertwined. "Every time you touch each other, or Rafael, the red at the center of his aura pulses and fills more of the darkness around him."

"And he sounds less like Hector," Claudia said with the microphone safely away from her mouth, or maybe she'd turned it off. Either way the sound didn't carry.

"Can we prove he is Padma's creature?" Pierette asked.

"It doesn't matter," Rafael said.

"But if we can prove he's Padma's rat to call, then you won't have to fight him," I said.

"Who told you that?" he asked.

I stared up at him. He looked back at me, face serene as if what he'd said made sense to me. "If we can make him go all vampy, then you won't have to fight him, right?"

Neva said, "Challenge has been given and accepted—Rafael must fight."

I looked at her and she was far closer than I'd realized. Her eyes were still black with the gleam of silver starlight in them. Did her eyes ever look normal, or were they permanently stuck like this, the way Micah's eyes were to leopard?

"But Hector is like a Trojan horse, he's not here to fight Rafael and be king, he's here to destroy us all."

"He must kill me first and that is no easy task." He was so confident now; the doubts of earlier in the day were like an illusion he'd shaken off.

"If he used vampire powers, is that cheating?" I asked.

"It would depend on the power," Rafael said.

"That's crazy," I said, and let go of Pierette so I could touch him; what I wanted to do was grab him by his shirt and shake him, but since he wasn't wearing a shirt, I settled for touching his arm and the top of his shorts on one side. "Rafael, you've felt his power before and now he has even more power. We can't let him use that here on you, on the rodere."

"He called to my beast and I could not refuse him, but now he is in our inner sanctum and we have power here that we do not have in the outside world."

"What power?" I asked.

Neva came close to us and spoke low. "I believe the reach of our magic will go outside of here now."

Rafael turned to her, sliding an arm around my waist without thinking, as if it were just the natural thing to do. I wasn't sure it was natural, but I slid in closer to him as if I agreed. Frankly, I was too tense to cuddle well. We were all in terrible danger—didn't he understand that?

"We have small magic outside here," Rafael said.

"No, my king, not small, not tonight, not with her power inside you, and the power of a goddess similar to ours inside her."

I started to open my mouth to argue that Obsidian Butterfly wasn't a goddess, or that I was a monotheist, but honestly, I was more interested in her saying they had a goddess similar to Obsidian Butterfly. I knew they didn't have a vampire as powerful as her hidden away in here, so what did Neva mean?

"What do you mean about a goddess power inside Anita?" he asked.

"All women have the power of the Goddess in them," Neva said, as if she were telling him something he should already know.

"Of course, but you were not speaking in generalities," he said.

"Get away from me, all of you!" Hector yelled.

"He is done talking to the rest of us," Claudia said, and handed the microphone to Rafael.

The young bruja that Neva had called *mija* came forward and said, "Carlos texts that Hector smells like a stranger, and Abuela Flora says he smells like a *tlahuelpuchi*."

"Isn't that just another word for *vampire*?" I said.

"Young people think so," Neva said.

"They are born, not made, and their desire for blood only arises at puberty," the young bruja said.

"It is good to know you can listen as well as talk, *mija*," Neva said.

"*Gracias, abuela*," she said, and looked pleased with herself. I wondered if *abuela*, which I knew meant *grandmother*, was an honorary term or a familial one. I'd ask later; the last time I'd seen my own *abuela* I'd been fourteen.

Rafael said, "If all supernatural blood suckers are defined as vampires, then yes, a *tlahuelpuchi* is a type of vampire."

"Can't we use that to just take him into custody?" I asked.

"You cannot be here as a marshal, Anita," Rafael said.

"I don't mean me taking him into custody, I mean you guys jumping his ass and capturing him so that we can use him to find Padma."

"Challenge has been given and accepted, Anita," Rafael repeated.

Benito said, "I'd like nothing better than to jump his ass, but once inside the fighting pit there are no excuses for canceling a fight."

"Even the fact that we know he's a Trojan horse for an evil vampire?" I asked.

"A Trojan horse is only dangerous if you don't know that it is full of enemies," Neva said.

I looked into her black eyes and realized that the other bruja with her had normal eyes; only Neva's stayed in power mode. "What are you planning to do?" I asked.

"Win," she said.

"Rafael," Hector yelled, "are we going to fight, or will you talk the night away, old man?"

Rafael raised his arm so that the brand on his arm showed clearly. "If you want my crown, little boy, come and take it."

"You first, my king."

Rafael gave a slight nod. Hector did a deep bow that swung his braid forward over his head, which meant he was doing it wrong. For a real bow you bent at the waist, not the neck; I'd been learning protocol for bows and curtsies for the wedding.

Rafael handed the microphone to Benito, then ran down the steps toward the railing, put one hand on the top of it, and vaulted over. The crowd cheered.

"That's a twenty-foot drop," I said, my heart beating a little too hard just watching him go over.

"Yes," Benito said, as if it was no big deal.

I glanced around, but everyone was chill with Rafael jumping, so I tried to be cool about it, too, when what I wanted to do was run to the edge and see if he'd broken his leg. Instead I stayed where I was and watched him walk toward the middle of the sand. He hadn't broken anything; in fact, he'd taken the time to dust off any sand that might have clung to his black shorts.

Fredo stepped out into the sand below us, walking toward Rafael. Fredo was slender with his salt-and-pepper hair cut short and neat; the equally short and neat mustache and beard that he'd added recently made him look like a stranger almost. I wasn't sure I'd ever get used to them. He looked even shorter than the five foot six I knew he was as he met Rafael in the middle of the sand. It gave me some idea of how tiny I'd look out there. Rafael was still unarmed, as Hector had been, but the overhead lights gleamed silver in the banderillas and small knives across Fredo's black T-shirt. Some of them were throwing knives and some were just small blades. He was one of the few people I'd ever met who was truly dangerous with a throwing blade. If there was any way to use a blade for lethal purposes, Fredo could do it.

Hector backed up the steps between the benches and did a running start, on stairs, before launching himself into the air, where he rose higher as if he had invisible wings. I'd have fallen on my ass just running on the stairs, but Hector lengthened out his body, his arms tucked in tight, his legs long and graceful together as he flipped himself in the air as if he were on a high dive over a pool instead of solid, unforgiving ground. I honestly thought he was going to crash-land and the fight would be over before it began, but at the last second he bent his body over and did a shoulder roll across the sand like Rafael had done, except Hector rolled farther and faster from the extra momentum he'd gotten from his fancy airtime.

He came to his feet with an almost balletlike leap, arms up and out, when he landed. He smiled at the crowd, waving an arm again; there was that echo of dance or gymnastics or something that you didn't learn in martial arts.

The crowd went wild, fickle motherfuckers. Flashy bastard, but my stomach was tight as I watched him glide toward the center, where the other men were waiting.

27

FREDO PATTED HECTOR down, tracing the edges of the fight shorts and even making him open his mouth to check that he wasn't hiding anything there. He did the same for Rafael. He even checked their bare feet and hands and ran fingers over their hair. It was more like a prison search then even a cop pat-down.

When Fredo was satisfied that neither fighter was carrying anything but what God gave them to fight with, he literally drew a line in the sand between the two men. Then he reached back and hit the switch on something at his waist that I hadn't even seen until he touched it. I realized it was a cordless microphone setup when Fredo spoke into the tiny mic by his mouth. I could see it as a thin black line almost lost in his beard now that I knew what I was looking for.

"Our king and his challenger have agreed to single blade and claws until one of them is dead."

Rafael spoke low to him, but Hector wasn't having any calming talk. He did a little bounce on the sand and it was just a little too high; again I thought dance training with his fight training maybe?

Hector held his hand out for the microphone, and Fredo passed him the tiny wired piece. "After I kill you, I will carve the crown from your skin, old man!"

Rafael just reached his hand toward Fredo, who pulled a blade from one of the many on him and handed it hilt first to his king. Hector threw the tiny microphone toward Fredo, who didn't bother trying to catch it, he just let it dangle from the other half of the wire. Fredo pulled a blade that looked to be a match to the one he'd handed Rafael and offered it to Hector.

They took a stance on either side of the line in the sand. Fredo moved back from them toward the edge of the pit, and then Fredo must have shut the microphone off, because he shouted something that I couldn't understand from here. Rafael saluted Hector with his knife. Hector returned the gesture, but with the blade pointed at the ground; in practice it points up or a little to the side, never at the ground, because that means it's a fight to the death, as in *I'm going to put you in the ground*. I hadn't been able to see Rafael, but I guess he gave the same salute. This wasn't training, or practice, it was for real. The men moved in a blur too fast for me to follow and the fight was on.

28

IN THE MOVIES knife fights last a long time, because it's supposed to be good cinematography, it's supposed to be pretty and exciting. In real life they're fast, because you're fighting for your life and you don't give a damn about pretty, you want to survive. Rafael and Hector moved forward at the same time, but the exchange of blades and arms blocking and moving them each past each other was so fast I couldn't follow it with my eyes. It was like special-effects fast and then Rafael was bleeding from his lower arm, but Hector was bleeding from his side. Blur of movement and blood. The side wound bled more, dripping down in a bright red wash I hoped meant it was deeper, but wasn't sure. They both ignored the wounds as if they were nothing; neither of them even hesitated. Most people will when they get cut, and a lot of them die in that moment, because the person who isn't cut takes advantage of it, but neither of the men on the sand was going to make that amateur mistake. The first exchange had turned them around so that Rafael was facing us and all I could see was Hector's back.

Rafael's concentration was all on the man in front of him. I'd had all his attention on me in the bedroom, but not like this; this truly was the world narrowing down to the person in front of you. People think sex is the only intimate physical act, but they're wrong. Intimacy implies pleasure to most people; those people have never experienced real violence firsthand. It's incredibly intimate when someone is trying to kill you up close with a blade or their hands, the kind of intimacy that will give you nightmares.

They blurred past each other on the sand, and again I cursed myself for not being able to tell what they'd done. I was supposed to be good with a blade, but their speed made me blind to the intricacies of what they were doing. They glided and spun and used the empty hand to block and pass each other past their bodies. Suddenly blood flowed down Hector's upper arm. The blood on his side had flowed down until it was darkening the edge of his orange shorts. That wound seemed to be bleeding worse than any of the others on either of them. Was it deeper? In a worse spot? I might have asked Claudia, but Hector launched himself at Rafael, who had to back up suddenly. I didn't see the wound at first, because his longer black shorts hid it, but the material of the shorts themselves was cut open over the thigh. The color of the cloth covering so much skin made it hard to judge how bad it was, but it was a new wound and that was bad enough.

I thought, *Rafael needs to finish this soon*. The longer a knife fight went on, the greater your chance of being hurt or worse. Only the two of them being incredibly good and well matched had made it last this long, but they were whittling each other down; if something spectacular didn't happen soon, the small wounds would accumulate and force a mistake.

I heard Claudia whisper, "Finish him." I didn't have to ask to know she was thinking the same thing I was.

Hector committed to a blow that tried for a liver shot, Rafael used his knife and free hand to move Hector past him, and I knew the blade was used because blood spilled out to shine in the lights. Rafael did something with his leg, and Hector was on his knees and Rafael still had control of his arm trapped across his chest with the knife. It was his empty hand that was going for Hector's throat. What the hell was he planning to do?

Rafael's hand touched the side of the other man's neck, and blood welled dark and rich. Hector's arm blurred out toward Rafael's groin but hit his outer thigh instead, and blood welled there, too. "What the fuck?" I said.

"Claws," Claudia said, before Rafael ripped them out of the front of Hector's throat, and Hector did the same to the side of Rafael's thigh. It ripped open his leg, so that the long shorts hung ragged and blood poured, but it fountained out of Hector's throat, staining the sand in a wet, splattering arc.

Rafael was having trouble putting weight on the leg, as he kept control of Hector's arm against his chest where he'd flayed the man's arm open with the blade and was still using it to control and cut him more. If they'd been human, the fight would have been over, but they weren't, and I'd seen powerful shapeshifters heal throat wounds that bad.

"His hand," Pierette said, "Rafael's only called claws on one hand. That's very rare."

"I've never seen anyone do that," I said.

Rafael still held his knife, but when Hector called claws, he'd had to give up his blade even if his arm could have held on, because once the long claws came out, they wouldn't wrap around a hilt.

"*Rafael es muy macho*," Benito said, and I knew he meant it in the best sense, as in strong and powerful.

Rafael used the arm as a lever to put Hector on his stomach. The blood gushed into the sand so fast it turned black. Rafael used the braced arm and body to steady himself, or that was what it looked like as he moved the extra step to Hector's side. He broke the arm at the elbow, a wet meaty sound that carried in the sudden silence, before he let himself collapse to one knee, pinning Hector's lower back, the injured leg held awkwardly off to the side. It was bleeding bad enough that he'd need to heal it soon before he lost too much blood. He used his claws to grab Hector's hair and pull the head back. I expected more blood to fountain out, but it didn't; maybe there wasn't enough left? With his knee pinning the body, he lifted most of the chest upward with the hair, as he moved the knife into place to tear out the other wells of the throat.

Hector's eyes were still open. I wasn't close enough to see the dead stare, and then I saw him blink. I had time to say, "He blinked."

Claudia said, "His eyes."

Hector used his working hand to fling sand up and into Rafael's face at the same time he twisted and bucked underneath him, using his undamaged legs to send Rafael sliding off his back, but Rafael still had Hector's hair in one hand and a blade. He used the hair to flip Hector with him, so that Rafael's own body weight brought Hector's back down to Rafael's chest, and he plunged the knife into the side of the neck he hadn't cut before. His good leg was around Hector's waist so that he was holding him against him as he plunged the knife into the neck and tore it outward, the blade version of what he'd done with claws to the other side, but this time blood didn't fountain out.

Power breathed like the faintest of winds, trying to hide what it was, but I knew. I said, "Vampire."

"What?" Claudia asked.

"Vampire; Padma is pumping more power into little Hector."

"What kind of power?" Benito asked.

"Healing," Pierette said.

Hector drove his good arm up to block Rafael's knife

hand, and the broken arm had claws again. They dissected Rafael's lower leg, so the muscle and tendons fell away from it. The leg couldn't pin Hector anymore, so he rolled out and away from the other man. Hector got to his two good legs and showed his claws like brandishing ten switchblades.

Rafael lay in the sand with a blade in one hand, but the claws were gone in the other, which meant he was even more injured than it looked from here, and it looked fucking horrible from here.

"We have to help him," I said.

"The vampire has used too much power. He has left us a trail," Neva said.

I looked at her and found all three brujas looking at me with black eyes that were full of the cold light of stars.

"Time to die, old man." Hector's voice carried, and it shouldn't have. Wereanimals don't do voice tricks like that, but vampires do.

Rafael just propped himself up as best he could and made a come-ahead motion with one hand, like *bring it*. Then he half collapsed back to the sand, propped up on one elbow, the hand with the knife in it free to use, but use for what?

Hector charged him in a blur of speed.

I screamed, "Rafael!" but the sound was lost in the roar of the crowd.

29

IF RAFAEL'S LEGS had been working, he could have kicked out and maybe dislocated Hector's kneecaps, but if his legs had been working, he wouldn't have had to lie there on the sand as the other wererat came at him, slashing with what amounted to ten switchblades. But because Rafael couldn't get off the ground, Hector had to go to the ground to finish him.

As hurt as he was, Rafael still raised the blade in his hand and tried, but Hector used his arm to brush Rafael's arm and the blade aside and leaned over Rafael with a mouth full of razor-sharp fangs. He was going to tear his throat out with them.

Someone near us screamed and it wasn't me. I wouldn't let myself scream, or look away, I just prayed for a miracle, for something, anything to save him. Rafael tried to bring the knife in around Hector's arm to stab him, but it was never going to work, it was just one last defiant gesture. Fuck.

Hector's mouthful of teeth was going for his face, not his throat. The bastard was going to kill him slow. Rafael managed to slide the knife that was still pinned outside Hector's body inside the arm, which made Hector have to turn toward it and use enough attention to slice Rafael's hand and force him to drop the knife. Then Hector's body shuddered, then froze for a moment; his face, which had begun to shapeshift, began to sink back into human as blood gushed out of his mouth. Heart blow, but how?

Hector went up on his knees, still straddling Rafael's body, and Rafael used the weight of the other man to give him the leverage that his ruined legs couldn't give him, so that he sat up and started digging with the blade that he'd plunged in under Hector's ribs, going under the sternum for the heart. It was the knife that Hector had had to drop to call claws. Rafael must have found it in the sand. The hilt of the blade was kissed as hard against Hector's skin as it could go, but Rafael was digging for the heart—no, he already had the heart on the tip of the blade. Now he was trying to rip it to pieces while it was still in the other man's chest, and it would be game over.

I cheered without meaning to, and then Hector levitated straight up and off the knife point as if by an invisible hand. Hector ended up on his knees, coughing dark blood and thicker things out on the sand, but it started to slow almost immediately. He was healing again, damn it.

"Go to him, Anita, keep our king alive until our magic finds his master."

I turned and looked into Neva's darkling shining eyes. She motioned me toward the arena.

"Anita can't help him fight, none of us can," Claudia said; her voice was anguished.

"Hector's vampire master levitated him off a knife blade, that means that Rafael's master can help him, as well," Neva said.

"I don't know what Padma is doing to keep Rafael from healing, or how to rapid-heal him myself."

"Then do what you know best, Anita Blake."

"I don't understand."

"Fight for him."

"Only if I go with her," Pierette said.

"Anita is your vampire queen, of course you must fight at her side."

"If you are going to fight, do it now," Claudia said.

Hector stood up on the sand. He shouted, wordless, joyous. He flexed his healed hands and arms above his head and stretched luxuriantly like a cat as if he were clawing at the air with just his human fingertips. The blood was still drying on his body from all the injures. His fighting shorts were black on the front with it.

"There are weapons behind all the barriers," Benito said. "Since there was no negotiation, you can use any of them."

"But so can Hector," Claudia warned.

Hector started walking across the sand toward Rafael. We were out of time. "Jump and go to him," Neva urged.

I looked at the railing and thought about jumping twenty feet and didn't know how to do it without breaking an ankle or something.

"I will go ahead of you, my queen. Join me swiftly," Pierette said, and she took off running like Hector had, except when she got to the railing, she used the railing to vault over like Rafael had.

I was already running for the railing before she vanished from sight. I realized as the railing got closer that I was afraid of making a jump this high. It was like the heavier weights; I still felt too human to do it. Claudia yelled after me, "Treat it just like a tuck and roll in practice."

I heard the clang of metal sharp and sudden, and just by the sound of it I knew it was swords. My hand hit the railing and I launched myself up and over. I had a moment to see Pierette with her swords from the sheaths on her back, one in each hand. Hector had double swords, too. My seconds of hesitation had given Hector time to grab them from behind the wooden barriers. Then I couldn't see anything but the whirl of my clothes and body, as I had to start tucking and turning in the empty air. I prayed that Pierette would be okay for the seconds the fall would take and that I wouldn't twist or break anything important when I landed.

30

THE FALL WAS both too quick and too long and I had to fight not to come out of the tuck too soon, and then I was rolling on the sand, but the momentum of falling that far meant it wasn't just one or two rolls and I didn't come smoothly to my feet the way that everyone else had. I ended on one knee, feeling vaguely dizzy. I was as surprised as anyone to realize I had a knife in each hand from the wrist sheaths. I was so far away from the fight that I might have not bothered pulling a weapon yet. They were on the far side of the arena, blades flashing in the light. Pierette was standing in front of Rafael, who was still bleeding on the sand. Hector was trying to fight his way past her to finish the fight.

I could see the weapons hanging on one of the wooden barriers. There was a pair of kalis swords with their combination of straight and that one swelling curve like a bigger wave to all the small waves of a kris. It was my favorite blade in practice and they were hanging right there. I put the knives back in their wrist sheaths and grabbed the swords. They were so much heavier than practice blades. I tried their weight, whirling them in my hands as I started across the sand toward the fighting. One of the reasons that the wererats practiced with live blades was that the difference with practice swords wasn't just the dull edge versus sharp, but weight. As I started jogging over the sand, tightening muscles to hold myself steady over the shifting surface so I didn't twist an ankle or a knee, I was really happy that I'd practiced with real swords. It would be a terrible moment to have to swing a real blade for the first time as I came in at Hector's back.

If you expected me to give him a chance to turn around so it would be a fair fight, then you've been watching too many movies. In real life it's not cheating to survive.

Hector heard me coming, because his swords came swinging out toward both of us as he whirled in a circle, clearing us both back from him, so that he could move to face somewhere in between us. I recognized it as part of the Archangel series. Pierette and I both moved toward him at the same time, and then Hector had to defend against both of us.

I ducked under his arm, the sword whistling over my head, and I might have been scared of that sound so close to me, but I was moving too fast and trying to slice open his femoral with one sword, while raising the other up to guard myself just in case he tried for my throat as I whirled past him.

He turned so I cut the front of his thigh instead of the artery, but I cut along his side as I went past, because some damage was better than none. He bent a little forward, but I was at his back and didn't have time to wonder why as he tried to turn with a sword swinging toward me, but Pierette moved in closer in front of him, and I came up behind him, aiming for the side of his throat.

He moved his head just enough that I missed the kill shot, but blood still showed on his skin as I moved past him and was in front of him again as Pierette glided around him from the other side, so that we traded front for back, and I was suddenly facing Hector on my own.

One blade came for my throat at the same time that

the other blade tried to slice open my stomach and pierce my liver. I swayed my upper body out of reach and brought my own sword up to block the liver shot. Hector stumbled, but I still had to block one of his blades as I spun away from his second. He collapsed to his knees, and my blade was coming for his unprotected throat when another sword was suddenly there saving him.

I stepped back from Hector where he knelt in the sand, swords up, ready to defend against the new threat. Pierette was moving with me. It was Claudia and Benito, both forcing us back from the kill.

"What the hell are you doing?" I asked.

"Neva says we need him alive," Benito said.

"To find his master," Claudia added.

"You have betrayed our laws, the duel is forfeit, I am king," Hector said, but he spat blood on the sand. It wasn't from anything I'd managed to do to him. I fought the urge to glance at Pierette or ask what she'd done at his back to make him spit blood.

Fredo came to stand between the two fallen fighters. He was still trying for an appearance of neutrality, but he turned the mic on and spoke for the almost silent crowd. "If we heal no matter what is done to us, then our fighting skills mean nothing. A vampire has violated our holy of holies; the vampire would put a king of their choice on our throne. Those closest to him have smelled the vampire on the traitor's skin. It is not enough to kill the traitor; we must slay his vampire master."

The crowd cheered, and some of them made a high, guttural hissing noise, which I think was the rat equivalent of cheering, or maybe it meant something else altogether. As long as they agreed that we could do what needed to be done to Hector and Padma, I didn't care what it meant.

"We must end this threat in its entirety," Neva said from much closer than I'd expected. All three of the brujas were on the sands. How had I missed five people coming down here? That kind of carelessness could get you killed in a fight. Oh hell, I'd been listening to Fredo and the crowd. I couldn't even blame the combat.

Hector got to his feet. He'd healed whatever Pierette had done to him. Claudia, Benito, Pierette, and I went down into a fighting stance. "Four against one, is that what has become of the honor of the rodere?"

Neva yelled a word I didn't understand and stamped one foot hard on the sand. I felt something rush past, and then Hector stumbled on the sand as if someone had tripped him. Claudia and Benito were on him before he'd regained his balance. I didn't know what had just happened, but they did. Pierette and I moved up, but Benito and Claudia had disarmed him with nearly identical flourishes that drew more blood, as they forced his swords to the sand. They kicked them out of his reach. Hector rushed Benito, sweeping one arm and sword past him, but Benito hooked Hector's leg and sent him sprawling backward, fighting for balance. Claudia drove her elbow into the side of his head, which staggered him more, and then brought her other elbow to the other side and hit him again. He swayed, eyes rolling back into his head. Benito was there to catch one arm as he sank to his knees. A man I didn't know came across the sand with a pair of special shackles. Not a single voice from the crowd rose in protest. When they had him secured, Neva said, "We will work our magic upon this one. You see to our king."

"Can the doctors come help him now?"

"Not yet," she said.

"Can he shapeshift and heal himself?"

"Not until Hector has left the sand."

"In vampire duels between masters, if the human servant kills, it's considered the same as the master vamp doing it."

"We need Hector alive to work our magic on him and his master," she said.

"But afterward if I strike the blow, does it count as Rafael's kill?"

"No, because Rafael is not your master, you are his; if you kill for him, he will still lose his crown."

"Shit," I said. Jean-Claude whispered through me, "We can give him energy to heal as we have shared with our other halves in the past."

"What does your master say to you?" Neva asked.

I wasn't even surprised that she could sense Jean-Claude. "We could give Rafael energy to heal. Will your laws let me do that?"

"Normally, no power outside of each champion would be allowed to aid them."

The other witch who had remained silent up to now said, "Rafael carries enough power as our king to be able to heal better than this, especially here in the heart of our power."

"So why isn't he healing better?" I asked.

Neva said, "We believe that this Master of Beasts is preventing it, though that should not be possible, especially here."

"If vampire power is breaking Rafael, let me use vampire power to fix him, please?"

"We will have to convince the assemblage that it is a fair balance of power, or you could heal Rafael and still lose him his throne."

I wanted to scream my frustration.

"Nothing like this has ever happened during a challenge for kingship, Anita. Give us a few moments to search our law and lore," Neva said.

The younger one with long hair said, "Trade places with Fredo and send him to us. He is one of our lore keepers."

I could have asked what that meant, but it seemed self-explanatory, so I just turned and started walking toward Rafael, because Fredo was kneeling beside him. I'd send

Fredo back and I'd hold Rafael's hand, and this would all work out. I tried really hard to believe that as I walked toward them. I tried not to look at the blood on the sand around Rafael and do the math in my head of how much blood you can lose before it's too late. I had never dreamed that a shapeshifter could bleed to death, but the only thing that prevented it was their healing abilities; take away that and they were just stronger, faster humans. It was ridiculous that we would all let him bleed to death when regular first aid could give him enough time for us to fix whatever Padma had done so that Rafael's own power could heal him. I would not let that happen, even if it cost him his crown, I would not let him die because of rules, not if I could save him. I promised myself that as I walked across the sand and saw all the blood around him. I promised myself I would save him, fuck the rules.

31

I CROSSED THE sand with the borrowed swords still naked in my hand. I had no sheaths for them and until the fight was declared finished, I was holding on to them, just in case. I knew the idea was that by delaying Hector's death, we had a chance to find Padma and end the larger threat, but it still felt like the swords should have been soaked in blood, with maybe Hector's head to throw at Rafael's feet. *Here, here is your enemy dead; even if you die, he died first.* As presents went it probably wasn't very romantic, but for survival and shared rage, it would have been nearly perfect, or maybe I wasn't thinking clearly?

Fredo was holding Rafael's hand, and when he looked back at me, his eyes were shining with unshed tears. The moment I saw the tears, my stomach clenched tight. I'd never seen Fredo cry.

I concentrated on his face, not letting myself look at Rafael yet; that would come, but first I'd deliver the message. "The brujas need their lore keeper to decide some things."

Fredo nodded; he raised Rafael's hand to press it to his face, closing his eyes, which made the first tears fall. He kept his face averted as he said, "My king."

"It is all right, Fredo, go. I will be here when you return." Rafael's voice sounded almost normal. I finally let myself look at him. I'd been strong through all of it until I saw him lying there on the pale sand surrounded by a halo of blood, his and Hector's, but mostly his own. Sand was clinging to the wounds; normally they'd have cleaned that out first, because once he was able to heal normally, he could heal so fast the sand would still be inside when he did it. He couldn't get infections from it, but the body could encase foreign objects in tissue, sort of like an oyster does except you wouldn't get a pearl from it, just a nonmalignant growth that sometimes had to be removed.

I stood there and looked down at him and tried to keep my face blank like I would at an awful crime scene, but this wasn't some stranger, this was my lover and my friend.

Rafael managed a smile for me, but his eyes stayed pain-filled. "Your face, Anita, now I know how bad it is."

I fought not to cry; I could at least do that for him. I started to kneel down and then realized I would have to put the bloody swords in the sand, so I wiped the blood clean on my pants, so that sand wouldn't cling to the edge if I had to use them later. It probably wouldn't have made that big a difference, but one, they weren't my swords so I wanted to take care of them, and two, sometimes small things can make a big difference on how well an edge slices, or if it catches on things. You want a blade to slice clean, sharp, and even. It helped steady me to worry about the swords. It let me kneel and place them one on either side of me and not cry.

I touched his shoulder and he made a motion toward my hand with the other arm, but a shudder of pain ran through him and he had to close his eyes and focus on breathing not to cry out. He was king; he would not let them see him be weak. I had to swallow hard not to cry; if he could be strong, I could be, too. "Don't move, Rafael. I'll come to you." I took his hand in mine, the same hand that Fredo had been holding.

Rafael opened his eyes, smiled, and then closed them again, breathing through another wave of pain. His legs were shredded. The only other time I'd seen damage like this had been wereanimal attacks where the human victims were already dead before I got there to hunt the killer down and make sure they never hurt anyone else ever again.

"Jean-Claude says we could give you energy to heal."

He swallowed and tried to focus on my face. "What does Neva say?"

I debated lying to him, but I couldn't do that to him. If we healed him and it lost him his right to be king . . . Rafael had to know the risks first.

"She says that since it's vampire power keeping you from healing, it might be okay to use other vampire power to heal you."

"Will it cost me the throne?" he asked, voice hoarse as if he'd been screaming when I knew he hadn't been.

"They're checking your rules and stuff, that's why they wanted Fredo. I didn't even know you guys had a lore keeper until tonight."

"We are a complicated people."

I smiled. "You can say that again."

He smiled back, but his eyes were beginning to wander as if he couldn't see me or was having more trouble focusing. He was pale. He had a slight dew of sweat on his forehead. I touched his hand to my face, but it was still warm and then I realized that Fredo had been holding it. Had his shoulder been warm or cold when I touched it? I couldn't remember, so I raised his arm and laid my cheek against it. His skin was clammy. Shit!

I yelled back toward the waiting group around Hector. "Can I put a tourniquet on Rafael's wounds?"

Benito yelled back, "We cannot allow doctors onto the sands yet."

"Can I do first aid?"

Claudia came jogging toward me, her long strides making the distance nothing. "You may only use what you have brought with you onto the sand. We can't call in any of the medics."

I let go of Rafael's hand and said a prayer of thanks that I'd brought the tourniquet and combat gauze with me.

Claudia said, "You brought a tourniquet with you?"

I got the other rubber-banded pack out of another pocket. "Do you know how to use a rapid-application tourniquet? It's a Gen 2."

"Yes," she said. I handed the second package to her. I put three fingers through the loop of the RATS tourniquet, then realized I was going to have to lift Rafael's leg so I could slide the tourniquet under before I put it over my hand. My hand was too small to lift his thigh, so I knelt down and slid my arms underneath to lift. Blood gushed over my arms, and it was the usual surprise that enough blood was hot against my skin. His leg was too light, or too heavy, or just not weighted right. Nothing moved like it was supposed to, and when a piece of the meat of his leg swayed and hit my hand, I had to swallow hard. I would not throw up, damn it. If Rafael could endure it, I could handle helping him get through it. If he'd been human, he'd have lost both legs below the knees, but he wasn't human. If we could get him out of here alive, he would heal.

I put three fingers back through the loop and cinched it tight. Rafael groaned, which I took as a good sign. Claudia's bigger hands and longer arms were making it quicker for her to encircle his leg multiple times. It wasn't the blood that was slowing me down so much as the pieces of his leg swinging in against my body at odd moments. The amount of damage that Hector had done to his legs was disturbing. You never know what will bother you until it does. This bothered me. I swallowed hard and was taking deep, even breaths as I finished the last round

of the tourniquet until it was tight enough and hooked the
end into the little clip. The only thing the RATS Gen 2
didn't have that most other tourniquets did was a place to
write the time you put the tourniquet on. If you left it in
place, you could destroy the limb you were trying to save,
but the rule was life over limb, though I wasn't sure Rafael would agree. But I knew that for him and any shapeshifter, if we could just keep him alive, then they could
chop off the leg above the dead point and he'd grow back
the legs. There were options if we could just keep him
alive.

The blood trickled to a stop on the leg I was working
on. I glanced over at the other leg and the blood had
stopped there, too. I felt a moment of triumph and then
wished like hell I'd thought about the simple first aid
sooner. I started to open the gauze packet, then stopped
and asked, "Will this work on you guys?"

"Yes," she said.

I tore the packet open and then didn't know where to
put it. The leg was dismembered, so it was like there were
too many wounds. I was happy I'd brought two packets
of both gauze and QuikClot, but looking at Rafael's legs,
I wanted an armful of QuikClot. Jesus, I'd never seen
anyone who lived through wounds like this, and then I
realized that I'd never seen anyone who was just cut up
this way here; when a shapeshifter went bad, they didn't
stop at the legs. They didn't stop until there were pieces
missing that we'd never find. It's not like that scene in
Jaws where the body parts come spilling out of the shark.
Mammals digest things faster and have to chew them up
into smaller bites to eat them.

"Put it here," Claudia said. She guided my hand and I
let her do it, because I'd never tried to treat a wound with
this many moving parts. Rafael moaned as we shoved the
QuikClot gauze against his wound. Again, I took it as a
good sign. As long as he was reacting, he was still alive.

Benito came to stand above us. "The brujas need you. I will stay here with Claudia and tend Rafael. The tourniquets and QuikClot will hold our king on this side long enough for the brujas to work their magic." He offered me a hand and I took it, but my hand was so slippery with Rafael's blood that I lost my grip and Benito grabbed my arm to steady me.

"So much for being suave and debonair," I muttered.

He smiled and patted me on the back before he let me go. "Pierette and Fredo will have your back while you help the brujas."

I didn't question it, just walked toward the other little group on the sand.

32

HECTOR WAS STILL on the ground with his wrists and ankles shackled together with a long bar of metal. They were the new restraints that the police had designed for supernatural prisoners now that they were actually taking some of them into custody instead of just executions all around. Fredo and Pierette stood ready with sword and knife. When Neva and the other two brujas looked at me, their eyes were all black and shining with the cold light of distant stars, but Hector was still laughing. "The greatest magic the rats have at their disposal and it is not enough. You cannot defeat my master."

"Where do you want me?" I asked.

"Riding my cock," Hector said, and laughed.

I ignored him as if he weren't there and looked at Neva.

"Fill your eyes with the light between the stars," Neva said.

I did what she asked, and suddenly I could see the red aura around Hector like a wound, and that he had a real wound in his back. I could see him bleeding internally from where Pierette had pierced his kidney. It wasn't like X-ray vision, but almost like his aura had sprung a leak and the black and red were intermingling like paint spilling from two different cans.

"What do you need me to do?" I asked.

"We can use this one to find his master. We see him sitting in a hotel room, but we cannot breach the darkness around him. It is a piece of Madre de la Oscuridad, and it stands as a wall between us and what needs doing."

"My master had hoped you would have a child with one of your men by now. He says you owe him a son," Hector taunted.

"He gave up Fernando to save his own life, and he loved him a hell of a lot more than he loves you," I said.

"Only someone descended form Belle Morte's blood-line would speak of love and *moitié bêtes* in the same breath," he said, and his hazel eyes were solid brown and starting to shine.

"Do you know what hotel he's in, can you see a name, a notepad, a card, anything for the physical location?" I asked Neva.

"Once you join your power to ours, you will see what we see."

"How do we do that?" I asked.

"I am told that all your powers work better through touch, is that true?"

"Most of them."

"Then kneel and lay hands upon his skin, and we will lay hands upon you. You will be our battering ram against his castle wall."

"You carry so many of my beasts inside you, Anita, if you touch me, my power will take you over. You will be my creature as Hector is my creature."

"Bullshit," I said.

"The darkness will consume you if you touch me."

I smiled then, and he didn't like that I smiled. The doubt on his face, the confusion, was an expression I re-membered from his last visit. It was funny how facial expressions stayed the same no matter what body people were wearing.

"You got just a tiny piece of her power, Padma, I got the rest." And I shoved my hand through the blackness and the red until I touched the bare skin of his chest and stomach, and I could see the cord like a metaphysical leash from Hector leading down into the floor, into the ether, into . . . Neva spoke next to my face. "Find the vampire, Anita, find me the vampire on the other end."

My necromancy opened like a flower and the darkness parted before it, and I was suddenly seeing the room where Padma was sitting on the edge of a bed. It wasn't a good hotel, more motel—oh, how the mighty had fallen. I felt Jean-Claude's thrill of discovery before he backed off and hid his reaction. I knew without even thinking the question that he was telling Pierrot. The Harlequin would be hunting Padma. If we could hold him in place, they'd have him.

Padma looked up at me as if I were floating in the air in front of him. "So, you have found me; I will be out of this city before even the Harlequin can find me."

"The last time I saw you, you were wearing silk and real jewels. You're looking a little threadbare."

I felt movement, a great seething ocean of power behind me like I'd felt outside the warehouse. I didn't have to see to know it was the small rats again, but I looked all the same. The pale sand was black with fur, more than outside, so many more. Thousands of rats filled one half of the stadium floor. They sat waiting, watching, too quiet, too intent for just rats. The rat with the white spot on its chest and the one white paw stood up on its hind legs and looked at me.

"I survived the loss of my human servant and my tiger when I had to flee Europe. I will survive whatever you do to this one, too."

"I'm sorry for the loss of Gideon and Thomas." They'd been his tiger to call and his human servant. His own triumvirate of power. That he'd survived the death of them both would be like Jean-Claude surviving losing me and Richard. It was impressive.

Padma looked surprised. "Thank you, Anita Blake."

"You're welcome; they both deserved so much better than you."

Padma hissed at me, showing fangs, which was rare for the really old vampires. They considered it déclassé to flash fangs like an animal.

"Did you abandon them the way you're abandoning Hector?"

"He knew the risks."

"So, you're going to leave Hector to die, just like you left your son."

He stood up from the bed, glaring at me, hands in fists at his sides. There was a black wavering in the air around him. "I will wait for you to have a child of your own, Anita, and then I will return and extract my revenge."

"It was your choice to trade your son's life for your own, Padma. I'd have been happy to kill you instead."

"In all the history that Hector remembered, they had never allowed an outsider in the fighting pit on a night when they chose a new king. You were not supposed to be here tonight, Anita."

"Hector couldn't win without you cheating and saving his ass. Levitating him off the blade was too much; you gave yourself away, and you'd have done that without me here. Even if he killed Rafael, the wererats would have challenged him until someone killed him. He would never have sat the throne or taken the oaths that you need to possess the wererats. This has all been for nothing, Padma. You never could plan long term on your own."

"You are too young to know that," he said.

"I share a lot of old memories with people who saw you as the weakling you are."

"I was weak, that is true, but that was before the Mother came to me and together, we are so much more." The air around him wavered like dark mist, and then it was as if the darkness separated from him, looming at his back. I couldn't decide if it was black flame, or like a dark ghost, but it wasn't the darkness, it wasn't even the darkness between stars that filled all our eyes.

"I will be sorry to lose my rat, but there will be other rats to call, other animals to enslave."

"You're half-right," I said. I felt the darkness inside me move, liquid and alive; I had drunk down the night itself, and I had a second of fear that she had been inside me all this time, waiting to join with the lost pieces of herself, but I knew that wasn't right. I'd met another vampire in Ireland that had a piece of her power, but it hadn't been like this; they had gained one of her abilities to strengthen their own, but the darkness hadn't been separate from them.

"The darkness has moved aside for you," Neva said.

"It doesn't belong to him," I said.

"It belongs to itself," the one Neva called *mija* said.

"It's looking for someone to use," I said.

Neva whispered, "Our power will touch you, do not be afraid."

I didn't know what she meant until I felt something much smaller than a human hand touch my hand. It startled me enough that I looked down and lost concentration on Padma. The black rat with its white spots was looking up at me. The other rats had spilled around the island of all of us, but some had climbed the three brujas and the one on my hand. I stared into those black button eyes, and I swear there was too much weight of intelligence and personality for any rat I'd ever seen. I mean they're smart, but not that kind of smart.

"They will not hurt another rat," Hector said.

I laughed, and there was that uncertain look that I knew was Padma's and not the confident swaggering man that Hector was supposed to be. "Do you know anything about real rats?" I asked.

Neva said, "Make him look into your eyes, Anita."

I did what she asked, staring into the brown of Padma's eyes set in Hector's face. "I am the vampire here, Anita, not you." The eyes started to glow with brown fire like a brown glass with the sun behind it.

"Keep the Goddess in your eyes, Anita, it is not as vampires we need to tame him," Neva said.

I fought to hold on to the blackness that Obsidian Butterfly had taught me. I leaned over Hector and looked into Padma's glowing eyes with the darkness between stars in my eyes.

"They showed me their dark eyes and it availed them nothing," Hector said, but it was Padma's voice the way Pierrot's voice could come out of Pierette.

"This is not the same darkness," Neva said. "There is more than one goddess in the heavens, Master of Beasts."

"I don't know what you are babbling about, woman."

And then I saw the rats in the darkness, so that it wasn't the darkness between the stars at all, but a blackness made up of rats, as if the universe were connected together with them, or the universe was nothing but rats, black and warm, and the darkness collapsed into an avalanche of rats that fell through Neva's eyes and into my own and into Padma's eyes in Hector's face.

"What are you doing?" Hector asked, and his voice held the first hint of fear.

Neva answered, "She has opened the way for us."

I felt like I was falling with the rats and the darkness into the brown glow of Padma's eyes. Hector started to scream, and I wanted to join him. I repeated in my head, *I trust Neva, I trust the rodere, I trust their magic, I trust Rafael, I trust Claudia, I trust Benito*, and then the rats and I spilled through Hector's eyes and into Padma's hotel room, except the rats weren't metaphors or bits of space darkness—they were real squeaking, scrambling, wriggling rats filling the room.

"You cannot hurt me with rats, it was my first animal to call," Padma said.

The rats milled around the room and did not touch him, he was right, and then like an echo I felt the black rat with the white chest spot touching my hand, its whiskers tickling along my skin. It reminded me that my body was still kneeling on the sand and on Hector, and it reminded me of one more thing.

"Rats are my animal to call now, too," I said.

"You are a child playing with toys you do not understand," Padma sneered.

I felt the rat scramble up my bloody shirt and push its way through the mess of my hair with its drying blood, and the rat didn't care. It liked being near me, and I realized I liked the weight of it on my shoulder, the way it cuddled against my face. This was the first time I'd ever been able to interact with the real-life version of my animal to call—with all the others it was the wereanimal, but never just the animal part without the human in there somewhere.

It was as if I'd been holding my breath and suddenly, I could let it go. I could relax in a way that you can around your dog, or cat, because they aren't judging you like people do. The rat settled more heavily against my neck and the side of my jaw. If it was relaxing to touch the wereanimal you could call, touching the animal version of it was even more soothing.

And just like that was all right, it was all right to feel like the darkness was made up of a million rats. It was all right that the rats fell through me and were me, and weren't me, and filled the hotel room and began to swarm over Padma.

"I forbid you to hurt me," he commanded.

The rats didn't care what he wanted, and neither did I, because I wanted him dead. I did not want him haunting our steps and I never wanted him near our child. We needed him dead and the rats liked me better because he didn't like them. He didn't even like wererats, because they were just animals, after all.

The first one took a bite. "Stop, I command you! You will not hurt me. You cannot hurt me; I am your master." He sounded so sure of himself, but we could feel his fear, we could smell it on him, feel the trembling of him under-neath our feet and against our bellies as we climbed him. Fear meant food.

They started biting him, hundreds of tiny mouths tak-ing a bite, and then they began to feed. And he started to scream. "You cannot do this! I am your master!"

"You are not master here," Neva, the two other brujas, and I said in unison, "not in our holy of holies. You cannot win here when we have another vampire to call rats for us, another bruja to see the darkness between stars, another wererat to be a conduit for the Goddess. You only seek to steal power, Master of Beasts, but Anita seeks to share it. Someone who shares is always more welcome than some-one who takes." And all the time Neva's words poured from our mouths the rats fed. If Neva hadn't held me in her power, our power, their power, the Goddess, or the God, or something, I would have been horrified, shocked, guilt ridden, but he had threatened our child, one we didn't even have yet. He would have killed us all, enslaved us all, and that we could not allow.

Regular rats shouldn't have been able to hurt him, it would have been like a lead bullet, but the magic changed the rats into something more like a silver-dipped bullet that could pierce supernatural flesh. The fire died in his eyes while they were still tugging and slicing the flesh from his bones. And then we were back on the sands, and the light died in Hector's eyes while we were still pulling back from them. He hadn't survived the death of his master.

I half expected the rats all around us on the sand to fall on Hector's body like the other rats had on Padma, but the rat on my shoulder made a soft, almost chirp sound in my ear. *We aren't that kind of rat*, it seemed to say.

Neva said, "That is not how we dispose of bodies here in the fighting pit."

I knew because Rafael knew that there was a trap door that opened over the river and there was something not rat, not human, that had been there when the wererats first came to St. Louis. The wererats had built upon the power of this place and what lay beneath. The dead of the fighting pit were sacrifices to what hid in the river here, and in turn it had become part of the magic of the brujas, part of the power of the holy of holies.

I knew that Rafael was healing before I turned and saw him sitting up on the sand. My eyes were back to normal as I crossed the sand toward him. I wanted to run to him, but I still had the rat on my shoulder, and I wasn't sure how secure he was there. I'd never had a pet rat, and immediately in my head the rat was disgusted with the thought that he was a pet.

"Sorry," I said, out loud.

Rafael held his hand out to me, and I took it and knelt on the sand, keeping my shoulders straight so I didn't spill the big rat off. Rafael was smiling at me; his legs were healing all that damage like those fast-forward films of blooming flowers. It was wonderful and a little disturbing.

"You killed another master vampire for us," he said.

"It was a group effort," I said.

"A group effort that wouldn't have worked without you with us," he said, and raised my hand to his lips to lay a kiss across my fingers.

I wanted to say so much, ask so many things, but I let it all go to trail my fingers down the edge of his face. The rat on my shoulder started to walk down my arm toward him.

"And who is this?" he asked.

"He didn't like being called a pet, so I'm not sure I get to name him."

"He says you may choose a human name for him," Neva said as she walked toward us, "and he will let you know if he likes it."

"Fair enough," I said.

"I had hoped to take you up on your offer with Pierette tonight, but though I am healing I will not be able to do anyone justice tonight, let alone you and another lovely woman."

"That's all right, I think I'm not in the mood after all this."

"I am sorry that you found our world so harsh."

I shook my head. "It is what it is, but if Padma hadn't attacked us here, then we couldn't have defeated him this easily. He underestimated the power of the rodere."

"He underestimated more than that, Anita." Rafael leaned toward me as far as his healing legs would allow, so I moved the rest of the way to him.

"I told you before, I'd come to you."

"You did, but I know you like your men to meet you partway."

I smiled and we kissed.

ACKNOWLEDGMENTS

Thank you to Matt Stumpf for helping reawaken the warrior inside me, and to Guro Dan Inosanto for sharing his knowledge and skill with all of us. It is an honor, sir.